I0707582

TWYLA
& the
WARBIRDS
Family Lost

Book One

T. W. Bellen

Copyright © 2024 T. W. Bellen
All Rights Reserved. No part of this book may be reproduced, stored in a retrieval system, or transmitted by any means, electronic, mechanical, photocopying, recording or otherwise without written permission from the author.

For Wiley.
My Heart.

My granddaughter asked about my war—what I did and who I was. I said I would tell her when she got a little older. She didn't give up. She wore me down. Made me put it all in a box and label it. It took me a few days to realize this was my chance to tell the truth. To unwind it, un-juke-n-jive all the detours I had made around it. All of it.

Who am I? I am a fighter pilot from a family of fighter pilots. We fight and we die. This is the requirement of the job. We live with loss until we die. It is neither good nor bad. It is who we are. I am a fighter pilot. I am Twyla Campbell. I chase death for a living. And it chases me right back.

—Twyla Campbell
Circa 2000, Sonoma County, CA

Tale of the Hawk

he *audacity* of paved runways makes her smile.

She angles the steering yoke and advances the throttle of the little high-wing Taylorcraft. Rising over Iroquois Point, she slides up through horizontal rays of spun gold. Below her, big gray warships slumber like arrogant gunslingers in their tidy berths. A moment ago, driving past, they were towering walls of steel blocking half the sky. But just like that, she's five hundred feet up, and they are toy boats in a bathtub. She wonders if her eyes are playing tricks on her.

This week alone, she'd witnessed Pacific Island beauty in mystical force: birds, flowers, and fish in every imaginable color; arresting enough to slow her heartbeat and quiet her incessant head noise. She'd seen more beauty in one week than all of her previous twenty-three years. Nothing here was like the dark, rocky cliffs of the northern California coast. The little islands of San Francisco Bay had, at the time, struck her as the most beautiful sight she'd ever seen, a perception problem that worried her from time to time. *What does one do with an emphatic feeling once it's challenged or proved dead wrong? It seems there's no end to this, therefore, no end to being wrong—about everything. Are there islands even more beautiful than Hawaii? How is that possible?*

Does this mean truth is temporary or just geographical?

"Can you hear me?" The man in the copilot seat, Butch "Crusty" McCuskey—as he is known by the military fliers on the island—sports a scruffy brown beard, a grease-stained undershirt, and about thirty extra pounds.

"Yessir," she replies quickly, nodding. Her persimmon curls bounce, half-gathered in a sage-colored headscarf.

Butch motors on conversationally—because everything he says is interesting. "M'wife, Doris, thinks the islands need old folks. Oh, there's plenty of kids comin' and goin'. But she's convinced if you git them oldies comfortable flyin' over water, then *smack*!" He claps his big mitts together. "You got yourself one busy airline. McCuskey's Rabbit Ways? Rabbit Airways. Or, Winged Rabbit Lines. McCuskey's Rabbit Wings Lines. No, Flying Rabbit Ways! 'Cause yer hoppin' from one island to the other! See that?"

She smiles politely. "Aloha Airways or perhaps Bird of Paradise would be a natural name for—"

His expression stops her mid-thought and strongly suggests she's the stupidest girl at 155 degrees longitude. "Trim 'er out, I'm about to forfeit my breakfast, he says. "And let tower know we're headin' that-a-way." He points nowhere.

She clicks the mic switch. "Taylorcraft, November—" She turns to Butch.

"Two-one-one," he says. "He'll tell ya to drop anchor at two thousand. Double that."

"Hickam Base," she calls. "Taylorcraft November two-one-one, eastbound, sixty-five knots, request traffic over Pearl City and Honolulu, over."

The little bird scratches for altitude while the radio chirps out a reedy voice, "Good morning, girl pilot. Good morning, Butch. Look for a standard flock of Buffalos and Hawks, plus B-17s inbound from Hamilton. Maintain two thousand ceiling. Butch, I thought you moved to John Rodgers strip? Over."

"Held the admiral off 'til next month, over," Butch replies.

"Roger. Hickam out."

"Two thousand ceiling. Thank you, Martin."

"Thank you, Martin," She repeats into the mic. "My name is Twyla Campbell. Pleased to meet you. November two-one-one, clear."

"How's your beau feel about you flyin'?" Butch inquires without segue.

"What do you mean, sir?"

From the radio: "Tower to November two-one-one. Butch, stand by." Martin's voice bends in the static.

"Oh, not the damn Nene geese again," Butch mocks. "Martin's crimped 'cause he's missing church today." His oil-stained fingers flick. "All right, show me a stall."

"Yes, sir." Twyla throttles down and pulls the nose up. The plane shudders and spills over like a flour barrel tipped off a wagon. Despite her experience, she is nervous. Leaning forward to tuck her skirt under her leg, her necklace and locket get caught on the door handle, inhibiting her from pulling up.

"All right?" Butch's dull appeal is barely audible.

The silver chain snaps, and the locket lands open in the footwell. The little face of her fiancé stares out from under his Navy hat, his wiseass expression outshining the shadowy footwell. Twyla gazes at it momentarily, mesmerized by the alternating amber and blue light quivering on Lieutenant Haliday's face. The engine whines loudly in the steep dive.

"She's hardly a performance bird!" Butch barks. "And you ain't no Jimmy Doolittle."

"Just checking your new fuel pump's function in a steep angle," she bluffs.

"Well, check your airspeed, Jackie Cochran. And those clouds, what type?"

She finally gets the nose level and glances up. "Cirrus?" she answers, embarrassed at being frazzled.

"Without looking at the compass, what approximate heading are we on?"

She scans the horizon. "We should be between two-fifty and two-eighty—"

"Two-one-one, clear the area!" the radio chirps.

"Martin, unhitch your brai—"

"Clear the area! Stay off the radio!" Martin's voice is sharp, all friendliness vanished.

"Martin, not one goose." But he stiffens, brow furrowed.

"Clear the area and the radio?" Twyla repeats. "What's that mean?"

Butch scans all the way around. "Whatcha got out your side?"

"Um, clouds and water," she replies, stealing another peek at the locket.

"No! Look for planes!" he shouts, suddenly agitated and fidgety.

"Do you mean Army pla—"

A deafening roar, extremely close, engulfs them. "Oh!" Twyla jerks away from it, tossing the plane ass over teakettle.

"What the—?" Butch twitches around, and they both see flashing propellers, streaks of silver, and red disks painted on tails and wings. Twyla wrestles the tiny craft level.

"Whoa! That—that…?" Butch stammers. "But where the hell did that come from? Better be some mock exercise!" Butch clicks his mic. "Tower! Damn it, Martin! Tell me there's some kinda practice invasion this morning! Japanese planes up here!" He turns momentarily to Twyla. "I'm takin' over!" He grabs the wheel, but she pushes his hands off. "Martin, we're comin' in!"

The radio blasts in a rushed garble, "Butch, don't come back here! Don't come back!"

Twyla fights hard to turn the plane. Butch's feet push on the rudder pedals.

"Jiminy! Heartworms!" Twyla hears her mouth shout.

Butch tries again to push her hands off the wheel. "I said I'm takin' over!"

"Not in your condition! Pick up your feet!" she yells.

"My condition is tip-top!" he shouts back, but his eyes turn wild as he grabs his wrist, then his throat. He lifts his feet.

"You okay?" she asks.

He calms himself and shoots her a dull look.

"I'm climbing," she explains and pours on the throttle.

Altitude is time. Gain altitude, gain time, gain options.

Six silver torpedo-slingers overtake the Taylorcraft, beelining for Ford Island, the warships, and Hickam Field.

"Jiminy Cricket!" Twyla gasps.

"Oh, no! No! No! This can't be! Pearl! Where the hell are our flyboys? No one's flyin'!"

"They don't seem friendly," Twyla says, unable to stop her mouth.

"No kidding, Inspector?" His eyes bounce quickly around the island and track the smoke rising from Wheeler Air Field.

Directly below, flashing detonations seem to pulse the air around the little craft. Fire and smoke launch upward in black, reaching ejections. "This just can't be." Butch jerks around. "Look at that!" he screams.

Twyla whips her head around to see a Japanese Zero coming out of the sun, straight for them. "Lewis," she murmurs. Butch grabs the wheel and pushes it forward. "Dive!" he yells from the very fungus of his toes.

"No!" She slaps his hands. "No, turn!" Instead of firing, the rapidly closing Zero must nose up to avoid a collision. Twyla covers her ears as the bigger aircraft rushes by the tiny plane, hurling them into a sidelong skid. She wrestles the plane back under control. *Inches!* She banks steeply around and shoves Butch's hands off the wheel again.

"We're still alive! Ha! He didn't fire!" The enemy races away. Butch rubs his face.

Twyla's head bounces back and forth, scanning the island below where ships and aircraft are on fire at Ford Island, Hickam, and Wheeler. Streaking silver birds drop black eggs onto the massive port; flashes and fireballs race skyward out of breaking ships. *Does sleeping Honolulu think the military is just practicing?*

"Hey, there's our boys!" Butch shouts. "Come on, Yanks!" He changes the radio frequency. "Taylorcraft to… 47th! 44th! Bravo five!" He darts a glance at Twyla. "Is that yer beau?"

Her head whips around. "I can't really see over there."

Butch snorts and wipes at the side window. "Two, at least. A 40 and a 36… I think they're trying to form up. Nope, they're going after the devils! Is that yer beau?"

Twyla gasps, imagining Lewis in the middle of all that violence. "I know his plane has a star on the rudder," she says.

"Useless!" Butch barks.

She thrusts the wheel forward.

Ships tilt. Charcoal smoke boils upward like burning foothills climbing one another, up and up. *Wiley is down there, too*, she thinks.

"I see three Yank birds, hairball! Too much smoke." Butch's voice suddenly modulates. "Come on, Yanks… Is that yer beau?"

Twyla's face screws up with concentration and sweat. She doesn't want to see it. If she doesn't look, she doesn't have to see how bad it is—Lewis and Wiley can still be alive.

"Hold on!" he blurts. "My wife is down there!" He shakes his head. "Planes everywhere! Too much smoke. Too far away. Shit to heaven!"

Twitching with focus, Twyla frantically scans away from the harbor, looking for—

"Hey, we got one of them! Maybe two! Nip devils! Oh, no! Poor Army bastard… Whoever that is, he's goin' in!" Butch clicks his microphone. "Martin, I have my eyeball on an Army pilot who just became Navy! Martin? Martin?" Only static comes back on the radio. "Jesus, all the ships… They're in pieces!"

Twyla is silent. *Martin is already dead.*

She finds her spot and cranks the plane over so severely they are briefly upside down. "Jesus, doll, I'm afraid your boy is… I'm not sure… Nip devils. Wait! Where are you taking us? You can't land, for holy fucking shit! Are you out of your Shirley Temple-headed mind?! They'll kill—"

Ear-splitting metallic snaps interrupt them.

"Oh!" Twyla shouts.

"What the—?" Butch screams. "We're hit!"

A Japanese torpedo bomber and two fighter escorts roar past them, juddering the Taylorcraft. Butch hits his head on the low ceiling. Twyla jams her rudder, adds more power, and straightens them out.

"They're killing Americans down there! Why the fuck would you go there?" Butch screams. "Any other island! Any other island!"

Twyla absorbs this, swallows hard, and holds her breath against her hyperventilating lungs. "My man is down there! Doris is down there!" She plunges the wheel, nosing them steeply down. The little engine whines fiercely.

An image comes into her peripheral vision then snaps into sharp focus: leather flying cap perched over goggles and a sneer.

What would Hawkeye do?

France 1918

Hawkeye Campbell's eyes are certainly playing tricks on him. He leans forward and squints at what he would swear is pink mist spraying from the neck of his wingman only yards ahead of him, inverting, diving, and on a collision course with a Fokker Triplane. Hawkeye sits back and pushes his control stick forward, plummeting with the enemy, his brain simultaneously calculating the moment to engage the fighter (if his bleeding squadmate's guns jam or if he passes out) *and* puzzling over why he's able to see such a fine mist of blood within the prop wash and whipping wind of a 120-mile-per-hour dive.

Hawkeye notes—again—his mind's capacity to lie to him about his capabilities, adding another notch on his mental thrashing stick. He considers his wingman, Chance McClean, who has flown at his elbow for almost six months—an eon in this vocation. McClean held the squadron record for most assisted kills, a frustrating curse for a fighter pilot, especially a rail-thin ginger named Chance.

Chance's dive slackens. His guns don't fire. Hawkeye swiftly sideslips onto the tail of the triplane. On the enemy fuselage, a black dragon breathes fire. Hawkeye clears the chambers of the twin Vickers machine guns, guesses the next three maneuvers of this well-trained pilot, pulls the trigger, and pours his last eleven rounds into it. The enemy swerves away smoothly. Hawkeye sucks at his teeth, presses his thin lips together, then banks toward Chance. He watches his best pal, Happy, swing his French Spad XIII fighter close on Chance's starboard side.

Though famous throughout northern France for his sunshine smile, Happy's leather-capped head now recoils at the pink mist from Chance's neck, which quickly disappears into the slipstream.

Hawkeye, Chance, and Happy are the Flying Musketeers, Bark Beetle Boys, Rusty Rivet Ravens, and countless other titles that changed depending on the mood. "Hole in the Wing Gang" suddenly comes to Hawkeye's mind as he throttles toward his mates, the last survivors of his ten-man squadron. He glances over at the escaping fighter, trailing smoke as it rolls onto its back and oscillates downward like a tailless kite toward a bright green square of farmland. He slants in on Chance's port side, observing puffs of black smoke belching from his engine as his left wing sags, tossing Chance's head to the side. Hawkeye peers at Happy, who stays close but slightly astern, and glances down again in time to see the Fokker crash into a French farm in a fireless thump of dust.

Chance's Spad is now upside down; he is held in place by a thin rope across his lap, his right arm dangling and flapping in the rushing air. Hawkeye sees only one arm and takes this as a good sign—the other hand is likely still gripping the control stick. He signals Happy with a twist of his flat palm. Happy nods and slips in close to Chance's plane. Hawkeye maneuvers his own starboard wingtip under Chance's wing, measures his unconscious friend through his smudged goggles, and lightly touches the wings together. He has one venture to get this right. If he lifts his wing weakly, he'll tip Chance into a knife-edge angle followed by a corkscrewing spiral of death. If he lifts too hard, he'll damage the canvas and wood wings of both planes. Happy gives Hawkeye a knowing nod.

The three French fighter planes, locked wingtip to wingtip, would be, only a few years later, a flying circus trick at polo fields or fairgrounds anywhere in the world. Yet, on this day in 1918, they are hurtling at one hundred miles per hour and four thousand feet above the fourth year of World War I.

"*Ici ne va rien!*" Hawkeye cries (something like, "Here goes nothing!"), holding fast to his self-imposed challenge to *parle un peu Français* each day. His engine quits with a backfire and a wheeze, and his wings promptly lose touch with Chance. He's out of fuel and begins to drop back. Before he can think, Happy takes his place under Chance's wing, carefully making contact. After a brief moment to align, he banks right, slinging Chance's starboard wing upward, rotating the plane.

Hawkeye continues to drop away. Chance rotates around in his cockpit, one arm sweeping in a hasty arc, as if excitedly identifying a perfect spot on the beach to stage his towel. As Chance's plane rights, his own hand smacks him in the face, and he jerks to life, then jerks, and jerks some more. Hawkeye assumes he's coughing in the dense vortex pouring from his engine. Chance's elbow sticks out, probably pressing his hand to his leaking neck. Next to him, Happy is frantically waving him down. Chance's arm drops out of sight, and his plane sags away from Happy, who quickly closes the gap, resuming pressure on his wingtip and leveling the damaged fighter.

"Brilliant!" Hawkeye yells into the void. He knows Happy will stay with Chance. He just doesn't know what more he can do. Hawkeye's propeller stops altogether, adding even more drag to his quick descent. The Spad XIII's thick nose plows the cold air like a riverboat on a sandbar. Without the brain-vibrating engine, however, he is suddenly able to see much more clearly and sharply the multicolored squares of—cherry? Plum? Pongs of hot engine and gun oil are momentarily brushed aside by fragrant, sweet-sour… *But it is autumn? Foulage, then. Grape crushing… and something else? Cider!*

The American volunteer combat pilot is ensnared by an alien future world as piquant particles insinuate foreign ideas onto his reason. But he never liked wine. *Pomme cidre! Be an apple farmer.* The utter softness of the idea of apple farming unhinges his battlefront resolve, though it is hastily overrun by anger at the gaping hole in his fruit orchard knowledge. All of this temporarily masks his fury over this morning's aerial warfare debacle. But what is to be done? He is purposefully avoiding pointing his eyes just a few degrees east. He knows what is there: The German High Command is making a mess at the Sambre Canal. A last, desperate lunge for momentum. Clobber the British Expeditionary Forces before the French and Americans, freed from the Argonne Forest, can reinforce. Enemy machine gun specialists were holding the flooded canal. A thousand bloody bodies floated in the water or were piled upon the shell-cratered moonscape, the nearly lifeless shoreline from the same battle four years earlier.

He gives in. His eyes flick up and take in the line of smoke and puffs of artillery fire behind shattered hedgerows less than two miles away. He spins his dead warbird toward a cart trail along the River Sambre. His failed mission has brought them directly into the path of the driving enemy.

With his engine quieted, Hawkeye peers up into the great blue parasol, streaked with horsetail clouds and two miniature aircraft trailing a black ribbon. To starboard, at the eleven o'clock position, the planes are merged as one quadraplane, and he hears the report of Happy's guns. In this piggyback formation, his main wheels are surely straddling Chance's head. There's another flash from his gun muzzles. *That'll wake him.*

Hawkeye imagines his two mates diving on him, reforming in a tight "V," and successfully landing together at the river. Instead, he watches Happy's plane rise like a raptor clamping a dark fish in its claws and slowly roll over, while Chance's plane dips and tips into an uncontrolled spin, his smoke trail making it easy to follow. Hawkeye turns away from his friends. *So, that's it.* A shimmering fury sears his guts and burns in his throat. He quickly clenches his jaw shut.

He will not give even this to the enemy. *They get none of me.*

He gazes down at the Bosch's trenchworks zig-zagging below. The battlefront soldiers are blind to the machinegun nests just yards in front of them. He glances up one last time, hoping to see Happy, but he's gone. Happy's words ring in his ears, "Hundreds of thousands of men wasted to gain and lose useless tracts of dirt! Useless! Hawk, don't you see? We, as fit aero pilots, should coordinate a two-squadron attack, leapfrogging, guns blazing down the enemy trenches, pouring unrepentant slugs into them while our men advance unmolested! A no-shit cover fire." Hawkeye admires his friend's imaginative brain and knows he's right. But also, field commanders are not taught to have imaginations.

Seconds later, Happy zooms up from behind Hawkeye and slows right next to him. Hawkeye, coaxing his nonexistent glide slope, steals a quick glance. Twenty feet starboard, Happy is half-twisted in his cockpit, his arm stretched out behind him, gripping Chance by the collar. The rest of Slim-Ginger is draped spread-eagle over the rear fuselage, his boots flapping in the wind. If Hawkeye weren't busy crashing his bird, he'd be hooting with laughter.

Sixty feet over the canal, Happy's engine quits. The Spad biplanes slam hard into the French dirt, bouncing, weaving, tipping, and spinning. Hawkeye and Happy tangle wings and slide sideways, ripping canvas and wire as they careen over the bank, catapulting Chance belt over boots into the water. Happy's red-hot engine hisses and puffs out an enormous white steam cloud as he drifts out of his cockpit and swims for Chance, who is floating face down. Hawkeye appreciates the cold slap of the water while cursing his thick leather long-coat. He dogpaddles toward his mates, not unlike…

Circa 2000

The black Labrador named Fleawagon swam, snorted, and slobbered all over the tennis ball, dropping and re-biting it as he splashed past the eleven-year-old girl with ginger hair and a water skier's vest bobbing in semi-brackish water.

"Gram?" the girl called. "Gram Gram?" She slanted her head and stared at the thin yet durable woman slumped awkwardly in the child-sized wheelchair. Her Gram's head of thick white hair, still sporting amber speckles from her youth, was tilted back, her mouth open. The girl didn't believe her grandmother was dead, though she had nothing on hand to throw at her to test this, and Fleawagon's attack against the beleaguered tennis ball wasn't doing the trick. From a crow's point of view, the two humans and the dog were noisy pests in a large pond set in twenty-five acres of neon yellow mustard flowers overrunning rows of Pinot Noir vines.

The girl could paddle back to shore only twenty feet away, pull herself up onto the weeds, yank Gram down from the wheelchair (careful not to let her fall, crush her, or pin her down), roll for Gram's car, and… As she pulled toward the embankment, the girl realized the flaw in her plan—she was too short to touch the gas pedal of Gram's giant station wagon, and her own legs didn't work anyway.

"Yes, dear?" Grandma said, suddenly sitting straight up and smiling a perfect denture smile on a perfect day in West Sonoma County. "I think I swallowed a fly. Did I nod off with my mouth open again?"

"You did," the little girl answered, staring at her expectantly.

"I might lie to you sometimes, but it will always be interesting," Gram said.

"Aaannnd you don't think that's weird to tell your granddaughter?"

"Did you figure out who Hawkeye is yet?" Gram continued with mock impatience.

"But you didn't finish the story! They just crashed at the river! The enemy is on top of them! And how did Chance get into Happy's plane?"

"Do you know where Belgium is, pond frog?"

"*Oui, madame, das tue ich.* It's between France and Germany. But Gram, how did Chance get into Happy's fighter plane?"

"Right, dear." Gram flew her flat palms one above the other. "You see, Happy positioned his wheels over Chance's head so he could grasp the axle between them. It's known as a strut-pluck. But that's not the hard part." Her hands twisted. "Happy rolled his plane over so Chance could get his feet onto the underwing and grab a wing spar, stretch for the edge of the cockpit, and pull himself up. Where it usually goes wrong is while the plane is turned sideways, trying to fling you off. Once Chance reached the cockpit, Happy clutched him and slowly rolled upright. I think poor Chance just ran out of strength. You okay in there?"

"I'm fine. Get your hat on, Gram."

"Smell that cut grass? That'll ambush me later." Gram plucked her floppy hat out of the dirt. "Shall I continue?"

"If you promise not to fall asleep again," said the little girl.

Gram stuck out her tongue. "I can neither confirm nor deny warm-sun-cool-breeze narcolepsy." The soggy Labrador brought the ball to Gram, and she wrestled it out of his teeth. He bobbed and juked, happy as a new car salesman. She threw it surprisingly far for an eighty-two-year-old. Fleawagon leapt with joy. Gram adjusted her hat, smiled at her granddaughter, sucked in a deep breath, and…

Hawkeye and Happy dogpaddle Chance out of the water, lay him down, and unbutton his coat. A halo of glistening burgundy quickly forms in the dirt around his head. Small-arms fire cracks arrhythmically, like the drums of a novice marching band, overlaid by the ruptures of big artillery not a quarter mile away. Suddenly, Hawkeye stands straight up, his lungs endeavoring to keep up with his raging brainpan, one fist jamming his hip and the other shielding his eyes from the low autumn sun. He scans the scrubby riverbed surrounding them. No time! All the planes are busted; even if one is flyable, they have no fuel. He smacks himself in the forehead. *No time!* "Fuck *cet enchevetrement*," he spits, unable to believe he is out of options, searching for the impossible. He scans his surroundings but anger fogs his concentration. They are way out of position, too close to the front, too far from the rear, and miles from an intact village. Chance's only hope is a vehicle. *It has to be now.*

A new sensation grows in his gut, past his hunger, past his world-record thirst—always thirsty—past grief and loss. His head falls, sure Chance is a dead man. He takes a deep breath and tastes the bitter root of *powerlessness*.

He jerks toward a rustling sound coming from a ruptured hedgerow behind him. The ground shudders, and something immense comes crashing through. A spooked, riderless horse of at least seventeen and a half hands bursts onto the river road and stops. A black monster of bone, muscle, lashing mane, and keen eyes locks right onto Hawkeye, who glances to his two friends. The horse flinches and gallops away in a cloud of pitched dirt. Hawkeye falls back onto his ass and, without thinking, gives a sharp whistle. The sprinting horse disappears.

Gone! That was his moment, lost now. "Dammit to hell!" he screams. He wants to run after the horse but can't bring himself to leave his wingman. Hawkeye couldn't explain to Hap why he whistled again. But how else does a boy round up his ranch dog?

The earth rumbles again. In a sudden cloud of snorts and twitches, the monster is upon them, towering over them—wild-eyed, uncertain, but in apparent need of a master… or food. They observe his English-made saddle and tack, and Hawkeye slowly approaches Monster, murmuring soothing sounds. He extends his left hand, his right hand pulling limestone grass from the ground. Jittery and ready to bolt, Monster, his black coat glistening a gunmetal blue, cautiously sniffs at Hawkeye's fingers, letting him stroke his long, broad nose, but more interested in his other hand. They hoist Chance up onto the saddle. Happy holds the Royal Army horse's bit. As they mount, Hawkeye murmurs, "Neutral on the reins, Hap. I wager this fellow knows the way."

The field ambulance is located in an abandoned German dugout, ill-equipped for serious injury, yet serious injury is all they see. Hawk and Hap gently lay Chance onto a horse blanket and fold a long coat for his head. A gaunt medico, no older than a teen, bandages his neck wound.

"In toe-curling pain, he is," Hawkeye whispers. "Please give him morphia."

"Och aye," the medico blurts. "We've not laid eyes on morphia in a damn dooble fortnight."

Hawk pulls Chance's head onto his lap as the kid tilts brandy into his mouth.

This longest of days finally doffs its cap to night, and Hawkeye pulls his flying helmet off to rub his head and loosen his shaggy black hair. He would never be able to adequately describe the shape and texture of his wartime exhaustion. But this moment, seeing Chance tended to, that they *were* able to get help, was a disproportionate relief against the innumerable desperate moments that never gained such. It was enough to push the powerlessness problem back a few rows and had been delivered by the biggest horse he'd ever seen. Yards away, the full moon rises behind Monster, who gobbles grass like a starved madman.

"He'll barnie oan," says the medico with a Scottish smile as he plucks the brandy from Chance and escorts it to the next dark patch of dirt and man.

"Hawk?" Chance mumbles in a blood-gurgling whisper.

Hawkeye bends close. The command, *You must defer*, comes cleanly to his mind, as does, *Dear Mrs. McClean, it is with sorrow I inform you of your son's…*

Not now. Defer.

Chance raises his bloody left hand, something hidden in his fist. He opens it, and Hawkeye clasps a tin yo-yo.

"Lefties only," Chance says with a wink.

The manifold layers of war-bonded love between them are well-represented in that wink. That night, Hawk's brain, without his permission, will retrospectively calculate this moment as Chance's last seven heartbeats in all of creation. Abruptly, stretcher-bearers lift Chance and turn him toward surgery. Away they go, unaware that, within two steps, Chance is not of this world.

In the darkening woods at the army rear, Hawk and Hap watch their comrade disappear. Hawk's ticker-tape brain floats a sophisticated argument for why *he* must be branded unlucky. *Who loses six wingmen?* He pushes this aside and replaces it with memories of Chance's excellent flyer's instincts and the humorous, dirty things he would do with that yo-yo. The two American volunteer pilots don't need to discuss what comes next.

Dragons.

The pilots jump from a Yank-built Liberty lorry and march off the field at Rembercourt Aerodrome, now under the command of the American Expeditionary Forces. Happy watches Hawkeye bury the yo-yo in his coat pocket and pull goggles from his oil-smeared forehead. The day the 95th Pursuit Squadron formed, the pilots and crew took one look at Ernie Campbell's keen blue eyes and slightly hooked nose, and it was a nickname gimme.

Muddled twilight smears into the rough-hewn ready room, where the men are bent over a small table. The square-jawed bomber pilot, Wally Schirra, offers a scrap of paper and a chip of black lead to Hawkeye. Hap rolls a cigarette, and a dark brown bottle is passed between him and Wally, who says, "The morning is wiser than the evening."

Hawk and Hap fly their hands in arcing gestures, muttering schemes. Wally tips back the bottle, swallows loudly, and sets it down in the middle of the paper. Hawkeye traces its outline. Hap snatches the bottle as Hawkeye bisects the circle with a long dark line. They will kill the Black Dragons—they just lack machines.

The squadron adjutant officer appears out of nowhere, his hat pushed back above beady black eyes and a pencil-thin mustache. *"Capitaine, il y a quelqu'un ici pour vous voir."*

Hap turns. Adjutant presents him a folded telegram. *"Merci,"* Hap says.

Hawk croaks out, "Who?"

"RAF Commandant du 47 Escadron," Adjutant announces to Hawk.

"De rien," Hawk says. Then, to Happy, "Here?" but they are interrupted by a fire wagon in bootstraps and patterned breeches stomping through the doorway, approaching, saluting, and extending its hand. It says, "That's the spirit, ol' boy. Name's Collishaw, of 47 Squadron, Royal Air Force." Words spit from his lipless mouth fast as a twitchy cat.

Hawk and Happy share a look, but Collishaw's brakes are busted. "Appears I've caught you in the nick. At this ripe hour, a few long cigars and brass caps are stinking up the inside of a hidden rail carriage poised to scribble their indecipherables on a parchment that will finally end this bloody business. The Allies don't need you here, Mr. Campbell, Mr. Arnold. This war's all but over.

We need you in Russia. Bloody Bolsheviks have some loony ideas. Count you in, what?"

Hap's considerable eyebrows arch as he absorbs Collishaw's astounding news. He shares another glance with Hawk and offers the telegram. To Collishaw, he says, "Here's your man," and jabs a thumb toward Hawk.

"47 Squadron?" Hawkeye inquires.

"Defenders of London." Hap nods, genuinely impressed.

"Sopwith Camel jockeys," Hawkeye adds.

"Just so. That's our bird." Collishaw beams.

"Fine bird, Commander." Hawk gives him a wily smile.

Hap squares up to the stout Brit. "War's over?"

"By midday tomorrow," Collishaw pips, a sudden weariness slacking his face.

"Time enough, then," Hawk starts. "Listen, Commander, the Hole in the Wing Gang is busted up and could use a couple of Sopwith guns for one last sortie. After which, you can count me in. If, that is, I'm assigned to Odessa."

"Not so fast, Captain." Happy claps Hawk on the back while holding fast on Collishaw. "Hey ol' boy, wouldn't you know it, Hawkeye here is going to be a papa, which means we're also regrettably low on cigars. Count you in, what?"

"But Grandma, the Scottish medic said Chance would make it!" Little Twyla complained.

"Not yet," Gram said. "I'm full emergency war power, high-speed compression! Diving brakes fouled!" At the water's edge, Grandma Twyla bounced in her granddaughter's wheelchair, one shoe held high in her hand, the other lying neatly in her lap while her bare feet remained submerged in 1918. She relented, interrupting her tale, "He did. You're right. You'll pardon my trench French for some of the above?"

The little girl silently chewed on that. "Poor Chance. But Gram, how high is seventeen and a half hands?" she asked while performing a lopsided pirouette.

"Almost as tall as your papa."

"Six feet!" Twyla convulsed, spinning.

"That's right, super-soaker." Gram cackled, then sneezed like a tortured goose.

"Bless you. Who *was* Hawkeye?" she asked with a shiver in her voice.

"Oh, you ready to come out?" Gram teased.

"No!"

"Okaaay."

"Poor Chance," the little girl mumbled again and poked her fingertips out of the water like a shark fin, her eyes fixed on the cattails ringing the pond. "Th-they h-h-have to k-kill the Dragons," she added with a shudder. "What's a Bolshevik? Wait! C-c-captain Campbell? Isn't that… th-that's your name? Wait. Wait—"

Gram pulled her feet out of the water and rose from the child-sized wheelchair. Little Twyla's chin quivered. "W-what? You-you c-c-can't s-s-stop n-n-now?"

"Right. Come on."

"Awww. Hawkeye was your uncle? No. Your brother?"

"My brother was—no. Hawkeye was much older."

"Wait! Great-Grandpa?"

"Bull's-eye."

The girl's eyes widened. "Your dad… was Captain Hawkeye of the Hole in the Wing Gang?"

"Yep. My papa had a sense of humor once. I was told."

"Hawkeye was Great-Gramp Gramps?"

"That's right," Gram said. "Welcome to the Western Front. Fighter pilot swagger was invented right here." The elder Twyla smiled at the younger Twyla and decided she was old enough to hear more. *She's small, but not of brain or heart.* She pushed the wheelchair forward. "See, sometimes an angel is a horse."

"Angel of death, you mean."

"That's why we had a big horse on our farm named Magpie or Maggie or Pie-face, depending on how she was minding you. She was my very first love. Papa thought she was good luck."

Her granddaughter squinted. "Good luck? But Chance died."

"True, but not before Monster rescued all three of them."

Little Twyla stopped spinning, bobbing only slightly, not a blink or a fidget. "Did you ever crash your plane, Gram?" she said, now pulling toward the shore, shivering in the purple shade of the vines.

"A few times, little bitty, but that was a war of a different color."

"They really hated the Dragons, huh? What did Great-Gramp Gramps name his fighter?"

"Wild Bill."

"Did your plane have a name?"

Grandma Twyla's eyes sparkled. "She sure did. My bird was a thing of beauty. Fast, agile… She really took care of me. Annie Oakley was her name."

"Annie Oakley. Annie Oakley." Little Twyla singsonged it a few times while Gram's eyes focused on the middle distance and its leafy, converging geometry.

"My people. My land. My fight." After a dozen memory bricks restacked, she blinked back to the present. "Someday, you may feel that way about someone, or a cause, or a man, little bits."

"Tell me about your war, Gram Gram. Please!" she begged through chattering teeth. "Please?"

Grandma Twyla pushed the wheelchair into the water, stopping when it reached the top of her shins. Her namesake twisted herself up onto it, and Gram backpedaled her onto the shore and wrapped her in a towel.

"Mmm, you're slicker than snot on a goat's glass eye!"

"Eeew-uh, Gram!"

"Your Aunt Cornelia had a hundred sayings like that. She liked to pretend she wasn't a proper Southern belle. C'mon, we'll pick this up tomorrow at daycare."

At daycare, Gram woke next to a large window overlooking the freeway-split town of Santa Rosa. The afternoon sun slammed into the whitewashed room, scarcely slowed by the beige vertical blinds. She watched Little Twyla survey the long row of overstuffed chairs fitted with old people reading, listening to stories through headphones, or snoring, while colorless fluid dripped into their arms and chest ports. She supposed her granddaughter was working up some kind of fable about this place. *She'll have a new name for it in no time.*

"Ya know," Gram said, startling Twyla, who had been sure she was out cold. "I've lived so long, Doc says they have to replace my replaced hip."

Little Twyla rotated her chair and played with the tape near Gram's collarbone, where the line of poison inserted. "Dad said you could get a bionic hip from the VA if you don't mind mad scientists experimenting on you."

"Just think how much faster I could limp!" Gram chuckled and groaned in equal measure, pulling on the curls hanging over her granddaughter's ear. "Where does the pole vaulter world record stand these days?"

"I'll look it up!" Little Twyla said, reaching for her laptop in the saddlebag hanging behind her.

"Rhetorical bluster." Gram made the "time-out" gesture. "Stand down, Dora. Okay, before you nod off again, I'll tell you about the most famous Marina now and my Marina later. Two Marinas. Just like there are two Twylas."

"But why was she famous?"

"The *most* famous," Gram said, nodding her head, feeling a tinge of guilt for such easy manipulation. Little Twyla volleyed back a sheepish smile, which Gram figured meant this smart little one felt the same in reverse. "You see, Russians are creative people, tough and lovely," Gram started. "So, on this day in 1938, exactly twenty years after Hawkeye found out he was a father, three of the most robust Russians you've never heard of were attempting the impossible. Flying over the Far East—not flying well, mind you—their ANT-37 converted twin-engine bomber, named Rodina, was going down. The long-distance world record was at stake! If they crashed now, nothing but a desolate wilderness awaited. But Marina Raskova was bone-tired, her blue eyes were red, swollen, dry, and itchy, and her five-hour dehydration headache remained sharp and vengeful. On top of all that, her cheeks hurt from a prolonged navigator's squint. She suddenly knew if she didn't get out of the Rodina right then, she would be the first to die."

"But why?" Little Twyla asked.

"Because of no fuel! Because of bad weather! The plane was going down. Marina was in the navigator's nose bubble. She would die on impact."

"Get out, Marina!" Little Twyla said, bouncing in her chair.

"I know! So, she blew a kiss to her best friends, opened the hatch, and they would follow. They were all devastated. They had almost done it! Nearly accomplished the first nonstop, trans-Siberian flight with an all-female crew." Gram sat up straight, eyes wide. "Twenty-six hours and six thousand kilometers. No fuel, no visibility, no world record. That meant they would *not* celebrate that night in Komsomolsk, *not* drink a superior vodka or bathe in a steaming hot *banya*. *Not* sleep twenty hours in an actual goose-feather bed. *Ni za chto!* Instead, they would look forward to years of explaining their failure to an endless committee of committee members, how they came up short in aviation technology, bravery, and squaring with the West."

Little Twyla squeezed her head between her hands. "But it's not her fault!"

"Mmm, in the Motherland, everything is your fault," Gram said with a knowing smile. "Marina Raskova leaped into the frigid Far East gloom, plunging at historically disappointed-Imperial-Empire velocity—no warm rising air to slow her descent. Then it struck her!"

"What? Something hit her?"

"No. Worse! She panicked."

"What?"

Gram stood, patted invisible pockets, and looked up at her lost friends. "She forgot to grab her emergency kit with its compass, knife, rations, whistle, torch, Lyster bag, and vial for water purification. The thought of crashing, of quitting the Rodina, of her personal failure in the world record attempt, wasn't as infuriating as not being able to find her crew, her friends! That kit would have helped her do that."

"Ahh, naw!"

"After crashing through a tree, she unbuckled her pack and, in her pockets, found a watch, smashed sunglasses, and her prized Dr. West's Miracle-Tuft toothbrush, which she'd bartered for and won at the aircraft factory from a comrade's traveling spinster aunt. As she cut down her parachute, a wolf cry rang out and echoed off unseen rock walls."

"What the—?"

Gram pivoted around, eyes wide. "*Good reminder*, Marina thought. She considered her parachute. By night, it would be her warmth, and by day, when she stopped to rest, her ground signal."

"Um… the wolf?"

Gram sat down and grasped her I.V. stand. "It would take Marina Raskova ten days of hiking, climbing, sheltering—with only scant food and water—and running from werewolves and zombie bears to find her friends. Who, it turns out, did not bail out behind her…"

Little Twyla was seized and breathless. "Instead, they crash-landed the Rodina *and survived*!"

"What's that?"

"All three aviatrixes would be awarded Hero of the Soviet Union medals."

"Wait! Medals for crashing?"

"Can you believe it? They were the first women in all the history of the Great Russian Empire and Soviet Union to receive such an honor."

Little Twyla pinned her bouncing knees together, her eyes fixed on her grandmother. "The most famous Marina!" she cried, clapping her hands.

Gram grunted back to her feet. "Roll with me to the loo."

"How do you know I have to go?"

"Because our bladders were assembled on the same factory floor."

They shuffled and trolleyed along the length of the poison distribution center.

"Zombie bears," giggled Little Twyla.

"I know, that's ridiculous. I meant zombie moose. So, for her failure and shame, Marina Raskova was a national hero."

They stopped at the door to the bathroom. Gram caught her breath and kissed her granddaughter. "That's how you become the most famous Marina. Next Wednesday, when we come back to… what did you call this place?"

"Pick Your Poison Wrinkle Pharm with a p-h," Twyla quipped with a giant smile.

"Close enough!" Gram said. "The P-Y-P-W-P? Hmm, flows about as well as a Ukrainian argument. Then, I'll tell you a story about a nobody girl who talked to animals and wore a dirty pair of Livvie Campbells."

"Livvie Campbells? That's *bahl gorm*," Twyla said happily.

"Your Boontling is improving!" Gram said. "But you just said, 'Shoes are good eating.'"

"Close enough!"

*

Little Twyla scanned the Revolutionary War wallpaper covering Gram's dining room. The women depicted wore long dresses and worried faces; the men and boys all carried rifles. She rolled past a snoring Fleawagon toward the refrigerator and stopped in front of the calendar hung by dogface magnets. She read, "On this day in 1922, the BBC began broadcasting radio in the United Kingdom, and Lt. Harold Harris made the first parachute escape from a stricken aircraft, establishing the Caterpillar Club." She flipped pages. "And in accordance with the Treaty of Rapallo, the Germans instituted the first postwar flying school in Lipetsk, Russia. In 1925, Benito Mussolini became the youngest premier in Italy's history." She gasped theatrically for breath. "In 1941, President Roosevelt signed the Lend-Lease Act designed to supply England, China, and Russia with weapons, warships, and planes."

"You're a good reader!" Gram hollered from the living room. "Now come here and look at this."

"That's a weird calendar. What's the Caterpillar Club?"

"An exclusive club to which no one ever wants to belong."

"Why?"

"Because it means your airplane was doomed and you had to bail out and survive so they could present you with a pin."

Little Twyla smiled. "Like Marina Raskova."

"Precisely."

Gram handed her a brightly painted wooden doll no more than ten inches tall and shaped like a squat bowling pin.

"Oh! What is it? Is it new?"

Gram turned to the fireplace and lit kindling under small oak logs. "Oh, yes… no. Not new. I've had that for eons, from your long-lost auntie. Just pulled it out of the closet this morning."

"Aunt Anna." Little Twyla turned it in her hands. "Pretty." She felt its weight. The round top was painted with a red headscarf above the woman's face in blond wood and an intricate folk dress of green, gold, and black.

"Russians love dolls. They remind them of their history. That's my family," Gram said. "Well… your family, too, Twyletchka."

"Twyletchka?" the child repeated with a genuine smile of surprise. "Twyletchka, Twyletchka, Twyletchka!" she said, like licking a new hard candy. She rattled the doll. "I like it!"

"Have you never seen a Matryoshka doll? I'm sorry, I just swear I've shared—"

"It feels like she has insides."

"*Da, harosho*. Grab her bottom and her top and twist."

A big smile grew as the girl twisted, unstacked, and fit the halves back together, creating a row of eight dolls from tall to small, each with a distinct gender and face.

"That one is my mother," Gram said, putting the second smallest doll in front of Twyla. "That's Ernie—"

"Hawkeye!" Little Twyla cried. She placed the great-grandpa doll into the great-grandma doll's bottom half, then put on his top.

Gram pointed to each doll. "Anna, Lewis, Marina, and that's me. Those are the people inside me. I am me because I am them. Your family are those inside you. This little one is so small, but it can open, too."

"Does a baby go in there?"

Gram hesitated and unconsciously thumbed an object in her pocket. "That's for another time. Let's get your things in a pile so we don't have to rush about like headless chickens when your papa gets here in the mornin'."

Twyletchka made clucking noises and stacked the dolls, turning each face toward her just as they disappeared inside the next.

*

"Gram Gram, what if sloths had invented timekeeping?" inquired Twyla's granddaughter as she wheelied her wheelchair back at daycare.

Gram hooted and coughed in the PYPWP. "They'd be right at home in this place, huh?"

"Roger!" Little Twyla pipped.

"Roger! Drip slow, talk fast. You ready for a sloth-less tale of adventure?"

"Almost. Just need to stand up and stretch my legs for a minute," Twyletchka said deadpan, a wicked smile close at hand.

"Heavens! You've got your great-aunt's disturbing sense of humor."

"Who?"

"Shut yer Pop-Tart slot, and I'll tell you!"

The child snorted, and tears of laughter sprang forth.

Gram leaned down, hugged her, and whispered, "Twelve years to the minute before the Rodina crashed and made Raskova the most famous Marina, Twyla Campbell of Boonville, California was eleven years old."

"Hey, that's you! Finally! Jeeeeeez!"

Gram laughed anew. "Is it okay if I tell this in third person? Makes the hard parts easier to recount."

"What's third person again?"

"Well, like I'm tellin' someone else's story, not mine."

"I don't mind. Just make the move, Gram Gram!"

"Of course, my mini marsupial."

t w o

Who Are You?

The leafless Gravenstein apple tree cradles the eleven-year-old girl, her mop of persimmon curls tilting and bouncing as she scans the Milky Way for any movement among the sparkles. Though the stars are cheerful, they are too weak to render color upon the pitching black hills, oak and redwood groves, sheep, and barns of Anderson Valley. She's waiting for a shooting star, her usual prompt to go to bed—though she isn't sure she'll ever sleep again.

Eucalyptus, bay, and rosemary particles drift and mingle with smoke from a neighboring trash fire, tamping her growing anxiety. *Where is Llewellyn? He had said someone would be back to get me before sundown. Papa, Mr. Haliday, or maybe Doc Hyatt is what he meant?* In the field today, Llewellyn had yelled at her, screamed at her, to fetch Doc Hyatt. *But that was only this very afternoon. How can it already feel like a dream?*

Indeed, only hours ago, she'd stood next to the field, breathing hard in the late afternoon sun. A forty-pound can of avgas toppled from Llewellyn's handlebars and glugged out noxious fumes in waves. He had grabbed her, hollered at her, while her face was clamped between his hot, calloused hands. Her eyes darted across the field; images before her twisted in strange undulations. She was unable to turn the shapes into meaning: rows of low alfalfa; Papa's aeroplane in a smoking heap on its back, the landing wheels stuck straight up like the feet of a stiff dead bird. She remembered two lumps, one with Papa's white t-shirt and another, smaller one Llewellyn had covered with his jacket. *Where is Tommy? No, that's not right… I saw it all later, when I came back with Doc.*

The sound she remembers is an insistent mourning dove or the crackling of dry leaves. Llewellyn was so upset. He was furious. *Was he scared, too?* His face stretched in a jerked spasm of teeth and spit, pressed like small photographs under high pressure and flicked with an unyielding thumb. No. *That wasn't*

Papa's white shirt today; it was his flying scarf from his war. Llewellyn had pulled it out of the ground, and it leaped up and twirled, fluttering and snapping, as if trying to escape.

But now, in her dark apple tree, the trace of eucalyptus thins and threatens to dissolve away. Two owls query the monochromatic, breezeless landscape. Shortly, they are joined by the *yip-yip* of coyotes and the rustling of either Lavender the skunk or the Robbers, a family of obstinate raccoons. This was her lullaby every night since she was five—when the unpruned apple tree just beyond her window slowly stretched to her, inviting her out.

At first, she would climb into the tree, play with her doll, and listen to the owls and bats until she got sleepy. She needn't worry about Tommy tattling on her, as he was out in a blink; he slept like Polina, her apple-head doll. She would sometimes put dead crickets or buttons on Tommy while he slept. He would be mad at her in the morning. It used to take hours for Twyla to fall asleep.

Then, when she was nine, Papa pointed out all the constellations available in this hemisphere and their names, but now she could only remember a few. Her favorite targets were Sagittarius, the half-man/half-horse archer who never missed his mark, and the bright red star called Mars, which she considered her sister star, as they were both made of red stuff. Though her sister was not a star at all. "She's like Earth," Papa had said, but Twyla didn't really understand the difference. And there was big Jupiter, which gave her butterfly belly because, "Jupiter has many secrets."

"Polly, look at Sister," she had whispered and squeezed her Polina. She'd considered the distance to Mars and decided it was just as far as the moon, which was big because it had animals, while Mars was small because it had insects. She'd thought about the Big Dipper and couldn't decide whether it would look bigger or smaller from Mars. She didn't remember the archer's name, only that he was called a bridge between Earth and heaven. She could only imagine the log bridge across Anderson Creek and wondered why no one at church or the general store talked about these exciting places.

A flash had caught her nine-year-old eyes. A bluish-white streak came out of the center of the Milky Way and crossed to the western horizon, turning blue, to white and red, and broke into many little stars. "*Yink!*" she'd yelled and quickly covered her mouth, wishing Lavender or the Robbers were there to share her excitement. There were only owls and their one-word call.

Now, the last eucalyptus trace surrenders to the trash smoke. Twyla kicks against the images that come, forming with more and more force. The thought that her entire family is dead, abandoning her here so she is now a sudden orphan, is so ragged and bottomless of construction, she cannot seem to shape it into the wooden box she feels must hold all of it. A dozen ranch chores come at her in a rapid-fire shuffle, a blurred deck of cards: all the things Papa and Tommy did that she wasn't yet strong enough to do.

"Orphan?" she croaks out loud. She can't gauge the true meaning of it, only that it has caused a sense of inward spiraling. She begins to hyperventilate against the fear of tears one could only measure by Papa's long-legged strides. Behind this is the roar and push of a distant, black wave. *But they will be back.* And where is *Babushka* with her stern manner and comforting stories? *They will be back!*

She wants to be five again.

*

"*Dobroye utro*, dragonfly," came an elderly voice, whispered from somewhere behind her.

"*Utro, Babulya*," little Twyla said, when she was five.

"Did you dream?" said the voice.

"Gold egg. Gold egg."

"Oh, and who were you in this dream? Tsar Vyslav? Ivan? Perhaps you were the wolf himself?"

Wriggling from the small bed, Twyla said, "I hear the morning birdie."

Grandmother smiled softly from her rocking chair, wrapped in a wool blanket. Her herb-colored headscarf collected her hair away from her nearly wrinkleless face, save for deep forehead lines. Twyla gazed through the wavy glass window, searching for the insistent bird. Grandmother inquired in Russian, "*Golub', chto ona govorit*, Twyla?" (The dove? What does she say?)

Twyla shrugged and rested on her tiny heels. "*Ya ne znaju, Babulya.*" (I don't know, Grandma.)

Grandmother rose and seemed to get closer without moving her feet or making a sound. She explained that, "Every new day, the mourning dove asks a simple question, but the answer is most difficult. She expects no reply."

Twyla rose back up on her tiptoes. "*Chto, Babulya?*"

The dove continued its insistent query. "Who are you? Who… Who?" Babushka whispered. The birds cooed. "Do you hear it? Twyla, who are you?"

Hunched next to the window was a dresser of drawers upon which stood a photograph of stoic Hawkeye and broad-smiling Happy next to a crashed aeroplane. On the fuselage, a long black dragon bared its teeth and spat flames. The pilot lay on the ground, dead. Twyla concentrated closely on the bird's words and stared at the dragon.

A sawing, thrumming sound suddenly filled the air and shivered the window, collecting her attention. A royal blue biplane sparkled brilliantly in the early autumn light as it turned sharply just above the trees. She was down the stairs and across the orchard faster than any other five-year-old in Anderson Valley history.

He rose up from the cockpit of the Curtiss JN-4 biplane like a conjuring wizard in his black leather war coat and goggles. Ernie "Hawkeye" Campbell lifted eight-year-old Tommy out of the front cockpit and set him onto the lower wing. Tommy vomited down onto the grass. The top of his head looked like a brown duster being shaken of its dirt. When his face tilted up, his bright green eyes focused squarely on Twyla. Tommy glared. She smiled.

Ernie hopped off the wing, his greatcoat billowing as he landed on the grass with a soft thud. Tommy retched out the last of his apple pie breakfast.

"*Sortir de l'avion*," Ernie said, gesturing for the boy to back away. Twyla happily bounced toward them. Ernie pushed her away. But this was a mistake. She came back. Tommy shoved her hard.

"What wrong?" she asked.

Ernie ignored her and grabbed the tail of the plane, lifting it and pushing it forward. He was the strongest man in the world. Twyla waited for reasons, waited to be picked up, hugged, or set into the magic flying machine. She got none of these, not even a glance.

Ernie turned the plane and settled the wheels in worn divots between two baby pine stumps while tears tumbled down his daughter's little cheeks. She ran toward the house. Tommy wiped at his mouth and chased after her.

"Twy? Twy?" Tommy yelled.

She stopped. "No, Tommy!"

"Ya *backdated chuck*! Papa ain't in no mood!" His face was screwed up, and he had a wheezy cough. "Don't be such a dumb girl." But his chin quivered. His eyes became glassy, and his face flushed. "Slow-witted and ignorant," he spat.

These words bounced off the dry leaves and embroidered directly onto her brain. She felt heavier than a flour sack and wiped at her eyes. Tommy ran to the house. Chain clanked, and Ernie grunted as he tied down each wheel and said, "Twyla, go tell your brother *se lavez pour le dejeuner…*" but he stopped short, straightened up, and looked at his leather flight bag. He removed his coat, revealing his plain white T-shirt and overalls, and motioned for her to carry the bag. She missed this. He pointed to it. It was ordinary and brown, but attached to it, there was a red ribbon threaded into a shiny ornament upon which a pointy cross was engraved.

"Oh," she leaked out, dashing forth. He didn't move while she gathered the bag's handles in her tiny fists. She really wanted to play with the ribbon.

"Twy, *c'est juste...*" he stammered, "You're a girl... and girls don't... well... girls are..." He turned directly to her and, for a brief windblown moment, managed a smile. "Anyway... these machines. Men will... insatiable men..." His eyes unfocused for a moment, and he became still as a statue. "This bird will help me carry the post to Ukiah and Fort Bragg and Santa Rosa and beyond." His head tipped forward. "My girl, flying machines'll just break your heart," he finally said softly.

It was a narrow set of words she wasn't sure was meant for her. It would be many years until she understood that his World War's worth of tinnitus hid his own voice from himself, *and* his disappointment with Tommy often landed squarely on her.

With all her might, she lifted the bag and looked up at her father. Right then, only seconds after he smiled at *her*—no one else in all of her giant two-orchard world—an idea sprang onto her tiny chalkboard brain. "Poppy, Poppy? I can help not break Poppy's heart. Then I still a dumb chuck?" She smiled up at him, happy to have an idea. Happy to be helpful. Happy to be five.

Ernie looked at her, pushed his fingers through his hair, and stammered, "Why—why must you look so like your mother?"

*

"Orphan?" Twyla shivers in her eleven-year-old body. Her back hurts, and her bladder is near bursting. She turns tentatively on the branch, peers into her bedroom window, and recoils. The window is black. The house is black and quiet and empty, and not just of her family—no sounds, no lit lamps, upstairs or down. No signs of life at all. The only house she's ever known is a sudden and worrisome stranger. She doesn't want to go in there if her family is really... She cannot go in. She wants to sit on Maggie's back in the spring sun, on Tommy's birthday when Llewellyn constructed eighteen-foot stilts for stringing hops on Porter's farm. When Papa had stunned everyone and challenged Llewellyn to see who was the fastest hop-row stringer. Pies were brought out, and smiles formed on cement faces.

She climbs partway down the tree and jumps the remainder, landing hard on frozen-needle feet. She yanks the overalls off her shoulders and squats in place. Suddenly, shockingly, she remembers, "Oh, Maggie!" *How could I be so stupid?* She curses her searing guts, impatient to be done.

She runs to the stable one hundred yards north of the house, sidestepping the tractor and curved orchard ladders in the near blackness. A whinny floats out of the darkness. "I'm here, Maggie!" she calls. "I'm here!" Maggie snorts and brays out a directional beam all the way to the barn.

Twyla opens the paddock and flings her arms around her horse, willing herself not to cry. She pulls her out to a water trough, where Maggie takes an enthusiastic interest. "Someone'll get us soon, Mags." She glances around the dark ranch and grabs onto Maggie's neck, her eyes finding the dark house. The lifeless tomb.

Maggie yanks her nose from the trough, snorts, and flings her head side to side, flipping water all over Twyla's back. She pays no mind. The big horse bobs her large head while Twyla unconsciously siphons warmth from her. Maggie stomps her hoof and snorts again, demanding an explanation.

In the dim starlight, the oversized raccoon family ambles by, a settling rhythm of normalcy. Twyla finds Mars and is comforted by this red sister. She grabs Maggie's tail and, using the edge of the trough as a step, jumps up onto her haunches. She scoots forward and lies down, grabbing coarse mane hair firmly between her knuckles, then buries her head.

I'm no orphan. I'm no crybaby. Tommy will call for me any moment.

*

Circa 2000

"Non-small cell lung cancer," the short, round-faced doctor said in a voice that reminded Gram Gram of Kermit the Frog or Yoda. He flipped through her chart while she sat on the edge of an examination table, poised like a prison escapee moments from launch. Twyletchka sat quietly in a recliner in front of the hospital window, her wheelchair nearby. Covering the walls was green paint of such a distinction as to encourage nausea from healthy visitors.

"I happily smoked my way through the 1950s and '60s right alongside everyone else," Gram said. "When I turned fifty, it just seemed stupid."

Round-face raised his chin a little. "That may have contributed. We don't have the cause narrowed down yet. It appears anyone can acquire this, smoker or not. I'll be back later today. In the meantime, a nurse navigator will visit." He turned and walked out.

"Navigator?" Gram pipped. "At this altitude?"

"Do you want me to call Father?" Twyletchka asked.

"Absolutely not. Let him finish his workday unmolested. Common story, I do believe I'm right. You come into the shop needing a wheel repaired, and you end up with dry rot throughout your whole cylinder block."

"You're mixing metaphors again."

"You are correct. Life is a mixed metaphor."

"Oh, I didn't realize—"

"Well, pay attention, roller girl," Gram said. "They'll tell me I can still get a new hip, but why don't I wait 'til after they've attacked my lungs? Might save them the bother. I'll proffer my fear of healing too slowly, they'll wait 'til my sass reaches terminal velocity and I lose all boundary layer control, then they'll knock me down with chemo and excuses."

Twyletchka transferred herself to her wheelchair, rolled over to Gram, and put her head in her lap. Gram snatched a deep breath. "Get comfortable. Next up, Gram solos."

"Wait… what? You can't do that!" she protested. "Apple-tree Twyla's in the dark with Maggie! Where's her family? What happened to everyone?" Twyletchka pulled her head off Gram's lap, defiance in her eyes. Gram imagined her granddaughter bolting up onto her feet, widening her stance, and crossing her arms. "Where's Twyla's family? You can't leave me hanging!"

"Okaaay! Okaay!" Gram shot back. "Sheesh, princess! I promise I'll circle back. I just can't… I'm going to jump ahead several years, but I'll come back. I will. I just need a little sunshine."

*

The autumn sunrise saturates the steep, round edges of the Marin Headlands. The Pacific wind weaves the tall grasses in restless coils. Cold air off the water makes the cockpit frigid and Twyla's hair more vermilion in the blue shadow light.

Southbound at sixty-five feet of altitude, she's wedged in a young man's lap in the rear bucket of a Fleet Model 2 biplane. Comforted by her tight confines and his warmth, she tracks a lone pelican skimming the wave tops of the rocky shoreline just below her. No flock or team or family, and only inches off the water, the expert glider surveys the shallows for breakfast. She wonders if pelicans leave their families forever.

The pilot tilts them away from the beach, adds throttle, and climbs toward the apex of a single hill, skimming the wheels across grass tips. When they clear a massive emerald mound, Twyla shrinks in her seat and covers her open mouth. Her entire field of view is overwhelmed by two massive metal towers—steel-gray monoliths of vertical superstructure on an impossible scale, easily a thousand times taller than the biggest stock barn she's ever seen. Slung below the towers on what seems like a spider's thread is a train-trestle-like beam spanning a dreadfully wide, watery chasm.

Her eyes tilt up the fjord and behold the entire Bay Bridge, newly minted just a year ago in 1936, connecting Oakland to Yerba Buena Island, then on to San Francisco, where stout buildings stand like cows on the sides of steep hills.

An empyrean wonder accompanied by a disorienting optical skew. It's too much to absorb at once. She quickly slips it into one of her brain flaps for inspection later.

Her pilot, Llewellyn "Lewis" Haliday, lived adjacent to the Campbell Ranch. He came to Twyla's home every week for two solid seasons when he was fourteen years old to get close to Ernie's flying machine. In a blue and white streak, he would zoom up her driveway on his bicycle while nine-year-old Twyla stood spread-eagle—one foot in her tree, the other on her bedroom window ledge—holding Polina. In his jeans and white undershirt, Llewellyn would *harp Boont* with her papa, who would sometimes offer the boy a *horn a zeese*. As he drank the coffee, he might sometimes glance up at her. He might smile his big teenager smile, sometimes. She could see his white teeth from fourteen feet high and what must have been forty yards away.

One day, after thanking her father for the coffee, Llewellyn saluted, jumped onto the pedals, perfectly balanced, and in three quick hop-turns, reversed the bike's direction and peddled away. From her perch, she giggled at his carnival trick and watched him go. And though he disappeared quickly behind the thick apple trees, she tracked him, knowing all along he must ride past exactly four gaps in the rows of trees.

"Teddy Bear, Teddy Bear, turn around," she sang.

He whipped by the first gap.

"Teddy Bear, Teddy Bear, touch the ground."

He blurred through the second gap. *Backward on the handlebars!*

"Teddy Bear, Teddy Bear, touch your shoe."

He whizzed into the third opening standing up, one foot on the handlebars and one on the seat, hands stretched high.

She giggled and lowered herself down onto her window. "Teddy Bear, Teddy Bear, that will—"

He stopped in the fourth gap, beaming right at her! He bent at the waist and took a theatrical bow. Twyla yipped, giggled, and clapped her hands. And he was gone.

This cloudless and shimmering morning, Llewellyn pilots just fifty feet above the north tower of the art deco colossus. Straight down, hundreds of men stretched all over the spider webs and great arcs of metal tubes wave their arms. The workmen seem almost to expect this aerial tourism.

Smoke, burning coal, diesel, and oil fill Twyla's nostrils. She waves to the men and suddenly remembers they are called the "Halfway to Hell Club." Until just now, she couldn't picture what this meant. Llewellyn waves, too, then points to the west, where dozens of naval vessels, a fleet, gather just outside the Gate.

Every kind of fighting ship is represented. He yells into her ear, "Hey, that's the *USS Pennsylvania*! And the *California*! The *Colorado*! *Indianapolis*!"

On the horizon, like ghost islands, are three immense ships. "*Taish*! Carriers *Lexington, Ranger*, and *Saratoga*!"

"How do you know their names?" Twyla shouts back.

"Every boy knows the ships of the line. When I was just a skeezix, I wanted to be the captain of the *Ranger*!"

She smiles in wonder and turns to take in the action down on the bridge road. Every inch is covered with speckles of black, gray, and brown fedoras; pink, white, yellow, and green parasols; and flowering and feathered hats in diverse shapes and colors. And people are... *Gliding*? Twyla wonders. *Ice skating? Stupid! Roller skating!* Twyla squeals with delight and squeezes Llewellyn's legs. They soar past the south tower and down along Crissy Field at the Presidio Army Base. The expansive grass field at the bottom of the towering superstructure is a lime-green blanket on the banks of the bay.

"Wiley said we can petrol here. I wonder where all the planes are!" Llewellyn bellows with a quick turn of his head.

"There's a few!"

Excerpt from:
SAN FRANCISCO CHRONICLE – MAY 28, 1937

The following is today's schedule of events for the grand celebration.

11:00 a.m. – Flight over the bridge by five hundred planes from Navy aircraft carriers Ranger, Lexington, and Saratoga.

11:30 a.m. – Bridge opening ceremonies at Crissy Field.

12:00 p.m. – President Franklin Delano Roosevelt will press a telegraph key in the White House, declaring the span open to the entire world. Automobiles will commence traveling over the bridge simultaneously from the San Francisco and Marin sides.

12:30 p.m. – The arrival of the United States Fleet—forty-two ships in total. Ten capital ships will be led by the USS Pennsylvania *under the command of Admiral Arthur J. Hepburn, followed by the* California, West Virginia, Texas, Maryland, Nevada, Idaho, New Mexico, Mississippi, *and* Colorado...

10:00 p.m. – A grand fireworks display. Fog permitting.

They descend over the Presidio. There are three familiar aircraft, plus one of a shape Twyla doesn't recognize, parked at the west end of the field. A steep bank to port sweeps their view across Alcatraz Island and Sausalito, completing a crop-duster-style, extremely short approach. On their left now, the massive spread of barracks and marching grounds slope up the hill to a line of eucalyptus, Monterey pine, and bay trees standing like watchmen over the Gate.

Twyla feels Llewellyn's excitement at being near anything military. While still several yards above the grass, the engine dies. She knows the hut with the windsock is his target. His game: coast all the way to it without overshooting or having to restart his engine, thus avoiding an embarrassing 180-degree turn. She wrestles her gaze from the bridge to someone moving swiftly past that sock, a skinny man in a fine, dark-blue uniform, walking at an energetic—or angry—clip.

Llewellyn's bright blue and borrowed Fleet touches down without the smallest bounce, tracks straight in, and waddles to a stop forty feet short of the sock. Pulling their helmets off, Twyla's smile is stuck in place by the wonders they just flew over and that remain stretched out before her. Llewellyn claps his hands together and says, "Hey, not bad, if I do say so! Was scheming inside fifty feet of the sock."

"I guessed as much," she says.

"I've never seen that many people in one—"

"You're really pushing it, Mr. Pilot, sir!" comes a voice from the skinny, definitely angry walker turned pimple-faced lieutenant.

"I'm sorry… uh," Llewellyn stutters. "Uh, Lieutenant… I—I was—"

"You here for the leaflets?" Pimples interrupts.

Lewellyn cocks his head, swings a leg over, and jumps to the grass. "Errrr. Yes? Yes! The leaflets."

Pimples shoves a thumb behind him. "That's your bag." A swollen canvas mailbag lies in the grass between the sock and the hut. "Now get the hell off this field!" He turns to go.

Llewellyn spins to Twyla, who is motionless in the cockpit, staring at the bridge, her face frozen and loony. He turns back.

"Yes, sir," he says. "Oh, sir?"

Pimples stops, half-turns, and shoves his hat a little farther down his forehead.

"Two things will make us *bahl*—uh—bird, sir: petrol. And why the hell do I need to get the hell off your empty field?"

Pimple's hat holder tilts, and his mouth opens. But before he can say anything, another voice hits Llewellyn like a shovel to the forehead. "Boy, who in all of Yankee creation said you could land your box of kite parts on my field?!"

Llewellyn turns to a thick, red-necked, towheaded sergeant, but before he can even sputter a reply, a third man in a matching uniform marches up to Sergeant's ear and, with just enough volume for everyone to hear, says, "Sir, Lieutenant Martin is puking his guts out again."

"General Lee's outhouse?" Sergeant murmurs, then turns back to Llewellyn. "You haven't answered me!"

Llewellyn ping-pongs his head off the mailbag and Twyla. "Leaflets!" he yips.

"Leaflets?" Sergeant convulses and glances up at the bridge. "Wap Ghirardelli!" he spits. "Get your fuel and get out of here."

Llewellyn marches toward the mailbag. Pimples mumbles about fetching the fuel wagon, and Sergeant retreats.

Llewellyn hefts the bag up to Twyla, who grunts it into the forward bucket and pulls out a sample. The leaflet is a golden color with black printing. She reads, "Del Monte Cannery invites you to enjoy Ghirardelli chocolate in full view of the world's newest wonder. Free chocolate bars all day! Hooray for Ghirardelli! Hooray for the Golden Gate!" Her smile manages to get goofier. "Look, Lewis, it's for the celebration." She waves the slip.

"Hold it!" thwacks Sergeant's voice as he drives a pointy finger directly toward Llewellyn. "I've got four planes to move and three healthy pilots. I'm conscripting you for the afternoon." He gestures over to the group of parked planes.

Llewellyn's eyes bug out, and his head jerks as if he's not sure he heard correctly. Two hundred yards up the field, he locks on to some kind of Jules Verne illustration—a Fairchild 45, a four-seat monoplane with a slick, white, closed cabin is being hand-pushed away from three Fairchild 21s that, in contrast, look like they're right out of a Bronze Age boiler room.

"Two hundred birds are about to land here," growls Sergeant. "Hundreds more at Hamilton and Mather in Sac'."

"Yes, sir," Llewellyn replies and turns to Twyla in a fit of restrained euphoria. He tries to speak and fights against the urge to laugh and shout. He's been asked by the military to fly a plane! There's been no greater moment in his life thus far. He clears his throat, smooths his jacket, and turns to Twyla. "Meet me in Sacramento." His voice squeaks like an adolescent despite being well into his twenty-third year.

Twyla sucks in a short breath and chirps, "But how do I get there?"

Lewis gestures to the aeroplane beneath her. An icy thunderbolt cracks through her body, nineteen years old going on eleven. *I must've heard him wrong… What's that noise? Can't hear him over that sound of… He can't leave me!* Twyla's racing heart seems to be stumbling upstairs in oversized boots, kicking every rib along the way.

"Twyla?" Llewellyn goes on, "Just like we practiced at Tuttle's."

But she can't breathe. She wants to help so badly. She wants to believe she can help, just like a grown-up man. Suddenly, she can't think of one preflight procedure. *Me?*

He plucks his map from the cockpit. "Back across the bridge, follow Redwood Highway out of Marin and all the way up to Santa Rosa." His excitement ramps up. "It's not direct, but all of it will look familiar. You'll have a clean shot of Mt. Saint Helena ahead—turn soft-east over the Mayacamas, and on for twenty minutes. That should put you on a course to intersect Sacramento and Mather Field. They asked me to help!" He beams, boyish and irresistible.

She wants to kiss him but doesn't dare in front of these men. He jumps down and runs directly toward the Fairchild 45.

"Hey, pup tent!" Sergeant barks. Llewellyn skids on the slick green. "Don't you dare touch that Fairchild 45!"

Twyla lowers into the cockpit and gawks at the instrument panel, which has lost all meaning, though there are only a few instruments and switches. The magneto, RPM, and oil temperature indicators seem to smear together. Standing at her portside wingtip, Pimples stares at her, his head bending under the weight of his last particle of patience. The only thing she's sure about is the curved spirit level that indicates when her wings are tipped or not—critical to know when flying in low clouds or fog. She plants her feet on the rudder boards and grabs the stick. Her left hand flips a switch; her right hand and feet check the control surfaces. She pulls out a plunger knob and nods to Pimples, who quickly moves to the propeller. Her fuel gauge reads full. *When did they refuel me?*

She taxis for a couple hundred yards toward the gorgeous, sculpted women securing the pillars of the Palace of Fine Arts building, perhaps eight hundred yards away, and turns back toward the bridge. Adrenaline spikes her heart. She sucks in the clean Pacific breeze, opens the throttle, and blasts up the green. Her wheels spin free, and she ascends toward the as yet unpainted bridge—so, the Gray Gate Bridge—and angles north.

She levels off at the exact height of the suspended roadbed, zooming along 220 feet above the water and only 50 feet from the 100,000 celebrants. The men in dark brown and black wool suits tip their hats toward her. The women wear colorful dresses, costumes, feathered hats, parasols, and smiling faces. She waves with what feels like someone else's hand. Crazy quilt laughter escapes her. It strikes her that, in spite of her nearly paralyzing anxiety, she probably appears the confident modern pilot graciously waving to the throng. Amelia or Lindbergh out of Oakland Field, except she's going the wrong direction—so more like a comedy routine of Lincoln Beachey.

She forms up with Canadian geese over Vallejo's Mare Island Naval Shipyard, where walls of steel hang on cranes and bright blue stars flicker beneath her from a constellation of welders. She suddenly realizes she's turned too soon and angles back to the west. She steers her undulating shadow over the chicken farm mecca of Petaluma, then just shy of Santa Rosa, she angles east. Twenty-five minutes later, the watercolor ribbon of the Sacramento River wriggles along, reflecting the sky and drooping trees. She finds downtown Sacramento and, ten miles beyond, a tremendous airfield.

One thousand feet below, sprawling Mather Field is covered in hundreds of planes of every shape and size. She's suddenly not sure which direction to land. *What does Llewellyn say? Look for anything indicating wind direction— bending trees, weathervanes, flags, a kid with a kite…*

Two crisscrossing runways offer four landing directions. She watches a twin-engine plane take off toward her. *That's it! Downwind approach, base leg!* The sun vanishes, an eclipse that drops her into instant deep shadow. She glances up into a falling metal grain silo scarcely yards above her. "Jiminy Cricket!" she shouts and jerks her plane down. "XB-15" is painted on the colossal vertical stabilizer of the four-engine heavy bomber. It dwarfs her little plane, shoving her around in its wake. *Would you look at that?* The pilot is waving at her. *Oh, that's nice. He's greeting me.*

A *get-the-fuck-out-of-the-way!* expression creases the bomber pilot's red face. She waves back and decides to follow him down. She fancies herself a flea on the back of a Great Dane as she slides in behind the behemoth. Later, from an astonished Llewellyn, she will learn this is the largest plane the United States has ever built.

Bucked, pressed, and juddered in the agitated air of the bomber only one hundred feet ahead of her, she concentrates: *Back off the power, but not too much. Easy. Keep your nose up. Not too much! More power. Rudder against the crosswind, less power.*

She absorbs the immense runway and shouts into the slipstream, "And that's the most cement I've ever seen by a million!" She lands very close to the bomber, surprised by how difficult it is to keep her plane steady. The moment her wheels touch the ground, a speeding Jeep flying a red-and-white-checkered flag careens toward her. She shouts into the wind, "I did it! I did it! Lew! Oh, Lew!"

The Jeep gets closer, and the driver gestures for her to follow. She zig-zags up the taxiway into a flight line bulging with military aircraft in colors of khaki green, navy blue, and flat gray. The Jeep zooms away.

Shutting off her motor, she steps up on top of the fuselage and turns 360 degrees. She is a speck in an ocean of military sheet metal.

"Hey, little girl?" a gruff voice floats up to her. "Where's your pop?"

Twyla spins around.

"And get that toy off my apron," says a sunbaked, shirtless mechanic standing between two beautiful Stearman Kaydets. He pulls a cigarette from his ear, jabs it in his mouth.

She says, "I'm looking for Lewis… Llewellyn. Do you know where he is?"

Sunbaked spits tobacco bits from his parched lips. "I know a dozen Lewises. What in the green Ganges is a broad like you doing here?"

She climbs down onto the radiating concrete. "I brought Llewellyn's plane… to pick him up. I just don't know where to find him."

"Welcome to the military, Red!" he barks around his cigarette. "Go to the ATC office below the tower. Ask for the officer in charge. His name is General Chaos." He spits again. "He'll fix you up."

Acres of heat-warped military aircraft with hundreds of men crawling over and around them strike Twyla as Llewellyn's perfect ranch yard. *He will be full of excitement tonight.* That she cross-country soloed, saw the new bridge, flew with geese, and landed behind a monster plane from the future would take a back seat to his day. *That's okay*, she muses. *There's room enough for both of us to have great days.*

She spots him one hundred yards away between two men, flying hands. Abruptly, she remembers the stolen mailbag of golden chocolate certificates and runs toward the men, shouting, "Ghirardelli!"

t h r e e

It's Far-Fetched

Excerpt from "A Family History" by Jesse Haliday

As a teenager, Llewellyn "Lew" Haliday was known as the Carpenter Bee King of the Valley, so labeled by his best pal, Wiley "Heelch" Felton. He milked, tanned, fermented, hammered, hefted, sawed, and sheered for fourteen hours every day. Interviews with dozens of folks here in Boonville revealed Llewellyn knew almost everybody in the valley and most from Bodega Bay to Fort Bragg. He was an action-first, sort-it-out-later young man.

"If Lew ever sat down, his jaw would be grinding, his knees bouncing," Heelch reported. "When he wasn't blabbering, he was eating bits of everything in sight. His world was fleeting, dusty, and edible. While charlin' in the dairy, he could easily drink a gallon of milk. Berries, fruits, and wild mushrooms were a few reasons to slow him down for plucking. I always knew when he'd just been with the cows 'cause he smelled like 'em, and his belly sloshed when he ran past."

Wiley told how Llewellyn had so many ideas and was so full of nervous energy, it manifested impatience with most everyone. He made his father, Gerald, crazy. How does it work? Why? Mechanicals, science, laws, traditions, and taboos all alighted in one of two possible apple bins: measurable fact or subjective opinion. He wasn't too fond of ignorance. If he couldn't find a taboo or tradition in nature, it was no more real to him than the color of wind.

Wiley suggested that everything changed mightily for Llewellyn in 1932, when he was eighteen years old.

*

Llewellyn jogs behind a two-horse wagon sagging with baled hay, his flying cap and goggles in hand, and jumps on. The slim ledge of tailgate is just enough to sit upon and lean his back against a prickly yellow-green bale. Seconds later, he jumps off and runs up the main street of downtown Boonville—population: several dozen.

A floppy hatted woman unties her Barb horse and backs away from the general store's hitching post, revealing a flatbed truck parked askew. Music floats into the street. Whispering Jack Smith's "The Song Is Ended" manages a commendable clarity as it escapes from the phonograph player set in the store's open window. Llewellyn squints at the truck and skids to a stop on the wide dirt avenue. He stares at its small rear window. His chest tightens, breath unconsciously held. A ginger ponytail pokes out the passenger side. He beelines toward it, slowing as he draws near. In the truck's tiny side view mirror, he spies a small freckled nose, dry lips, and fingers rubbing an eyebrow.

"Twyla?" he says. "S'that you?" His own freckles and rectangular face point toward her.

"Oh!" she starts, turning, her fourteen-year-old body recoiling at his sudden proximity. "What's that? Llewellyn?" Her voice is reedy and semi-hoarse.

"What are you doing here?" he asks. "What happened to you after… That is to say, I haven't seen you since the funeral… I mean—it's been three years… How are you? Where have—"

Twyla's head spins back toward the store. A large man clomps out into the sunlight, his eyes dark and his olive skin sunburnt. He carries a forty-pound box of nails in his gloved hands and says, "Boy, *tsit tsit!*" His Italian accent is obvious with just one word. He shoos Llewellyn with his fingertips.

Llewellyn backs away a step. Twyla straightens and tracks him in twitches. Llewellyn returns her attention, keen on her eyes, taking in the details of her face.

"Uh, my apologies," Llewellyn says. "Sir, I'm looking for ranch work. Do you need more hands in your orchard? I'm a good machine operator if you have any gasoline-driven mechanics."

The nail box slams onto the truck bed, echoing off the store windows like a rifle shot. The large man climbs into the cramped cab and jabs the air in front of him. Llewellyn jumps to the front bumper, catching Twyla's downturned eyes. He disappears below the hood and pops back up. "Where is your ranch, if I may ask, sir?" he says, sounding too interested. The man remains silent, his contempt for the boy crystal clear. Llewellyn, suddenly needing both hands, spins around, searching for a place to put down his leather cap. *Hood of the dirty truck? No. Hitching post? No, still wet with horse slobber.* After a none-too-manly panicky pirouette, he finally pulls his flying helmet on, grabs the engine crank handle, and whips it around hard.

Twyla peeks over the dashboard at him. The truck sputters to life, and Llewellyn jumps back as they drive away with a belch of lead smoke. Twyla stares back at him, receding into a cloud of dust. He pulls off his helmet; his brain has a new wad of thoughts to chew on.

"Capitan Llewellyn!" The booming voice plasters his ears. He turns to Wiley "Heelch (whole cheese)" Felton, all six-foot-five blond inches of his best pal, standing amongst wooden barrels at the curb of the Boonville Hotel, gesturing for help. "Tell me again, what exactly is it you do?"

"Wiley!" Llewellyn hollers as he turns and dashes the other way. "Hang on! I'll be right back!"

"What am I, new?" Wiley shouts. "The work is here, skeezix!" Wiley spits tobacco, hefts a massive oak barrel onto his shoulder, and walks it into the hotel, stopping short to admire his buddy's pluck.

Llewellyn crosses the broad avenue and bursts through lollygaggers in front of the white-steepled church. His name is hurled at the back of his head as he descends into the blackberries of Robinson Creek, then up onto Schoolhouse Road. He flashes across a quarter-mile of open field and climbs into a bright white biplane. From six hundred feet altitude, Llewellyn follows a rust cloud attached to Twyla's truck as it threads up Anderson Valley toward the even smaller town of Philo. She vanishes under thick redwood groves, appearing and disappearing in a painfully slow meander, forcing Llewellyn to circle around and spend his meager petrol to avoid outrunning her.

He scans the ranches ahead and realizes where they're headed: Edna the Witch. *Edna and Mr. Campbell were cousins or something.* His fuel gauge is forlorn.

*

Twyla's brain sputters with Llewellyn's image. *He looks like a man now, and he saw me. He saw me!* She stares at her hands and carefully glances at the large dark-haired man named Castor. They jostle up the valley through thick, slowing air. She hadn't been to town in months and tries to recall the last time— back through an endless stream of days, each a copy of the last. Dirty dishes stacked to the kitchen ceiling, her chapped, withering fingers pushing pounds of boot mud from beneath the table to the back door… Endless soiled laundry, bed sheets, and hungry animals. She reeks of the sharp, sour stalls, aches from moving pasture stones that appear by the dozen every morning. *The music from the store was so beautiful; grown-up music for other people, not meant for me.*

The Gultch Ranch is a five-hundred-acre sprawl of cattle, sheep, and hops. Standing behind the truck, Twyla glances back at the house. Aunt Edna rolls to a stop on the small dark wood ramp. Her black, stringy hair bends like bird nest twigs at her shoulders, emphasizing her sunken eyes.

"*Vieni qui*," the big man says with a "come along" wave.

Twyla grasps the box of nails with both hands. Grunting with all her body weight, she claws at it, letting the box fall onto her thighs. She jerks it up with a gasp and follows him.

One hundred yards from the back of the house, they stop next to a massive pile of split redwood posts, stacked six feet high by ten feet across. Castor pulls a dog ear of paper from the sternum pocket of his overalls and unfolds a crude drawing of the pastureland in front of them. To their left, two hundred yards away, is a vertical post. He points to it and sweeps his hand across the field to another post, two hundred yards opposite. He throws a thumb toward the pile.

"Lay each end to end. *Oggi*. Today." He smiles, baring yellow teeth, and walks away. "Return in four hours," he adds.

She runs to stop him. "Please. Castor. *Guanti*," she pleads.

He studies her for a moment, reaches into his back pocket, then hands her his gloves. "*Buona* idea."

She pulls on the big leather gloves, tucking the sleeve ends of her brown wool shirt into them and shoving the oversized shirttails into her stiff denim overalls. She circles the waiting redwood pile and pulls two wooden boxes in front of the heap. Climbing up, she grabs a post by its end, tugging it toward her. It's heavy, sixty pounds to her ninety. She takes a deep breath and heaves it quickly to the balance point of her shoulder. Teetering on the imperfect boxes, she missteps and crashes to the ground, the post bouncing off her head.

"Oh! Ouch! *Taish* it!" Blood flows from her ear. She pulls herself up and levers the post off the ground. She drives her shoulder into its center, lifts, and overshoots. Its momentum slams her onto her back. The post thumps next to her head, then falls across her chest. She rolls out from under it, collecting redwood splinters. Crows mock her from the tops of oak trees. She tries again, succeeds, and waddles like the town drunk out to the field.

At the future fence line, panting and shaking, she drops the post to the ground and immediately loses control, diving out of the way. It crashes next to her. She sucks air in rapid spasms and rolls onto her back. The field around her is neon green. Though it's now June, the soil here is so fertile the grass began poking up back in December.

Llewellyn looked like a man. Llewellyn! Right there at the truck! No chance to talk to him. He seemed... Didn't he know all along where I was? Does anyone know where I am? Is this why no one writes or visits?

She drags a post, no longer able to carry them on her shoulder. She pulls it along three or four steps at a time, straining against utter collapse, saturated in sweat, grunting, and willing herself not to cry.

A voice comes tumbling into her ears, bisecting the treble clef improv of crow scat and red tail hawk screeches: "Twyla?" Llewellyn runs up and stands in front of her. "I found you," he says, panting and sweaty.

She drops the post. They look at each other, both breathing heavily. She stares up and down the valley. "How did you—?"

"Where have you been? Here? This is your aunt's place?" he asks.

She nods and lunges at him, hugging him for all she's got.

"Twyla, what? What's gotten into—?"

But she grips him tightly. He pushes her away, and tears pool in her eyes. She wrestles them back and holds his gaze as he stares at her like he's trying to answer two or three important questions.

He looks at me like I'm an animal—a discarded animal.

Then his face changes, softens, and he smiles slightly, reforming her— transforming her. Now, he looks at her as no one has ever looked at her before. He finds the nasty assembly of reddening splinters at her neckline.

"Have you seen Maggie?" she asks. "Do you know where she is?"

He shakes his head and surveys her workload. "She was a good horse. So, that pile needs to be strung to that far post in a layout fashion?"

She nods.

"Awright, that's bird. We work first, then you're coming with me. Do exactly as I say, and we'll get to dessert in a crack."

Back at the post pile, he stands one of the posts up on end. "You pull 'em and stand 'em. I'll run 'em out to the line. Have them ready quickly; it'll be worth it." He snatches his gloves from his pocket, pops the post up on his shoulder, and runs.

Twyla blinks in disbelief. In the distance, he lays down the post and runs back. She rubs the scar on her eyebrow, bounces her palm off her forehead, and climbs the pile.

Ninety minutes later, what would've taken Twyla three days to accomplish is done. Llewellyn is a dirty, sweaty mess, topped with a stupid grin. "Come on," he says, grabbing her hand. They run up the valley, past happy-go-lucky cows and sheep.

"But I have to be back soon," she protests.

"Naw! You did your work for the day," he says with that same grin.

She glances up the valley at the white speck in the distance. "Whose... aeroplane... is that?"

"Mine! That is... if all goes well, it will be soon."

They reach the plane and fall into the summer grass, panting and thirsty—always thirsty. The fog line recedes up the valley, the air nearly ticking audibly as it warms.

"What are we doing… here?" Twyla pants.

"There's something I want to show you."

"What is it?"

He points straight up. "It's up there. Come on." He pulls her to her feet.

Her eyes widen. "I have to go back. I can't be here. I don't want to get in that."

"It's okay. You did your work!" He lifts her up onto the lower wing.

"No!" She pulls away and jumps down. "I have to go back!"

"Twyla, you're okay. You finished your work." He appears so earnest and single-minded. He has an idea for her, an idea of a troubling kind, though she is hard-pressed to reason it out. Her life is so closed, her movement so severely restricted, that his idea is like looking into the empty house of a dead family.

Llewellyn relents, disappointed. He scans up and down the valley. She thinks, *Maybe he really doesn't know what's happened to me, and…*

"Then I'll fly you back!" he says.

"I'll get in trouble."

"But you feel you're due back now?"

She nods.

"*Yink* it." He shrugs. "It'll take us twenty minutes to walk back, or we can fly in a flash."

She glances down the valley, back to the aeroplane, then into his glistening, sincere face. *Castor may already be looking for me.* She pulls on her eyebrow as her anxiety grows. *Llewellyn came. I'm* not *a ghost. That machine makes ghosts. He found me. He's not a ghost*, she reasons, her body shaking. She closes her eyes, crushed by a new problem: choice. An unfamiliar burden. *But I don't want Llewellyn to leave.* She takes a deep breath and climbs up on the lower wing, immediately feeling light-headed. *No, not this!*

"It's okay, Twyla. I know every wing nut and washer on this bird, and she does one thing really well. Squatting in the grass is not it."

Twyla's heart suddenly feels like an engorged watermelon trying to beat its way out of her chest. Imagining the faces of Aunt Edna and Castor constricts her throat. She turns away from them and squares up to the aeroplane. Her knees buckle, and she sits hard on the lower wing.

Llewellyn steadies her. "I know," he says softly. "The last time I saw you was… I don't mean anything, but… I just… wish I could… I feel all kinds of bad for—"

She wrestles her mind away from its fear and tries to bind onto Llewellyn. *He found me. Followed me here, did my chores, was always a good friend to my family before they…* Her watermelon heart is now half-hollow; its floor has a small round pool, where black water sloshes about in agitation as if it wants to bust a seam, form a mouth, and scream. She murmurs, "I'm not a ghost."

Llewellyn is close enough that she can feel his moist breath, warm with the faint scent of bacon, machine oil, and sarsaparilla. She looks him fair in the eyes. He meets her stare, unblinking and solemn. "Don't leave me," she says and jumps into the black water.

Twyla stands, shaking, on the cockpit seat, watching Llewellyn over the nose of the plane.

"When the engine catches, push that knob all the way in!" he shouts up while pulling the propeller around a few times. She hears the pistons plunging and rising and some soft clicking. Llewellyn jumps up and yanks down hard on the blade. The engine sputters and coughs. She pushes in the church organ plunger, and the engine eases. He grips a handful of grass, flings it into the wind, and watches it float southward. He plops down behind Twyla, essentially putting her in his lap, then smiles and nods. The noise and sudden blasting prop wash force Twyla lower. He guides the plane up a narrow path between bunching cattle as they accelerate over cow pies and gopher mounds. She turns to his goggled face, behind which an enormous cloud of dust billows away.

After a jolting dash across the pasture, the airship instantly smooths. Her heart corks in her throat. The craft angles up steeply so that, in seconds, they are four hundred feet above Anderson Valley. Twyla's face is full of wonder, her eyes darting back and forth, up and down, trying to see it all.

Llewellyn banks the plane around, pointing them back up the valley toward town. Twyla can feel butterflies thrilling her stomach. She covers her mouth while tears smear across her temples. He offers his goggles. Donning them, she's immediately drawn deeper into the dream. He points down to the hotel and Wiley's wide face looking up at them, waving his big paws. Twyla nearly jumps in her seat and waves back, excited to be seen. "Hello! Hello! Hello!" she shrieks and turns her glowing face to Llewellyn. He nods and gives a "thumbs-up" to Wiley.

She hugs her elbow to her face because if she lets go, she'll burst. They vault up to one thousand feet. Twyla traces the main road stretching out toward the little village of Philo and identifies a couple of ranches, when Llewellyn's hand guides her fingers onto the control stick.

"Fly!" he yells in her ear.

"What?"

"Fly!"

He squeezes her hand tighter around the stick and lets go. Her eyes widen, and she shakes her head. The plane slips left. Lightning cracks through her scalp; her watermelon heart clobbers her ribs. She grabs the stick with both hands and pulls it right and back, immediately correcting the turn. Her head ticks back and forth. A buried memory suddenly flickers into shape—the first time she "flew." It was the windstorm of '27, when she was nine and had a family.

When she had a family. When she was nine.

*

That March, the orchard had been tossed like a giant salad. The temperature differential between the cool and often foggy Mendocino Coast and the hot inland valley had summoned a bedeviling wind. Trees hissed, whistled, and wailed warnings. Anything light and loose—leaves, tarps, shingles, line-dried laundry—was in the air.

When Tommy stumbled into the clearing where his papa's aeroplane was tied down, Twyla was already there. "What are you doing?" Tommy accused.

"I came to check on Rocket!" she said.

"It's called a Jenny, not Rocket! Papa asked me to help, not you!"

The sturdy biplane's wing wires whined and moaned. Twyla thought Rocket looked nervous. Her wings shuddered, and the grass field before her undulated. They watched her for a while, and Twyla knew she wouldn't be allowed to help, to even touch Rocket. But she liked being out in the windstorm. She slipped away from Tommy before he could get her in trouble. Following an impulse, she flattened herself behind a clump of milkvetch and rosemary, like a cat, to watch her brother.

Before too long, the wind subsided and the aircraft stood undisturbed. Tommy declared, "The stupid thing is fine," and turned toward the house, already forgetting about Twyla. He disappeared and an assembling uproar of dried leaves and dust took his place. She watched Rocket rise from the ground like a kite on a three-foot string. Out of nowhere, Maggie vaulted directly over Twyla's head and landed in a conflagration of dust-churning hooves, flashing tail, and excited snorting.

Suddenly, Llewellyn fell out of the sky, rolled like a hoop, and popped up onto his feet as spiraling airborne loam plastered him in detritus. He leaped for the aeroplane's tail and attempted to hold it down while grasping for a length of rope strewn about his ankles. His grunts and curses tumbled through the agitated air.

The wind moderated again, leaving behind an odd quiet. Maggie calmed and strode over to Twyla, sniffing at her and eyeballing her for a treat. Twyla reached up toward her muzzle when a sudden gust crashed around them. Maggie bolted, catapulting Twyla away from flying hooves and landing her on her ass in the semi-prickly rosemary.

She watched Llewellyn wrestle with the plane's tail, give up, and dash for the cockpit. "Twyla! Get the stick!" he shouted.

But how does he know I'm here?

Another belch of wind, and Rocket twitched, her tail jerking against a poorly tied rope. The rope paid out, and the tips of the wings waved at her. Twyla rubbed her eyes and stood up. Rocket awoke like Maggie struggling to her feet after last winter's illness. They had made a new bed in the paddock for her. She didn't get up for four days. Then, on that fifth rainy morning, the Mag-Pie lurched, snorted, stumbled up, and sneezed. Sneezing animals always made her laugh. Twyla had giggled for a solid week. "There, there, Rocket girl, don't be afraid of the—"

"In the cockpit… push the stick forward!" Llewellyn hollered again.

"Oh!" she said, not knowing what a cockpit was, but perhaps it was where Papa sat. She climbed onto the lower wing and pulled herself up, slithering over the edge and down into the wooden seat, headfirst. She stood up, turned, and watched a small section of the tail flapping up and down and side to side. There was a walnut baseball bat between her ankles twitching fore and aft. On the floor, a wooden foot bar slid back and forth in quick jerks. *When you grab a horse's reins, set her bit square*, she remembered Papa telling Tommy, but this she already knew.

The plane rocked and tilted around her. Impulsively, she grabbed at the dancing bat and pushed it forward, tilting the aircraft's nose down, slinging herself against the small windshield, gashing her eyebrow, and plopping onto the floor of the cockpit. As she tried to stand, she elbowed the handle to the left. Rocket tilted left and threw her into the sidewall. "Oh! Ouch! Whoa, girl!" She climbed back onto the seat, steadying herself. Something was in her eye, and she rubbed at it. Blood covered her fingers. She reached for the handle.

Llewellyn was suddenly next to her. "Keep the stick forward!" he yelled.

"This?" Twyla squinted to hear better, but he was gone. "The bat, right?" Twyla let go of the handle and leaned over, but her view was blocked by the lower wing. *Did the wind just get stronger?*

"Push the stick forward! Twyla! Push it forward!" His voice weaved like meshing gears into the hissing gale. Rocket lifted again, and Twyla pushed the stick forward, then back, a little left, now a little right. She squealed with delight. In all of her nine years of life, she had never felt a direct connection to a machine.

Later, Llewellyn would detail to his father how Rocket dragged, flung, and dropped him. But to Twyla, even though she couldn't articulate it, this experience was so startlingly bright and appealing; yet it was so paper-thin, she was forced to transcribe it onto something familiar, a thing she wanted from the bottom of her soul but wouldn't be allowed to keep: the cutest piglet at the county fair. She gently sat Rocket down. A premixed melancholy soaked into her heart for the loss of a thing she did not yet own, could not yet articulate.

"Ouch! That's it! Keep her down!"

Llewellyn rolled out from under the plane and onto his knees, one hand holding his head, the other holding his elbow. He scanned the Jenny back and forth, measuring its rise and fall, then up at the trees and back to the amber hair spinning furiously around Twyla's face. He climbed up next to her and bumped his head. "Corpus Christi!"

"I think she's just scared," Twyla offered.

He looked at her a little sideways and reached for the control stick, pushing it forward a few inches and touching the main wheels to the ground.

"Hold her right here. Please. Right here! I'll cinch her tight!" He dove under the plane again and, in a moment, rolled back out. "Now," he commanded, "slowly pull the stick back."

Twyla did this, and Rocket's tail settled. Llewellyn clambered to it and wrapped the loose rope all the way around the fuselage, just fore of the vertical stabilizer. She said, "Rocket girl, your saddle is cinched," and wiped at her bloody eyebrow.

Llewellyn helped her down. "You okay?" he asked.

"Rocket listens to you. She likes you."

"She wants to fly; there's no doubt. But she ain't built for high winds. Don't know that any plane is. Your eye *bahl*?"

A spiral of loose loam and brush rushed about them as Ernie and Tommy drew up on Maggie.

"See, Papa?" Tommy quickly asserted. "I told you Jenny was okay."

"What are you kids doing here?" Ernie called above the din. "Twy, is that your blood?" But he didn't wait for her answer. "Get back in the house." Twyla pointed at Rocket and said, "I came to hel—"

"Llewellyn, how's your dad's place holding up?"

"We'd just got everything nailed down when I saw Maggie lightning-bolt through Doc Hyatt's orchard. I got her calmed down and came to lend a hand, but she spooked again when I dismounted. I didn't want to just leave without double-checking your bird, sir."

Ernie seemed suddenly somewhere else. He considered his aeroplane and the boy with extra attention, as if looking at a live memory, or a ghost.

"*Jeune homme… merci*," he muttered, hardly audible above the clamor.

Llewellyn nodded and glanced back at Twyla. "I'd better get back. See ya around." But he turned full circle in place and said, "Oh, Twyla, *bahl* hands with the aeroplane!" and disappeared through the genuflecting greenery.

Twyla's small body spasmed in place. *What? What did he say?* She watched him go, watched her papa watching him go. Papa jerked his head toward the house and barked, "Twyla, you have no business out here!" His nostrils flared when he was angry. "Not in this wind and not near the Jenny. Get the potatoes in the water!"

Twyla's heart flattened; a shot of heat went straight to her cheeks, and her chin began to quiver. *But I helped. I helped secure Rocket. Doesn't he know that?* She felt the urge to cry, but also anger—she had anger. It gripped her stubbornly. But she would not cry. Not this time. Not ever! She looked back at Rocket and slowly walked away.

It took 185 steps to get back to the house—120 of them were angry steps, the nettle accusation of her father sticking to the bottom of her shoes. At step 121, however, the neighbor boy's words became a puddle in her path, washing the pricklers from her soles. *I helped! I helped! And Llewellyn saw me.* Her father's piercing gaze and hurtful words stabbed her again, but not to the bone. Something new was there, something like the wind itself she could not color when she was nine—when she had a family.

"We need fuel!" Llewellyn yells over the engine noise and prop wash. Twyla looks back at him, inches from her face. "Turn left." She angles left. "There!" She noses down toward a square of dry grass. "Easy now." Twyla pushes the control stick left slowly. The plane tilts and starts to slip down. He can feel her push back against the slight crosswind. He nods. "Now pull back on the stick so you don't lose—" But she's already started to level out. He nods again. "Now back to neutral. You see that yellow field... Trowbridge's tractor?"

Twyla brings the stick back to center position. Unable to contain herself from adding her own vibration, she squeals out an animal noise, and a warm tingle spreads all over her body. "Crickets!" *I did that! No Aunt Edna. No Castor. No absurd labor or night demons.* The redwood splinters in her chest and arms don't bother her up here. Not even her dead family seems to reach this high. Her feelings for Llewellyn are so strong and at such odds with her brain. Not until she is much older will she realize what Llewellyn has done for her.

For her.

*

She just needs something nice done for her is all, Llewellyn muses while flying toward Trowbridge's farm, contemplating the small redheaded girl, inches from his nose. *I think I'm right.*

The engine dies, and they drop like a shot duck. Twyla screams. He grabs the stick and pushes the nose down into a steep dive, bartering altitude for speed and lift. "Trowbridge pasture it is!" he yells. Twyla turns a horrified face to him. The engine now silenced, he adds, "Everything's bird, Twyla. *Bahl* flyin'."

He circles the aeroplane around the field, turning it into the wind, putting her down firmly, and rolling to a stop not ten feet from the tractor.

The moment his feet hit the ground, Twyla crashes into him, clamping him in a bear hug. He's not sure if she's still scared or just relieved to be on the ground. She doesn't let up. Llewellyn's teenage mind has no waypoints of logic, not one idea about what goes through a girl's head. *Is she fourteen or fifteen now?*

"Okay… okay, there. Any landing you walk away from is a good landing, they say. Just need a little fuel. Sorry if that was a bit…" He feels her shaking, hears soft whimpering. He gently pulls her arms away and lifts off his helmet, tossing it under the wing so it won't get hot in the sun. He can't stand her crying. *Wasn't she just the strange neighbor kid who was always a little too fledgling to catch on, too young to fit in? Is she taigey? No. She's square, just been through a blighted crop of...*

Though there's not a soul to be seen in any direction, he's too embarrassed to put his arms around her, wishing that by will alone, he could make it all go away. In that moment, the something inside him that was excited to see her in the truck that very morning wanted to stop Twyla's suffering. End his own discomfort? No. It was more than that. A string of thoughts he'd bound up tightly for a long time started to unwind. If he were honest with himself…

He begins to add up the times he'd thought about her in the last three years. It was true: He had actually felt excitement when he'd seen her this morning— and sour guilt. *What is wrong with me?* he thinks and fails to reconcile two concurrent truths—how much time *she* has occupied his mind and the fact that *he* had made no effort to find her. *No effort, you neeble-headed harieem!* Nope, instead, he'd made assumptions and collected justifications: *She was probably sent off to some distant relative or an all-girl boarding school in the city. Her fate was none of my business anyway…*

He had done this in spite of his self-imposed imperative that fate should never be an excuse for inaction. He's ashamed of his laziness at the exact same moment he becomes aware of how important she is to him. *Guilty as charged! This is more than unacceptable; it's unforgivable. What the hell, Lew?* He smacks himself in the head and inspects the tractor. Feelings flood him, not the least of which is an intense self-loathing, and, *Lew, you will make Twyla happy. Why? Seriously, Lew, why are you suddenly such a prack? She's none of your business.* "Saturnine," his mother would've said about this girl.

But it's too late. Peering through newly spun glass, he wants to put all the terrible moments of her life in a box and set it ablaze, build her a new box of wonderful adventures to replace everything before. He has so many interests and curiosities—there's so much to share. *That's a bent stick, Haliday! What is wrong with you?*

The tractor's fuel tank is bone dry, as any tractor left this far from the barn would be. He tries, one more time, to stomp out his head's clamor. Fail. So, he picks up Twyla, who clings to him with trepidation, and carries her back to Edna's ranch.

*

When the aeroplane's engine quit, she was sure to die. She wasn't afraid to die, just afraid of everything before the *dying* part—the knowledge of what was coming and the pain if it wasn't sudden. But Llewellyn's quiet confidence had been equally startling. He'd interrupted her thoughts, the racket between her ears.

Instead of crashing and dying, she'd climbed out of the cockpit and spun in place, taking in the trees and fields around her. She had seen them from a new point of view, the perspective of birds. *I flew. I flew in an aeroplane!* Just a few minutes ago, ordinary, inert, and dead things vibrated to life: the grass, the tractor, the sky, and the clouds all looked… closer, brighter, as when the rain clears away at sunset. The inanimate world, dirt-covered and narrow, impersonal and as unreachable as a barn-top weathervane, had changed. Everything, near or far, had abruptly become possible playmates.

She had thrown herself at Llewellyn, tears spreading across her dirty cheeks. She longed for him to hug her back, but it was okay just to press into him. Now, on his solid torso, his breath is coming loud and fast, his face only inches from hers.

She resolves Castor's form from two hundred yards away. Just like that, all the new colors disappear.

At the fence line, Llewellyn sets her down in front of the large Italian. She flinches and steps back, staring at her feet. She steals a glance at the house, where the black smudge of Aunt Edna gazes from the back porch.

"Worked herself into a heat exhaustion, I believe I'm right," Llewellyn offers. "I mean to say, that's a mighty big fence job you're about," he adds on Twyla's behalf.

Castor flicks his eyes between the boy, the completely distributed fence posts, and Twyla.

Llewellyn studies Castor a moment. "The girl just needs some water, a batch of *loweezies*, and rest." He pivots and takes a few paces backward. "Like I said, if you need any help, I work as hard as three men."

Though her head is still tilted down, Twyla tracks him carefully. He gives her a wink, spins, and runs back up the valley.

That afternoon, Castor keeps a close eye on her. He is solicitous with fresh milk and forces her to eat two plates of dinner. She heats several buckets of water, and he carries them to the tub for her. She aches all over, and the scrapes and splinters sting as she immerses herself in the hot bath. She wonders if her aunt aches like this. Castor returns with his dog-eared copy of *Pinocchio* in one hand and a chip of soap in the other. He flicks the soap to her and turns to go. But he hesitates in the doorway, lifts his book slowly toward the window ledge, and props it there. His gaze settles on her adolescent body.

She does her best to ignore this, which 'til now had been easy, as she hadn't cared about herself. She'd shucked away any thought of comfort or gaiety a year ago when she'd started menses. The blood that had scared her to her core had gone unnoticed and without concern by her aunt. This basic women's bond was Twyla's last hope for connection to Edna. Just like then, she would not be rescued here. Tonight, it was different. New thoughts and feelings push up through the redwood slats beneath her, shunting her skyward, out of a choking dirt into clean salt air. Her hands still feel the aeroplane's instrument panel plunger as Llewellyn yanks the propeller, the machine responding to her fingertips. She covers her breasts and squeezes her knees together. Castor bothers her now—bothers her very much.

He stands unusually erect in the doorway with his hands shoved deep into his coverall's pockets. She glares at him, unaware of the rage she's transmitting. It surprises her how good it feels to allow her misery to occupy her face.

Castor abruptly jerks his hands from his pockets and strides toward her, his big boots smashing the floorboards, echoing off the walls. His face screws up in a way she hasn't seen before. She sinks lower into the tub, though there's nothing to hide behind.

He bends down and slaps her hard across the face, slamming her head into the tub's solid porcelain.

Her lower lip, abused by the fence posts earlier, bleeds easily. Her ears ring, and her skull hurts. She turns her stunned face away, overcome by a powerful urge to cry, but she fights fiercely against it. Pulling Llewellyn to mind, she blocks out everything else. Castor unclasps his overalls, pulls off his boots, and unbuttons his work shirt.

Urgent barking, followed by banging on the door, halts Castor's progression.

The moment he disappears from the tub room, Twyla runs to the window.

Elgin the Watchdog is in a fit of disputation with himself. The German shepherd's right paw pins down what looks like a massive beef steak, as if saving it from floating away, while he growls at the stranger in front of him. His simultaneous approval/disapproval is evident in the muffled barks that leak out while he eats in grateful confusion.

Heelch stands in the expiring rays of the day, still wearing his grocer's apron. He seems to nod his endorsement to Elgin and takes close note of the house's front windows, the front door, and *her*. He nods again. He seems tentatively interested in the back side of the house yet proceeds to the front door. Twyla quickly pulls on her clothes and sneaks out. She peaks around the edge of the kitchen, rubbing her throbbing cheekbone.

"*Buono sera, signore*, if I do say so," Wiley says, like a forty watt bulb in a mental ward. "Here are the items ordered."

Castor rifles through the box and snorts. Wiley, still smiling, turns to go, his eyes sweeping past Twyla's half-hidden face, assessing the layout.

"Stop there," Castor commands.

Wiley halts, his smile holding fast. "*Si, signore?*"

"These items not for Ms. Gultch," Castor says like a shallow plate of oil. He doesn't blink.

"*Bilch*," Wiley says. "Well, perhaps I misunderstood. Oh, Willis! Porter's place. I meant to go one ranch farther to Porter's." He keeps his eyes locked on Castor while slowly approaching the box and soundlessly lifting it off the counter. He backs out of the kitchen and turns to go.

"Stop!" Castor bellows. Wiley abruptly turns, his smile a half-second late. The *Ite* crowds him, his expression cemented under heavy, bushy brows as he pulls a gargantuan fist from his pocket. Wiley, to his credit, doesn't even twitch; his smile remains plastered in place. He glances at Twyla, one eye widening as if to say, *If he punches me, I'll get in a lick yet.*

Castor turns his fist and opens it, revealing a Buffalo nickel.

"*Your Italian is insulting*," the *Ite* says.

Much later, Wiley will tell the story of how, at that moment, his heart had diesel'd like a tractor missing all its motor mounts.

Twyla runs back to her bedroom and quietly shuts the door. Through her window, she can see Wiley swipe a few glances around the property on his way to the delivery truck.

Castor's boots clomp to the tub room with a smashing echo, pause, then stomp toward Twyla's corner of the house. She heaves her dresser in front of the door just as it swings open with a bright *smack*. Flinching and grimacing, she shoves harder, trapping his big red hand in the doorjamb. With her foot, she kicks her work shirt under the base of the dresser, where it makes a temporary wedge on the roughhewn floor. She leaps to her bed and jams her back against her blackened window. Aunt Edna's voice peals through the hallway. After a long moment, the thick fingers retract, and the door shuts.

*

Wiley steers the truck down a black road that very night. He shoves tobacco into his lower lip and offers some to Llewellyn, who ignores him. Wiley says, "The west side window looked *nonch*. And I would help you fix your bird, but I have no mechanical skills. You need the boys from Gasoline Alley. I ain't no Walt. He can fix anything. No, I'm more like Doc; I only prescribe righteous solutions at a distance. Or like a baby skeezix, who's cutest when he's asleep."

"Wy, I need girl clothes," Llewellyn says. "Size fifteen-year-old, or anything you can find in small lady. Oh, the horse! Follow up with Rand Cowell at the mill. I need to know if they have that horse. I've got honey, redwood, and apple cider to trade."

Wiley's eyes droop, half-lidded, and he plucks an invisible radio microphone from the trucks dashboard. "Shore to ship. C, Q… C, Q," he mocks. "This is Point Arena Lighthouse, are you receiving? Come in, Captain Llewellyn Haliday of the SS Daydream? Come in, Daydream." His eyes go wide, then half-lidded again. "Are you there, Daydream?"

"Oh, pinch it off, Wy!"

"Everyone," Wiley bulldozes, "but everyone in Anderson Valley has redwood and apple cider."

"*Adult* cider, Wy," he shoots back. "And don't call me Llewellyn. And not Louis, neither. That looks like a girl's name, Louise, when you spell it out. It's L-E-W-I-S!"

"Suddenly you're a backwood gangster English tutor?" Wiley snorts out a laugh.

"No, Heelch, pal. Think a moment. Work through the discomfort of cognizance."

Wiley's eyes cross, and his mouth stretches all goofy, like Bert Lahr as the singing aviator in that *Flying High* picture. Lewis ignores him and soldiers on. "The banks collapsed, the federal government couldn't be farther away from us, and people always have needs. I may not get along with my paps, but he's right about aiming toward the nature of what people really want. Everybody wants something. Why not be at the intersection of all that? And keep a lookout for clean petrol tins." Wiley is unmoved. "Snap yer switch, Wy! I need this stuff tomorrow night! And meet at Zurbroog's at twelve-thirty."

Wiley tilts his eyes moonward and moans, "St. Farmall, patron saint of tractor jockeys, help me!" He shoots Llewellyn a look. "Check your hat size lately, Lew?" Heelch spits tobacco out his window. "Just promise me when the next war comes and you're the new Ace of Aces, you'll be nicer. And take me with you."

"And why would I do that?"

"Somebody's got to porter your titanic pillow."

"Judge Zurbroog's at twelve-thirty," Lewis repeats.

"If I'm late, don't get mad," Wiley whines. "I'm tippin' ten stories in five directions at any given moment. You know how it is?"

"I do. I'll start walkin' at twelve-ten."

"Sure, Dreamy." Wiley is quiet and spits again. "Ya know, I thought the *Ite* was going to clean my clock this afternoon."

"Good thing he don't know about your glass jaw. But tell me something, Whole Cheese. Why did you do that thing with your eyes when you got on your invisible radio microphone?"

"What? Just then?" Wiley turns back like he can see the two of them a quarter mile up the road. "Oh, that. I was playing the role of the sleepy lighthouse commander. Lonely and sleepy," he says, satisfied with his character choice.

"Oh." Lewis nods. "I was too mad to laugh. But I wanted to."

"Next time you see the lighthouse commander, you will," Heelch says with a surefire nod.

*

Twyla wakes in darkness and confusion. A tapping noise right behind her head and the words, "death of the Campbell girl," echo in her skull. She bolts away from the window, freezes, and takes in the sounds of the house. All is quiet. She pulls the dresser from the door just a little to let some light in and strikes her oil lamp.

The tapping returns, rhythmic, familiar, the cadence of a jump-rope ditty. She pulls the long nail out of the sill, meant to keep her locked in, and lifts the window a few inches. "Twyla?" Llewellyn whispers. She pulls the window wider, but it jams, with only a six-inch opening. She leaps at the dresser, shoving it as tight to the door as possible. "Twyla? You awright?"

She covers her mouth and squeezes her face to hold it all in. The lamp puts Llewellyn in orange, flickering half-light. He pushes his face close. "I might have a crowd of stupid questions," he whispers. "Oh, y'ought to know there's squatters sometimes in and out of your papa's house during harvest. They only use the bottom floor, though. They say the upstairs is haunted. *Taish*!" He slaps his forehead. "For god's sake, Lew," he admonishes himself. He's fidgety, nervous. "Don't bother with the valley folk who think your family are ghosts. Jesus *bilch* Christo, Lew!" He runs a hand through his hair—pulls himself together. "But, anyway, what I mean is the upstairs is untouched… nobody goes there. So, I figured I'd go up and pluck you a familiar face."

Threadbear slides under the window. She grabs her stuffed teddy bear and buries her face into it. She whimpers, but only for a moment. Llewellyn steps away from the window, scans the moonlit valley, and shakes his head in… *frustration*? She can hear Elgin growling and eating something. He steps back into the light and takes a deep breath. "Did he touch you?"

Twyla stops breathing, moving, blinking. Finally, she says, "I want to go to school," and sobs in small hiccups.

"Don't worry, me 'n Heelch'll riddle this out. Oh, one more thing. Heelch— uh, Wiley—sent this for you." He carefully slides a pocket watch under the window, yellow gold, delicate, and feminine. "It's called a Molly Stark, or something." Twyla hiccups at it, her eyes narrowing. "Wiley found it at the hotel. He said it reminded him of you. He says it's far-fetched how many valuable items get left behind in this valley."

*

Excerpt from "A Family History" by Elizabeth Haliday

After many interviews, it became clear Llewellyn's biggest befuddlement was why his mother had died when he was eight (cancer). Beth, Elizabeth Eubanks, had been a sharp, resourceful, and witty woman from Cedar Falls, Iowa. Her parents had migrated to Anderson Valley in the 1890s and set up a farm. Corn was intermittently successful due to the foggy summer days. Barley and Italian wine grapes were much more successful.

Beth met Gerald Haliday at the county fair, where he earned ribbons and a modest day's pay on the backs of broncos. Apparently, too many tumbles from unhappy horses ended Gerald's cowboy days early, but not before his stubborn attention toward Beth and laughter at her simplest gestures won her over. They married in Santa Rosa and honeymooned next to the train station at the Hotel La Rose. After a miscarriage, Llewellyn was born.

Llewellyn thought about his mother every day. For many years, photographs of her stood on the low makeshift China cabinet next to the ice closet. "Beth was a mystery to Llewellyn and never far from his mind," Wiley Felton added. "She was there for him during his darkest moments and his greatest victories."

It was said Llewellyn mythologized Beth, shaped her into the perfect consoler of his uncertainties and champion of his successes.

Practical to a fault, Llewellyn's fantasies of his perfect mother were one of his illogical allowances. Unknowingly, Twyla Campbell became the canvas for Llewellyn to brush on his mother's perfect potential. This was likely the source of his encouragement of Twyla, which seemed out of place for the time.

four

Good, Good Men

Lewis withdraws his oily hands from the transmission case of his father's Farmall tractor, arches his back, wipes his fingers on a rag, and paces. His brain, flummoxed by the events of the previous day, grinds on like an automated thresher. "C'mon Lew, take your pot off boil." Running forearm across brow, he thrusts his hands back into the tractor next to his father, Gerald.

"Pop, you know Edna, wheelchair lady? Well, the late Mr. Campbell's daughter, Twyla, boards with her."

"What of it?" snorts Gerald.

"Well, it's just… shoot, I believe things're *jimheady* over there." Gerald doesn't respond. "Well, sir, I mean, she ain't in school, I'm told. And she's only been seen when the *bekin-Ite* Castor comes to town."

"It's none of your business, Lewy," his father finally says. "They've got a big ranch, much to do. Work comes before school. 'N stay clear of that Garibaldi—you'll get a *dreakin'*. You ain't no Charlie Porter. Check the release now."

Lewis traces the foot clutch linkage into the Farmall's transmission. "Did Carl replace this rocker link?"

"Nope, fuel line."

Lewis's attention wanders up the valley toward Edna's ranch. He tries a different tack. "I think, in this new accommodation, the release lever is squeezing too hard. It appears to be free; that is, its position is correct, having been released from its former pressure, but its new situation is even more bound. I believe I'm right."

Gerald responds instructionally. "The spring is there to push the pressure plate away from the flywheel. When the master operator releases, allowing the machine back into gear, the whole enterprise progresses forward, all her parts staying nice and close." Gerald slows his speech and glances at his son. "A natural sequence is followed."

"Yes, sir," Lewis says quickly. "But if you're pushed past the release point and into another bind?"

Gerald tilts back his dirty cowboy hat and glances up the valley. "Lew and your instinct for the regrettable… No farmer in this valley can afford a fight with Ms. Gultch, including me. Don't insinuate yourself into others' business. The Gultch Ranch is a goin' concern. She's got this valley tied up pretty tight. I'm sure she needs all hands on deck, even little hands. She knows what she's doin'."

Lewis grimaces. *But she doesn't*, he thinks. *Not Edna, not a single adult in the valley is concerned with one little girl. Not this one. Not this bad-luck, invisible girl.* At this moment, Lewis knows what to do.

That very afternoon in the general store, Lewis stands frozen among burlap bags of grains, flours, seeds, and powders. Though he's deep in thought, half his brain watches Wiley lift his britches, retie his apron, and rub his eyes while staring back at him out of his cocked head. The other half is unaware he is standing like a statue in the middle of the store, masticating his plan like a needle trapped in a record groove. *Have I miscalculated the Ite? Misjudged the cunning of Edna Gultch?* he wonders.

Wiley asks, "Do you think she'll show?"

Lewis wipes his brow with a kerchief.

"Lew, you're *skiddley*, flop sweating like Harold Lloyd hanging from that clock tower."

Lewis doesn't respond.

Wiley is undaunted. "Sweat lodgin' with the Pomo? Spreading tar on the Live Oak building again?"

"What?" Lewis jerks into his body, suddenly self-conscious. "No, Heelch, just standing here."

"Bird," Wiley says and waits again for his friend to climb all the way out of his stupor. He doesn't. "Well, gangster boss," he continues with enthusiasm. "Two things y'ought to ponder. *Uno*, you're all outta' apple shine and jackass brandy because that Campbell girl's horse cost every last drop, plus futures."

Lewis nods absently.

"And *dos*, I don't know how these things work over there in your Chicago town, but in this tiny village, it seems to me that, if Ms. Gultch and the Ite show up and you're standing in your nervous puddle in the middle of the general store, they might not come inside. This could go *Mert's sister*; you might oughta have your wits."

"Oh! Fine… fine," Lewis says, nodding to a woman and her children entering the store tentatively. The woman nods back, her eyes darting like a mule deer stepping into a clearing. Lewis turns and walks out the back door, where the mustachioed Sheriff Wilkes is talking with two local ranchers clad in matching overalls and brown hats. The sheriff nods to Lewis, who responds by lifting his pocket watch, giving it a tap, and saying, "Ms. Diekman is here."

Inside, Ms. Diekman, wearing a forest green dress and beige heels, shuffles her three young daughters through the store. Lewis and the twins spread out around the shop. Wiley quickly gathers flour for Ms. Diekman, who nervously glances back at the store entrance.

"Mr. Felton!"

Wiley drops his eighty-pound sack with a window-rattling *thud*. Half-silhouetted in the entrance, Edna points her black eyes and yellow teeth in his direction. Castor hovers behind, his hands resting on the wheelchair, eyes darting around.

"Uh, yes, ma'am, that's me, since 1914," Wiley says in a wobbly voice, color coming to his cheeks. He scolds himself, partially recovers, then winks at Ms. Diekman, who has ducked behind a shelf of Mason jars.

He plods toward Ms. Gultch, who says, "Castor, my foreman here, says you've botched my long-standing account." She accelerates toward him.

"Yes, ma'am. No, ma'am. Um, not me personally."

"Where's Gordon?" she demands.

"Oh, he's up in Eureka. Rats got into our accounts and ledgers, so we need you to resign your credit—"

"I've been supplying this store with dry goods since before you were born. How is there any question about my credit? Other way 'round, my boy! I'm owed money from Fort Bragg to Fort Ross." Her eyes are bloodshot; she seems to be roiling for a boil and actually hisses while plunging forward, her bony knees bumping into Wiley's shins.

"Oh, not a doubt, ma'am. If you'll just come into the manager's office, this will take but a moment," he says with believable contriteness. Any moment, she will spit in his face. He slowly backs up, turns, and gestures for her to follow.

Edna's eyes flick to Castor, who's ogling a pail of ice cream perched atop a rapidly melting ice block, then trollies after Wiley. Castor pivots toward the ice cream table, behind which Lewis stands, wearing a cobbler's apron and a smile. He tracks Ms. Diekman, who is peering fearfully at the Italian from behind a shelf.

Castor approaches Lewis. "Scoop of vanilla or vanilla with blackberries?" Lewis offers in his best Sunday polite.

"Berries," Castor growls.

"Sir, it's fortunate you're here. I've got news from over the hill." He smiles, harpooning a wooden spoon into the cream, and begins to stuff a wax-paper cone. Castor looks bored. "As it happens, there's a hundred men in the breadline over in Ukiah just waiting for your job." Castor's dark eyes slide onto him.

"That's right, sir. If you want to keep your pillow at Ms. Gultch's ranch, you will bring young Ms. Campbell to town every morning. She will attend school every day. You will then drop her at the Haliday ranch every other day, and you will never tell Ms. Gultch. If you touch her again, Sheriff Wilkes will come collect you."

The block of ice drips an accelerating cadence onto Lewis's boots.

"And if you ever bother Ms. Diekman again, or me or Wiley is beleaguered in any way, boss lady will learn all about your treatment of her niece. No, I believe I'm wrong. The *whole town* will learn of this. Then, one of them hungry Ukiah fellows will gladly make use of your pillow. I believe I'm right." He hands Castor the heaping, top-heavy cone. "*Bahl?*"

Castor finds the twins five steps over his right shoulder, the sheriff over his left. Melting cream runs over his knuckles and down his forearm. Lewis drops the spoon into the pail and straightens himself. "A man who's got nothing to gain tells a convincing truth over a man who's got everything to lose… just in case you're not clear on this. But tell me, what kind of man takes advantage of helpless women and children? That's no man. *Tsk-tsk*," Lewis adds with a mocking flick of his fingers.

Castor turns red, and his Adam's apple spasms. He crushes the ice cream cone and throws it at Lewis, who well dodges but can't escape a healthy splat across his neck and apron. Castor turns sharply into Sheriff Wilkes's face. Wilkes tips his hat and sidesteps. Castor can't clomp his way out of the store fast enough.

Lewis tracks Castor all the way out the door, exhales, and without turning around, says louder than necessary, "Sheriff, how 'bout a scoop?"

Wiley follows Edna out of the office, turning at Lewis's signal.

"Incompetent children everywhere!" Edna yells, wheeling herself out of the store. "Castor!"

At the sight of Lewis's apron, Wiley claps a hand over his mouth and shudders with pressurized laughter, then dashes forth to help Edna out of the store.

That night, the market truck's six-volt headlamps are no match against the valley's moonless gloom. Wiley squints into the amber beam that only seems to illuminate five feet into the future and piles of horse shit. Giggles bubble out of him.

Lewis pouts. "Can't you stuff it, Whole Cheese?"

"Ice cream, gangster boss!" Wiley cackles.

Lewis spots a dim porch light half a mile up the road. He chews his black fingernails. "Can't this thing go any faster?"

*

An anxious spiraling overtakes Twyla as each passing minute feels hard-shelled and irreducible in her shrunken room. She has jammed her door with a large redwood-splinter wedge, and her dresser of drawers is shoved against it for good measure. Her kerosene *glimmer* is lit, the window open. Elgin barks sharply, then quiets. Castor stomps to the front door. A moment later, his boots return to the hallway and seem to march up and down the door itself, pounding and reverberating.

Then nothing—a ludicrous silence. Slowly, she begins to hear Edna's and Castor's voices, but their words are scrubbed of all vowels by the stout walls.

"Twyla? Twyla?"

Lewis's voice startles her. "Oh! You're here." She squeezes close to the window.

"I've got a newspaper full," he says. "First, be ready in the morning for school. I don't have a place for you to live yet, but I'm working on the Tuttles'."

She covers her mouth while quicksilver tears assemble on her cheeks. This seems to thwart Lewis mid-thought as if he wants to smash the window and grab her. "Uh," he murmurs, "old man Tuttle is a grouch, but he likes to talk about airships. Mrs. Tuttle is nice, and well, you know, she'll be your teacher. In the meantime, dress like you're just doin' your chores so Edna don't get suspicious… 'til I can work it out. I think Castor read my telegram, but you let me know if he needs more readin' lessons. Also—"

"Twyla, git out here!" Edna's voice broadcasts straight through the door.

Lewis ducks out of sight.

"I've got to go!" Twyla whispers.

"Kitchen don't clean itself! Now!"

Twyla flinches away from the window.

"Twyla?" Lewis pops back up. "One more thing." He gestures her back to the window. The disinclined *glimmer* colors him in a faint orange pall. His hand pushes under the window, palm up.

She lowers herself, her eyes darting fitfully to the door. Lewis's face is close to the wavy glass, and he looks at her directly, steadfast. She resists the urge to turn, twitching at the force behind the door. She slides her hand on top of his, feeling warm calluses. He whispers, "The Tuttles are kind people," and slowly pulls her hand through the window, just enough to put his mouth on her fingers.

*

Beneath a stand of two-hundred-foot-tall sequoias, Lewis and Wiley take their morning tin of joe perched on a stump the size of a flatbed truck. The monsters above, having caught a thousand gallons of coastal fog overnight, drop quarter-pound bombs from their five-hundred-year-old branches. The boys argue the practicability of building a church twice the size of the one up the street from just a single tree. Castor's truck squeaks to a stop. Sitting next to the scowling *Ite*, Twyla is wide-eyed. The boys raise their mugs.

*

The one-room school is often fitted with thirty students from age seven to fifteen. The middle-aged teacher has thick glasses and pewter-brushed curls. She settles a dispute between two boys as the remainder of the class files in.

"Good morning, Mrs. Tuttle," Twyla says eagerly, even though she feels like a ten-year-old fraud.

"And good morning to you, Miss Campbell."

Twyla offers a small twig-and-grass bird's nest sheltering half a dozen chicken eggs in a well-worn rancher's hat. Teacher puts it on her desk and says, "Isn't that sweet?"

"I boiled them hard," Twyla says, raising onto her tiptoes.

"I warrant Mr. Tuttle will eat them in one sit. He and I had a brief telephone with Mr. Haliday." She puts her hand on top of Twyla's. "How was your first week of school? I know the children can be mischievous. Things will settle."

Twyla lowers to her heels, soaking in this simple tenderness. "I like it here so much," she whispers.

A moist, bakery-at-dawn aroma wafts in just before an apple box lands hard onto the teacher's desk. Doughy, yeasty *loweezies* poke up through pure white cotton. The box rams the hat and knocks the bird nest to the floor, cracking all the eggs and sending a few spinning away. A skinny, curly-headed girl with long elbows and a rather pretty dress says, "Oh dear, I didn't see that little thing."

"Oh, Lizbeth!" Mrs. Tuttle starts, but it's too late. Twyla scrambles after her eggs. Children entering the room kick them across the floor and laugh as Twyla scampers around like a headless chicken. It takes a few minutes for Teacher to get them all hushed and in their seats. The whole class sings "Good Morning To You." Mrs. Tuttle writes the words, "emotion," "rhythm," and "rhyme" on the chalkboard.

"Let's continue with the poetry before arithmetic," she asserts. "Miss Eubanks, it is your turn. Please stand." She begins writing the arithmetic lesson.

"Yes, ma'am," Lizbeth says, rising and smiling radiantly at Twyla. "The title of my poem is 'God Frowns' by Lizbeth Eubanks." She begins to recite,

"Who flies above the rows all summer?
The blackbirds sing at dusk.
The Flutterby family disappeared suddenly
among blackberries and dust.
Wings spun into the ground
Crunching wood sticks and wire among lifelessness found
No such life forgiven by God for the folly of the Flutterbys.
Without wings of feather or God's light-boned measure
Man is not meant to fly."

The chalk squeaks to a stop, and before Mrs. Tuttle can turn around, Twyla is up and four strides toward a curtsying Lizbeth. Twyla's labor-strengthened right hook crashes into Lizbeth's face, sending her sprawling across the floor and into the teacher's desk.

"Twyla Campbell!"

All the kids jump up, crowding around them.

A glimmering 1939 Greyhound Supercoach bounces southward on the Redwood Highway toward San Francisco along the Key System route. Twyla and Lewis travel shoulder-to-shoulder, three rows behind the driver. When they'd boarded the bus in Cloverdale a few minutes ago, the warm, yeasty scent of baking bread had drifted by. Twyla recalled the first week in Mrs. Tuttle's class; seven years ago wasn't the last time she'd punched someone in the face, but it was the most satisfying. She wondered if the aroma of baked bread would always remind her of Lizbeth's broken nose.

The bus chugs up the steep grade above Sausalito and summits through the Waldo Tunnel into view of an insatiable blue fog consuming the entire city of San Francisco. The red tower tops of the Golden Gate Bridge float high above the roiling vapors. The road before them curls down and disappears into the opaque ether. Chilled air slips into the half-opened windows, and Twyla tucks her pumpkin twists into her headscarf and nestles closer to Lewis.

Impossible is the word on her mind. In moments like this with Lewis, off to see something or do something new, something she would never think to do without him, she invariably settles on the word *impossible*. Because Lewis isn't afraid of the unknown. His confidence regularly exposes how much fear saturates her head. Her evidence locker is stuffed with exhibits as to why she, in fact, should live in fear, while his sure-footed stance toward fear is a choice to indulge or not, present at every given moment. *Confounding.*

His attractions are many. Tangibly, of course, he is tall enough, taller than her by three inches. His bright brown eyes are at once penetrating and soft, his dark shock of hair often concealing one of them. His tight, capable body is in constant motion, his brain, a steam piston of never-ending analysis of reason and outcome, cost and benefit. She swears she can feel his mental adding machine through his jawbone and skin. Lewis's skin, though often glistening with urgent, activity-driven sweat, never smells sour, or for that matter, rarely smells the same way twice. He is deep in so many efforts, she can tell his daily chores. Cow or goat *charlin'*; horse farrier at the Hyatts'; deliverer of lavender, bay leaves, tack leather, vegetables, or wine grapes for the Italian brood over the hill. When they kiss, there is often fuel oil or petrol mixed with citrus, the lemon juice he uses to clean off grease.

She scoops a handful of memory from the years following her bondage to her aunt. She would meet Lewis upstairs in her old room on the abandoned orchard. Here, she would focus only on him—barricade herself inside of him, train herself to ignore the loss that was much like a dream; the truth was too exaggerated. They explored each other as often as they could find an excuse. His skin was smooth and taut across his masculine frame. He was manly, yet gentle, the kind of gentle that is accompanied by confidence in one's body. His intense pleasure with her drove her to a temporary madness that was both thrilling and frightening. She would murmur how impossible this feeling was, almost convinced it was breaking some kind of law. Their geometry seemed turned of purposeful design. He would kiss her and stroke her hair, her breasts, and down into her folds. Then, he would move inside her, slowly, gently, and become even more excited as he slid in and out of her, pulling on her bottom, sliding his hands inside her thighs, turning her over, and pressing himself across the length of her. He would rotate her over again, pushing his mouth to hers. Sounds would fling out of her, cries he wouldn't let her express as he continued to kiss her. Quick breath through flared nostrils as the tension, the pulling and pushing, would finally force Lewis to arch his back and suck in a deep breath, uncorking gasps from him and rapturous wails from her.

Impossible.

Her nethers tingle, and she grabs the loose skin of his elbow. "What an impossibly beautiful day."

He bends his arm, the skin slipping out of her fingers. "Nope. Need all of it," he says. "Though I wish I could trade it for avgas."

"Rather have avgas than elbow skin?"

"That's right."

"I don't mind the bus sometimes," she says.

He pouts. "If I had money for gas, we'd already be there enjoying the sights."

"I'm just glad you took a day off."

"Happy birthday, Miss Bloom," he says and gives her a silent air-kiss and a wink. "One more semester, and I'm off to Pensacola."

"I go where you go, skeezix."

"As long as there's a telescope nearby?"

"That's not too much to ask, is it?"

"It might very well be in mountain-less Florida… You're a strange duck."

"Takes one to know one," she says, grabbing his elbow skin again.

"Ducks are worthy airships," he replies. "Lifting power, speed, and range."

She coos. "You have lifting power, I'll admit to it. And better lips than most birds." She kisses him.

"Hey, not in public!"

Three hours later, they arrive in the sleepy agricultural town of San Jose. Though she regrets her shoes, she's excited for the adventure ahead. From the bus stop, they walk for twenty minutes southward before arriving at a brick building at the town's edge. The industrial shop looks almost new, yet is filled with rolls of mostly old, ugly fabrics. Twyla rubs her feet and watches Lewis through the windshield of a blue two-year-old Ford sedan that reeks of cigar smoke. The ashtray is crammed with tightly wound brown stubs. Her eyes burn, and her throat tickles.

This brings to mind other excitements jammed toe-to-toe with nastiness. *How did I enjoy Lewis's body so freely after being so repulsed by Castor? Perhaps they are two separate baskets found only in very specific places? Maybe one is far enough away—like a sister's memory? Is my enjoyment of Lewis possible because Castor is dead?*

Lewis flings himself behind the steering wheel. She says, "So the owner of this car is Wiley's friend?"

"'Acquaintance' is more precise," Lewis returns. "He's the man who got us this special appointment."

"I'll be sure to thank him on our return. Is he a cigar salesman?"

"Upholstery man. Why?"

"No reason."

"Newest automobile I've ever driven."

"Smells so—"

"New?"

She pats his head.

In the late afternoon, the ever-reaching fog makes for an eerie soup that reduces the speed of their climb up Mount Hamilton. Lewis is impatient to make it before sundown.

"I wonder why *this* mountain for an observatory?" she muses.

After an hour of nauseating curves, the fog thins and dissolves. Vague points of light can be seen scattered across the mountaintop, dotted with small trees and large clumps of dark vegetation.

"To get away from the lights of the city," Lewis says. "And *taish*, it's above the fog line."

The main building of the Lick Observatory is an imposing block of faux stonework with large windows. Thrust up over its shoulder stands the white telescope dome, distinct and optimistic. As they climb the stone steps toward the building, tentacles of fog push in behind them. By the time they reach the entrance, the Ford is a ghost.

"Back in '88," begins Nicholas, a sharp-eyed, handsome, young astronomer wearing a modest tan jacket and tie, "this became the world's first permanently occupied mountaintop observatory. Mr. Lick himself is buried under the thirty-six-inch telescope."

Twyla stands in a paradox of wonder and fear. Lewis and Wiley's unaccountably ambitious idea for her to see Mars up close both excited and scared her. The big-words-and-concepts problem was a specialty here. How could she keep up?

"Then, in '92," Nicholas continued, "Dr. Barnard discovered the fifth moon of Jupiter, a miraculous accomplishment of observation and intuition. No moons had been discovered by direct observation since Galileo himself in 1610."

"If I may," Twyla interjects, surprising herself. "Callisto, Ganymede, um, Europa, and Io?"

"Quite right," Nicholas says, genuinely impressed. "Do you know the fifth sibling?"

"I'm afraid not."

"She's named after the Greek mythological nymph Amalthea."

"Amalthea," she repeats. "Such a beautiful name."

"She is a redhead, due to sulfur that likely originated from Io."

"I'll be your Io," Lewis says.

Nicholas and Twyla stare at him quizzically while a distant buzzing penetrates the stillness.

"It'll be dark soon," Nicholas says. "You've picked a good time to see Mars if high clouds don't form."

But the buzzing grows louder, turning into a definite thrum and whine.

"If that's a plane," Lewis interjects, "I've not heard one like it. And it's a little late to be flying so—"

The rising alien discord smears in pitch, so loud it is certain to be on top of them. The eyes of the aeronauts meet.

The abrupt explosion seems to happen in four sharp echoes. They flinch into crouching positions, covering their heads. A blast of brick, mortar, plaster, and glass flies at them from only yards away. The lights go out. The impact is so brassy, their ears ring as they cough inside a cloud of billowing dust.

"My heavens!" Nicholas cries, then calls out as he fumbles his way into a darkening hallway.

Lewis pulls Twyla back out the doors of the main entrance into blowing mists. In the waning twilight, they find a large jagged hole in the building only fifty feet from the main doors, with an airplane wing jutting out. Smoke boils from it—or dust.

Nicholas yells from the doorway, "The telephone is out!" The lights pop back on behind him.

"Do you have a flashlight?" Lewis shouts back. Nicholas disappears into the building. Twyla follows him and soon returns with a hand light.

"Wait here," Lewis says and runs toward the wreckage, Twyla right behind.

Lewis sweeps his light across the wing and into the jagged cave. Small lights flicker behind a cloud of something. It's quiet and still. He listens for any sound—a voice? Flames? Dripping fuel? Nothing but the hum of an electrical transformer. The broken craft is difficult to make out.

"I mean, I think it's a wing," he says. "Let's try from inside." Twyla pulls her coat tighter and follows Lewis back into the building and through the main hall. Nicholas talks with two staff members, who nod their heads rapidly, confirming their health. Lewis grabs the flashlight out of Nicholas's hand and gives it to Twyla as they jog up the hallway and into the debris.

Bricks and plaster are scattered in piles everywhere. A broken twist of propeller lies against a wall; flayed and buckled silver sheet metal have knocked huge cabinets of electric machines onto their backs. Lewis works his way over a rubble pile to what should've been the nose of this strange craft, so mangled he cannot identify its manufacturer. He disappears into the distorted mound and hollers, "This almost looks like a bomb mount!" Glowing shafts of light kick upward like nervous miniature searchlights. "I don't see the landing gear."

Twyla hears him tossing bricks. "The wheels are retracted… *Taish!* I don't know what this is." He falls into a coughing fit.

Everything is white with plaster dust. Then, Twyla's eyes land on a gloved hand at the end of a forearm protruding from a pile of bricks. "Lewis?" Twyla's voice pleads. "Please come back over here."

Flickering images seem to slap at her face: *sunlit field—her bicycle—a tumbling can of avgas…*

Lewis navigates back to her and catches sight of her face. He jumps into the heap and begins digging out the body. Nicholas and two staff members arrive and climb in to help. Twyla slowly backs up, turns away, and shuts down what's coming. *Not tonight. No way.*

Two hours later, Lt. Richard F. Lorenz and Private W. E. Scott lie on the floor of the observatory, wrapped in painter's tarps. Their bodies are mangled so severely, their likenesses are impossible to know. Two hours beyond this, reporters from the *Mercury News* and *San Francisco Chronicle* will arrive, and their myriad questions will bounce off Nicholas while flashbulbs bounce off the floor. Nicholas says, "One of our staff identified the craft as the Northrop A-17 attack plane of the USAAF."

"That's the A-17?" Lewis says with honest surprise.

"We hear it fly over all the time."

"*Bilch!* The A-17 is a bullet. That plane's been clocked at 220 miles per hour level flight!"

"But why was he flying so low?" Nicholas asks. "And why was there no fire?"

"*That's* why," Lewis says. "Out of fuel… Desperate for a landing spot, huh, Twy?"

"A horrible feeling," she says.

"Those poor men," Nicholas whispers. "The police will be here in a while. In the meantime," he gently grabs their arms, "please come with me."

They hike up a few corridors of stairs and emerge inside the observatory dome. Dominating the immense, dark room is a light gray cannon diagonally vaulting overhead under a great curved ceiling.

"Welcome to the Universe Explorer." The enormous telescope tube is partially hidden behind innumerable black levers, wheels, and gears. Nicholas steers them to a control panel on the wall. "Please." He gestures to a large lever. Twyla pulls it. Clanking echoes fill their ears, and a huge slit in the parabolic roofline yawns open to bejeweled velvet. Nicholas says, "See the spiral stairs?" He points to the thirty-foot twist of stairs leading to the telescope's fulcrum.

"Never seen stairs like that," Lewis remarks.

"We won't need them." He motions Twyla to another lever. She pulls it. A loud *hum* and *whoosh* caroms about the room, and suddenly, the telescope is dropping toward them. Twyla feels carsick until she realizes they are rising; the entire floor is an elevator. She and Lewis smile at each other. In a moment, they are positioned perfectly at the viewing end of the great time machine.

Nicholas makes some quick adjustments and offers Twyla the finder. She puts her eye to it, and Nicholas instructs her on the focusing reticle. The moment the red planet resolves, Twyla gasps, covering her mouth. Tears fill her lids, and she fights them off. She wipes her eyes, and the red alien world saturates her atmosphere.

Her red sister is careworn with canals and canyons spidering around; pockmarks and a massive scar cross her face. She is nothing short of thrilling, enchanting, magic of another order. *A live dream*, is all Twyla can rationalize. Her sister fills her with loss. *But why? She's so beautiful…* Sadness and wonder overwhelm her—as if she's lying at the bottom of a pit filled with lovely red sand.

"It's quite all right, miss," Nicholas whispers. "One of the most surprising things we astronomers have learned about faraway planets and stars is how personal they are."

Emotions high and low crash inside her. A spindle of adrenaline unspools. Soundlessly, images of women in uniforms tinted in futuristic colors form into groups of specialists… something technical in nature. They become amorphous, like the shape of dry soil under a wheelbarrow when it rains.

"No," she says and pulls away from the eyepiece. She wipes at her cheeks and makes her way to the catwalk at the wall.

"Twy?" Lewis calls.

"Go ahead. Take a look. I'll be out…" She runs from the room.

Sixty minutes later, Lewis and Nicholas reprise the incident to the police and several reporters. One officer standing in the blowing fog asks Twyla if she's cold. They return the borrowed car and are grateful to be offered a lift back to the bus station. The two sleep on each other so hard, the driver must wake them in San Francisco.

June 1939

Dear Journal,

I just couldn't take it—couldn't take any more that night. I hate the world sometimes. I feel angry at Lewis and Wiley for making me see the observatory. Why can't Amelia suddenly arrive in a fishing boat with a deep adventurer's tan, her flying cap in hand, a legendary tale, and a victory parade instead of this loss? Bitter world. Mars was the most wonderful thing I've ever seen. But this life, here… I'm not sure we are meant to know there is more. So, for now, my red sister will be the cutest piglet at the county fair.

Then again, I've seen her. She's seen me. She's mine now. Neither of us knows what to do with the other.

*

Wiley is waiting for them at the bus depot in Cloverdale. She hugs him, half-lidded and happy to see his big face. Wiley picks her up like she's a child again—small and safe. He deposits her into the truck. Lewis slides in next to her. "Wy, I've got a tale so tall it won't fit in your truck," he says groggily.

"No doubt you do," Wiley says. "Just unravel it slowly, and we'll tuck it into the corners."

Twyla can smell the bakery again. Lizbeth's face comes to mind, as expected. But what she hadn't expected, hadn't remembered, was what had happened that night after she'd clocked that long-elbowed girl.

*

Not all Anderson Valley nights are the same. Some shine silvery bright, some take on a leaden, hesitant luminosity, and some are like the bottom of a deep well.

Tonight, Lewis and Gerald stand in Edna's front yard at the bottom of that well. A scant window glow and half-hearted porch light reveal Gerald's discomfort. Elgin growls and barks at them from his tether.

Twyla stands on the porch, her arms wrapped around Threadbear. A canvas bag stuffed with her meager belongings hunches at her feet. Her eyes are down; she can't help staring at her aunt's curved fingers and misshapen knuckles. Edna's face is thrust in deep shadow. She says in a thin, raspy voice, "There is not one thing that happens in this valley I don't know about. Castor was here to protect you. That he did. You think I am a cruel person? I know. Work you hard, did we? Were we mean? Don't confuse the two; hard work prepares you for a hard life. Scarcely cruel. Huh! Cruelty? Cruelty, my dear girl, would be God taking part of your body by the affliction of polio, disabling you so you can't raise your child. Cruelty would be God following this by killing your brother and your child. Ernie is dead. Tommy is dead… Tommy, my son."

"No." Twyla gasps. "But he's my brother. Tommy was my broth—"

"Oh, your little head hasn't thought this through."

"But—"

"Your papa was at war when you were conceived. You were his only child. Tommy was my only child. I lost my baby when I gained this wheelchair. Then I lost them both. Yet, you live."

"Leave'r be now, Ms. Gultch," Gerald says.

Twyla can't seem to breathe. *Tommy?*

Lewis gently pulls on her shoulder, guiding her away.

"Mr. Haliday?" Edna's jagged outline calls out. "That was a weak harvest season. How secure does the Ukiah Bank feel about its loan to you these days?" Gerald's back stiffens, his knuckles crack. "Oh, don't be sore. I'll give you one hundred barrels of Parducci prune juice for the whole thing. You can quit your yard scratchin' and walk away."

Gerald strides quickly to the porch as Castor's hulking silhouette slides into the doorway. Gerald ignores him and walks right up to Edna, bending down inches from her face. She recoils, unable to hide her fright at his menacing proximity. Gerald holds his unblinking gaze on her, reaches down, grabs Twyla's canvas bag, and walks away.

Moments later, Twyla sits between the two Haliday men in the near blackness of their truck. The weak dashboard glow provides a dying ember's worth of luminance. She feels empty. Nothing left of her but a girl-shaped galvanized tub of dust. No family—*not even a brother. Never was. Nothing makes sense.* Naught from her childhood can tell her who she is. *What does it mean?*

"Mr. Haliday?" she murmurs.

"Do you need to see Doc Hyatt?" Gerald asks.

"I don't know."

"Llewellyn will fetch him over."

"I will," Lewis says firmly.

"Thank you, sir," she says.

"You can do me one favor in return, Miss Campbell," Gerald says. "Pay not one ounce of attention to anything that witch said to you. Do you understand me? Not one ounce."

"Yes, sir."

"That'll be thanks enough for me," Gerald says with a glance to Lewis, who, in turn, will never look at his father the same way.

They bounce along the road for several more minutes, the headlights recoiling off the potholes in an uneven pulse. Lewis takes her hand and whispers, "There's someone waiting for you at our ranch." But Twyla's imagination has been cut to the quick. She doesn't hear Lewis and just assumes his voice is directed at Gerald. "Twyla?" Lewis squeezes her hand. She turns to him. "Wiley found Maggie. She was over at the Navarro headwaters hitched to a team of draught horses, pulling log sleds from the river. She's roughhewn but awright. She needs you."

And Journal, there are good men. Lewis is one of them.
And so is his father.

five

God, You Can't Have Lewis

"A woman's place is in the goddamn home!" Gram said in her best redneck parody.

She stood in a garish, blue-carpeted room ringed with grab handles, crammed with weightlifting machines, and smelling of bleach and sweat. Young physical therapists with applied poise and polo shirts moved silently from station to station. Twyletchka listened while hanging from a bar above her wheelchair, occasionally commenting in smug Chimpanzee. Gram Gram hobbled back and forth in rising excitement or agitation. "'I'm a flyer,' is what Lewis told the man draining his beer," Gram continued, lowering her voice to correctly convey Lewis's pitch. "'And so is my fiancée! I taught her myself.'" She points a thumb at her head. "That's me!"

Gram spat onto the blue AstroTurf and grabbed one of the parallel bars to stabilize herself. Her other hand jabbed the air with a brightly striped cane of orange and blue fluorescent paint. "Right there in the officer's club during flight school. Then, Gramp Gramps said, 'Soon, I'll be flyin' for the United States Army Air Corps.' That's when the redneck belched, 'Youngster, I know a speck about the Army, and pilots got to be officers first. The Army ain't takin' no criminals for pilots. Girls don't need to know a man's work. Showing that girl how to fly is wrong.'"

Gram crouched a little and swung her cane like a hockey stick. "Lewis shot off his barstool and stood in the man's face. Redneck rose on his boots, towering six inches over him, his head stalk bulging like a double ham hock. Lewis was convinced he was losing teeth that day, yet he didn't flinch a half-particle. Instead, he looked that Neanderthal in his shaded walleye and said, 'Well, sir, your unused lard bucket may think it's wrong to teach women to fly, but there's no law against it, you backwood Mynah bird!'" Gram snorted and bent in laughter. But she recovered quickly. "But Lewis wasn't done! He said, 'Why don't you take it up with Katharine Wright or Amelia or Jackie Cochran while she flies past your cave at two hundred miles per hour, causing you to spill your stone bowl of sour grapes! And another thing. Which one of your cave paintings shows that the exploits of women flyers have anything to do with you?' At this point, Neanderthal seemed to grow taller and growled back, 'You've got a big mouth with too many teeth. It's man's work!'"

"Wait, Babulya! What's a double ham hock?" Twyletchka asked.

Gram bulldozed ahead, "Then Lewis chopped the throttle and put him hard on the deck like the carrier pilot he was about to become. He dropped a silver nickel on the bar for the man's beer and said, 'I apologize, sir. It's not your fault. Your pocket watch is sadly broken. Let me be the first to welcome you to the twentieth century.'" Gram Gram swung her cane down like an ax. "Oh, my! That was my Lewis. I miss him every day," Gram said and handed over her cane. "Poor Lewy. In reality, the very next day, he was turned away by the Army Air Corps after his eyesight was deemed insufficient. Can you imagine rejecting a pilot with a perfect flying record and over one thousand hours? Lewis was convinced that Army doc didn't like flyers from small towns he'd never heard of. Men in power…" she mumbled and kicked a trash can, sending a plastic spray bottle topsy-turvy onto the neon blue rug. Several polo shirts flinched from their clipboards.

"I couldn't calm him down. Double ham hock didn't know he was an inch from losing his underbite that day. Lew's dream had died in a fiery crash. He went on and on about how good his eyes were and what a quack that Army doc was." She rolled her granddaughter along a bright yellow wall of free weights. "I finally convinced him to try the Navy. He loved those ships but was unimpressed with their flyers. After many passionate letters and some squeaky-wheel luck, he got a chance with the Navy. Turned out, that Army doc was indeed an imposter—Lew had perfect vision." She spun a full rotation back to her granddaughter. "One more circuit." She offered her a five-pound weight, then guided her granddaughter's wheelchair back to the machines. Gramma Twyla sat on a bench, grabbed two handles, and pushed up. "Oh, those years in the 1930s and right up to '41 were like broken mirror glass in a sunlit stream. Dazzling surprises, quiet after sundown, and always dangerous to bare feet. A crusade of mercury in a California poppy bree—"

"Gram? You're daydreaming again."

"More iron-pumping, less sass," Gram said. "What was astonishing about Lewis was his willingness to talk to me, explore ideas. There was no other man in my life that could or would do that."

"Gram Gram, you're never going to tell me about the death of your family, are you?"

Gram lowered the machine handles, looked her in the eyes, and covered her face with her hands. "No, missy," she said softly, half-muted. "Not until I absolutely have to."

*

In the middle of the largest body of water on Earth, thousands of miles from any continent of rock, desert, or jungle, a black '41 Buick glides like a blot of India ink past Ford Island and onward toward Hickam Air Force Base, Honolulu, Hawaii. It passes hulking gray warships poised like arrogant gunslingers sporting massive sixteen-inch cannons and towering metal armor; though, at the moment, their hats are pulled low as they slumber in the nascent dawn.

Twyla's head rests on Lewis's shoulder while he steers the Century sedan in his fine Navy dress uniform. She smiles because last night he called her "prize-winning-apple beautiful." And they made love. She is regularly astonished at the way he sees her, and she's excited for the day to come. She catches her faint reflection in the side window. A few particles of brightening sky and the meekest of glows from the dashboard reflect Bakelite and tortoiseshell hair combs and wave bones controlling her auburn mane. They create large loops and spilling curls, with a shock falling across her eyes. She has learned her femininity lowers Lewis's anxieties. She's surmised well what relaxes him and what injects him with excitement for evenings with her. She tucks her locket inside her pale pink blouse and pulls a needle and thread through the shoulder seam of his flight jacket. Back in their tiny duplex, while dressing, he had eagerly ticked off the day's events: a final check flight with some fresh-faced pilots around the island, then hacking away at his new favorite game of golf with Wiley. But mostly, she knows Lewis can't wait to join his new squadmates on the *Lexington* when it returns to port.

"Goodness! At what point do a man's shoulders stop growing?" she mutters.

"That's a good trick, sewing in the dark," he says, cocking his hat. They pass dim rows of planes, primary trainers, P-40s, P-36s, and B-17 bombers poised in sprinters' blocks, impatient for the starter's pistol shot.

"Killdevil Hills, North Carolina," she wonders aloud and glances at his muted aspect. "Kitty Hawk, Kill Devil Hills?" she continues. "Mmmmm. Kitty Hawk? Some bird of prey? Kill Devil Hills? Oh my, such a womb-to-birth flight." Lewis isn't really listening, but she forges ahead, "Ya know how people say the Wright brothers were born to fly? That Babe Ruth was born to swing a bat? Abe Lincoln born to be president? Do you think they knew it?"

Lewis absently nods his wooden cranium.

"And if so, what does that feel like? Can you feel something like that?"

Lewis sucks the ear strut of his aviator sunglasses. "Most folks are stingy about others' success, is all. If you have too much success, then God help us, it must be explained. Got to be typeset under some categorical heading. Born to it? No! More'n likely worked like a pack mule for it. I believe I'm right. Lack of imagination is a scary town to be from. Then, the poet of time does the rest." Though he is patronizing and distracted, she appreciates he still manages to find a kernel.

"Well, I believe I realize that," she says. "Poetry isn't very good unless it's woven around truth."

"Then you should exclude ol' Abe from that list," Lewis adds. "He didn't have an easy go of it. Wasn't remotely born to it. He failed beyond reason but never quit."

"He was compelled," she says.

"Compelled. That's a good word."

"I wonder what that feels like."

"You really think they'll let you fly this morning, Nina Clock?"—her favorite character in the Gasoline Alley comics—"You're just a girl, is all."

She raises her chin. "Get that worked out, Lizbeth, and I might not punch your nose on our honeymoon," she says.

Lewis tries to hide his laughter within a coughing fit as he slows the car. The headlights illuminate several small planes parked in a semicircle in front of a tin shack. He hops out, loops around, and opens her door.

Twyla knots the thread at the jacket's shoulder seam, bites it off, and snatches her little logbook from the visor. Behind Lewis, enormous palm fronds unsuccessfully hide the scrap-wood roofing and oxidized siding of the diminutive structure. Amber light leaks through its slats in the retreating darkness.

"You take advantage, Twy," he says, extending his hand. "My childhood being bare of any female example, you enjoy my rickety reference beam for girl behavior." He takes the jacket and pulls her toward him.

"Hey, watch the goods!" she protests.

The moment they moved to Honolulu, they felt out of place, like half-formed hillbillies stepping out of the bramble and into the big city for the first time. Lewis waits for Twyla to pick up her cue, but she's already batting her eyes, enjoying her part of their ongoing joke.

"Yes? You, that young man there in the front row, with the single suspender and missing teeth—you have formed a thought?" she says as if she were a school teacher. "Mister Llewellyn, is it?"

"It's Lew. Just Lew." He shakes his head at her.

"Of course, fewer syllables. Go on, Llewellyn."

"Uh, yes, ma'am," he says, jutting out his jaw and splaying his feet. "It's just, well, ma'am, you lick a dog end to end means you gotta lot of fur to get off your tongue."

"Just so, Mister Llewellyn."

"And my fee-uhn-cee, she's called Twolla Campbell from over in Billygoatville; I'm not sure what's to be done about yonder problem she heve. You see, I think she only lubs me for my brains and that I can fly a aeroplane. But I feel this is enough… You know why?"

"Why don't you tell me, Mister Llewellyn," she says with an oozing smile. "Just keep the words small so yer water jacket don't burst from heat expansion."

He stifles a laugh, determined not to break. "Because, ma'am, because no matter how many flight hours she gits, boss man ain't allowing no broads in no military wings. This means she will never fly a better plane than me." He crosses his eyes, and she loses it, hits him on the arm, and tries to pull it together.

"That may be a fact, Abercrombie, but saying it out loud means tonight, after dessert, there will be no dessert."

His face contorts into mock shock. They kiss anyway.

The sky seems to brighten, revealing their tropical-industrial surroundings in a humid, gauzy glow.

"If my Buffalo's runnin', I'll fly my very last briny-island-rookie tour, make sure the noobs are square, and we're ready for a *bahl chapport*. I'll pick up Whole Cheese, shoot nine holes, and be back about 1300."

"And by 'ready to fight good like Charlie Porter,'" she interjects, "what you mean is you, Wiley, and the other grease monkeys will sit in the 'O club' bumping gums, *bucky dustin'* for six hours, and call that your duty? Please tell me you don't *harp Boont* in front of your men?"

He doesn't look at her, exposing her direct hit. "Well, I've heard old man McCuskey is mean." He says, quickly changing the subject. "'Crusty McCuskey,' as he's known by said greasy monkeys. Fly level, Miss Bloom." She smooths his cheek. He kisses her hand and adds, "You meet anyone named Lizbeth, just keep your fists to yourself!"

"Don't worry, Lizbeth doesn't work here. She's over at HQ in charge of your botched fleet paperwork. So now I have to thank her!" He snorts and circles around the car. She adds, "Your offenses *may* be pardonable tonight; you could *possibly* get some pie… If we *harp* more, in English, about our wedding plans."

"Pie?" He bounces around theatrically. "Get some pie? That's the secret? I'm tellin' the guys! There's a wingding!" He hoots and hollers and throttles the Buick away in a tire-screeching wiggle-waggle.

One hundred miles east and forty thousand feet high, the new sun bounces off a pillar of clouds, suffusing Twyla in white-blue warmth. She giggles and turns toward the small planes. A yellow Piper Cub, a red Staggerwing Beech, and a white Taylorcraft with its cowling removed are chocked in front of the shack. Its roof sign spells out MCCUSKEY'S AIR SERVICE.

A chesty male voice lobs over the aircraft, "Your cousin needs driving lessons."

Startled, Twyla glances around. "What? Who's there?"

"Little early for an island tour, ain't it?"

She looks again at the Staggerwing. "Um, aloha! No, thank you," she half-yells. "I mean, yes, it's early."

"Then you're here for a flyin' lesson?" the voice says.

Twyla bends down, peeking under the planes. "No, thank you," she answers.

"Roger. Clear skies. Go away!"

She doesn't move, then spots a large head hanging down from the far side of the Taylorcraft. "Oh, there you are!"

"Curious behavior," the head mumbles, and a bare foot stretches from under the Taylorcraft. "Tail-draggin' miscreants."

Twyla ducks under and puts a rag in its toes.

"Twyla Campbell, sir. Aloha."

Sixty years old, overweight, and wearing a scruffy beard and grease-stained undershirt, the man appears on the far side of the engine, a small chunky box with wires dangling from it in his hand. She gives the box a quick peek and asks, "Are you adding a fuel pump?"

"Isn't that what I said? Name's Butch McCuskey," he says, introducing himself without offering his hand. "Still here, huh?"

"Well, it's very nice to meet you, Mr. McCuskey," she says, grateful he didn't offer his hand. "And pardon my saying so, but who makes a fuel pump for such a small plane?"

"My own design."

"Motor driven or electric?" she asks.

"Don't want vapor lock at high altitude… What?" He eyeballs her and squints. "Hey, what gives? Shouldn't you be servin' drinks at the Speako? Tell me you didn't come here lookin' for an instructor job?"

"No, sir. I mean, yes, sir. Sir, it's a fine insight you mention—"

His hand shoots up, big and greasy. "I have a powerful deductor. Yer father is an admiral here or captain on one of these Navy boats… No, wait." He looks her up and down again. "No, you're not royalty. Beau's stationed here, met in the States while you learned to fly; he enlisted, and you came for a holiday. You read a book about the Wright brothers. You expect Amelia to make a surprise return at any moment. And you got ten flight hours logged in a paper kite certified by King Kamehameha. And now you're ready to flight instruct?"

Before she can answer, he plucks her logbook from her hand, plops the pump into her palm, turns, and marches inside the hut.

"Oh! Sir, I get along natural with planes, and my flight hours are—"

But he's gone. She bounces the pump in her hand, spins back to the Taylorcraft, and picks up a wrench.

Twyla enters the hut, wiping her hands on one of Butch's rags. Inside, small snapshots of obsolete airplanes and a portrait of Glenn Curtiss hang on the corrugated walls. The hut is orderly and decorated in Polynesian furniture. She has successfully avoided getting her blouse dirty but failed her cheeks and forehead.

From behind a diminutive teak and bamboo counter, a woman wearing a yellow and aqua muumuu stands next to Butch, who peers at Twyla. He hands the logbook to Muumuu.

"Aloha. Welcome," Muumuu says with a soothing voice and very kind eyes. "Aren't you a beautiful girl?"

"Aloha. Oh, thank you. Twyla Campbell, ma'am."

"Doris McCuskey. It's a pleasure." She offers Twyla a clean rag.

"Thank you."

Butch washes his hands in a small sink behind the counter and mumbles, "M'wife, Doris. Well, she loves the pilots but hates the planes. I feel much the other way 'round." He flips water off his hands and walks out the door.

Doris observes Twyla watching him go. "Dog barks because he can't fly anymore, commercially," Doris says.

Twyla steps closer. "Why is that?"

"Heartworms." She winks. "Butch tells me you're a flyer. Father in the Great War?"

"Why, yes, ma'am."

"Where did you take instruction?"

"Northern California."

"On the level, or did you sneak 'em?"

This catches Twyla off guard. *Did I sneak 'em?* In this thick and humid island air, she finds it hard to recall just how many hours she spent in and around airplanes on dry dirt fields like those of Willits, Mendocino, Clear Lake, and the ranch strip in Ione. The latter was just a stone's throw from Sutter's Mill, where ninety-two years earlier, flecks of gold put California on the top of the world's to-do list, altering the U.S. economy and the outcome of the Civil War. Lewis said these little towns were home to enthusiastic consumers of Anderson Valley jackass brandy and apple shine. No finer apples anywhere, except Sebastopol.

Maybe. And though distribution costs created an unsustainable business model, Lewis insisted it was an investment in customer satisfaction.

Twyla refocuses on Doris's curious face. "Both, ma'am. I had to sneak flight lessons at first, then on the level," she finally says, wondering how long she stood there in silent thought.

"Was it your father?" Doris asks, picking up Twyla's logbook.

"Fiancée, ma'am."

"Bless his soul," Doris says. "You think you should be up there with him right now, don't you?"

"Uh… no, ma'am. But I… I think there's a lot we can do if just given the chance."

"Katherine Wright thinks so, too. No one talks about her. She was with her brothers the whole way, kept them patched together, risked her own life…" Doris turns the pages of the little logbook. "Katherine would tell you aviation is so young, anything is possible. Just don't mention Glenn Curtiss." She smiles. "But men and clouds have disparate cares," she adds, handing Twyla the book. "Butch will take you up."

"He will?"

Doris leans in and whispers, "He's never met a girl with four hundred hours. Blue skies, Ms. Campbell."

"Yes, ma'am."

"Do call me Doris."

"Yes, ma'am. Aloha, Doris." Twyla walks out of the hut and into a glorious Diamond Head sunrise. She smiles at the bewitching sight, warm light spreading over Honolulu's shoulder, and thinks how wrong Lewis is about Crusty.

*

Butch pulls his head out of the Taylorcraft's engine, his face screwed up in puzzlement. "Hope she holds together," he says. "Don't want to be up there with no teenager screaming for dear life because your new pump don't work." He snaps the cowling shut.

"It's not my pump, sir," she replies with a sincere smile.

Butch's oversized melon tilts, and she guesses he's elevating her intelligence from primary school brat up to, but not exceeding, teenage smart-ass. He spits out a wad of tobacco. "Preflight 'er!"

The audacity of paved runways makes Twyla smile. She angles the steering wheel and advances the throttle. They rise over the harbor, sliding up through horizontal rays of spun gold. She remembers clearly thinking the little islands of San Francisco Bay were strikingly beautiful when she first flew over them, a perception problem that worried her from time to time. *What does one do with an emphatic feeling about something once it's challenged, or dead wrong? It seems there's no end to this, therefore, no end to being wrong—about everything…*

Butch screams, "We're hit!"

A Japanese torpedo bomber and two fighter escorts roar past them, juddering the Taylorcraft. Butch's head hits the low ceiling. Twyla jams her rudder, adds more power, and straightens them out. "They're killing Americans down there! Why the fuck would you go there?" Butch screams. "Any other island! Any other island!"

Twyla absorbs this, swallows hard, and holds her breath against her hyperventilating lungs. "My man is down there! *Your wife* is down there!" She plunges the wheel in, nosing them steeply down; the little engine whines fiercely.

Skimming low across the Waikiki shoreline, she angles around the breaking waves, body surfers, and horseback riders enjoying the otherwise empty beach. A few beachcombers seem frozen in place, their heads pointed east toward rising columns of smoke. Ignoring Butch's bawling, she flares the plane.

The little bird lands hard at the water's edge, nearly tipping over as the wheels sink into Waikiki Beach just in front of the Moana Hotel.

"Fuck this mess!" Butch yells.

"Can you run?" Twyla shuts off the engine, slams open her door, and grabs the locket from the footwell.

"What?"

She jumps out and runs. Butch staggers behind. Three enemy fighters scream twenty feet over their heads.

"Christ almighty!" Butch bellows as he hobbles up into the hotel yard, across the spacious lanai, and into the main courtyard, where he ducks behind a massive banyan tree next to Twyla. "We're in it now," he says, panting like a pug dog. "Leave it to a dame to go flyin' on this day! Grabbin' the wheel! Trying to kill us! Four hundred hours in a puddle jumper is *not* combat flying! No idea what yer doing! Thank yer lucky stars I'm a fighter hero! You owe your ass to me, little missy!" His rant is cut short as a four-engine bomber screams by so closely, they flinch lower. It has white stars on the wings and the name *MARY ANN* near the cockpit, and oddly, no gunners at the ready—not in the nose, the top blister, ball turret, or waist.

"Goddammit! The cavalry is here!" He turns back, and Twyla is gone. "Hey! Where the hell—?"

After thirty minutes of running uphill away from the harbor, toward the big Army-Navy hospital, she slows to a jog in a flowering neighborhood of small houses. She carries an impossible hope that Lewis is already at their special place—where they had stopped during a recent walk, had talked for the first time about having children… As their tiny house is under attack near the harbor, this is her only idea. She can't help watching the planes zooming across the ships.

She stops at an open lot, her chest heaving, sweat dripping. She is surrounded by flamboyant flowers and plants with huge rubber leaves. Brute force metal-on-metal explosions tear the steel ships as if they were plywood. An alien ugliness has plastered itself onto this postcard of paradise. Hundreds of people in shorts and colorful muumuus stand on rooftops and in the streets stretching down the hill. Smoke drifts up to her, carrying a nostril-flaring mix of burning oil, machinery, and flesh. Klaxons peal, machine guns fire, and roaring airplanes dive down as desperate voices rush up the hill to her. She can barely stand straight.

"No," she commands to no one. *You can't have Lewis. You cannot have Lewis!* She covers her face with her hands. "Find me!" she screams. *Get yourself clear of that mess and find me!* She looks down at her hands. The ground pulses with each detonation, though she is more than a mile away from the ships. Yellow flashes, and three seconds later, the booms reach her ears. She scans over to Waikiki, her brain mechanically identifying the popular Lau Yee Chai Chinese restaurant with its tall, pointed, tiled roof. Chaos and civilization. *But where are our fighting men? If Lewis doesn't—*

Suddenly, hot, wet hair fills her palm. Lewis's arm wraps around her waist. Her heart stops, and before he can disappear again, she pulls him tightly to her body. Covered in oil and sweat, Lewis sucks in the thick Pacific air.

"They got to my plane… before I did… never got off the ground," he pants and slowly stands. She hugs him harder.

They turn their eyes toward the madness, the very first hour of a four-year world war. Ships blaze, swamp, and sink. Smoking rows of airplanes melt in place. Men burn in oily water. The violent pandemonium of this heretofore peaceful Army-Navy base is nonsensical.

"Poor… damn sailors," he says.

"We're in it now…" Twyla mumbles. "Where's Wiley?"

"Wiley is… we pulled a few guys… out of the water. I ran up here… he's still down there. Didn't know if you'd be here."

She puts her hands on his face. They look at each other for just a moment, then down toward the day that would live in infamy.

To: Lt. L. Haliday, #19057847 Naval Fleet USS (censored) Postmaster Honolulu

Dearest Husband,

Saw the most wonderful notice in the Honolulu Star-Bulletin today. The Air Transport Command, Nancy Love, and Jackie Cochran are interviewing ladies for a ferry pilot training program. Women will transport planes for the war! Now that's bahl ghorm if I've ever ate it! I ran to the post office with my letter of interest and flight log. Fight speedily and come back so we can have a proper honeymoon.

Bird of Paradise kisses,
Twyla

The warm-spun air curls and pulses around a small lagoon at sunrise. Roughly three hundred yards across at its widest jagged curve, the surf rushes through its mouth on the east side and cross-threads the momentum right out of the waves, creating a superb swimming and fishing hole. She thinks she's windward but seems to have asked all the wrong people. Halona? Toilet Bowl?

He'eia Pond? Even Turtle Bay way up on the North Shore was suggested. The locals don't seem to mind that she remains confused.

After an hour of alternating freestyle and backstrokes in this semi-deserted cove, Twyla stands on the dark, curved hull of a capsized fishing boat. A dozen basketball-sized green glass balls with thick, blackened rope wrapped around each of them knock gently against the boat. Her bright yellow skirt-panel swimsuit drips seawater onto her feet. She watches sunbeams sparkle off the crashing wavetops at the mouth of the small bay. Beauty and destruction. She doesn't dare take up an interrogation of God's design—not enough church, not enough education, just… not enough.

She squeezes out her hair and sweeps her gaze across the clouds to the west, locking on a low-flying flock of B-17 bombers heading straight for her. *A murder of crows*, Wiley would say.

*

Excerpt from World at War Digest, Volume 1

Sixteen million American men would eventually enlist. Tens of thousands of men and women would build 300,000 planes, 40,000 tanks, 10,000 ships of all kinds, trucks, guns, and unknown billions of bombs and bullets. The United States would add its might to the Pacific Theater, Europe, North African Front, and China. Spread thin with astronomical attrition rates, the pressure wouldn't let up until deep into 1944.

*

Dearest Husband,

I have spent the last six months helping new friends dig out of the harbor wreckage, their broken hearts reanimating their loved ones' every detail. Many graveyard promises cracked out of trembling voices in tear-soaked repetition. I am waiting for a reply from Mrs. Love, Ms. Cochran, or the ATC. Every day I'm greeted with silence from them and you.

Don't be a Wiley! Send me a scrap of paper with an "X" on it.

Sour grape kisses,
Twyla

The four-engine B-17s cleave the air at only two hundred feet off the water, their rumble and roar easily overtaking the surf. Twyla waves to the flyers as they pass. She watches them skim the slim palm trees on the hilltops and twist out over the sea as they disappear. The crashing surf slowly resumes the sound bed of her swim hole.

Days blend together.

Dearest Husband,

I spilled my guts to poor Doris today. Again. Newspaper and scrap metal drives, war bond rallies, and spy talk leave me empty. I want to be tougher. It's been almost a year since the call for female flyers went out. Seems every girl aviator is going to train in Texas but me. After we cleared all the airfields, I traded instructing time for twin-engine training and gained another hundred hours.

Please come home.

Forlorn kisses,
Twyla

Lying on her back, stretched out across the capsized boat hull, she stares at the clouds assembling into massive towers to the east. Her skin is tan, her swimsuit faded. Two old men cast fishing lines from the shore. Overhead, thirty bombers fly east to west while twenty fighters flow southward and crosshatch the open sky. She says, "Come on, T. C. Haliday, let's go ambush the postman!"

Dear Skeezix!

Bull's-eye! The day has finally come. I'm shaking with excitement, so I can hardly write. I'm off to Texas! I'm going to fly for this country! I hope. If I can pass the test. I'll likely have a criminal record when you return because I mauled the postman.

I miss you and love you beyond Mars.

Lone Star kisses!
Twyla

The morning before she would board the *SS Lurline* for the mainland—the same steamer that brought Amelia and her Lockheed Vega to Honolulu eight years earlier—Twyla swims out to her boat hull island. Glistening in the contoured, humid air, she rubs the scar on her eyebrow and, with distress, must admit this horrible war may be good for her—perhaps a peek into an Abraham-Lincoln style gripping force compelling her toward something quite unreasonable. After reading about the adventures of the RAF women's auxiliary pilots, she desires to be a military pilot more than anything else, or at least equal to her yearning to visit Mars—they feel similarly impossible. *Lincoln gave in to no one.*

She scans the shoreline around her, finds the two old fishermen, then spots a diesel trawler a mile out to the east and a bomber formation on the horizon. She tries to imagine actually meeting the famous flyers Jackie Cochran and Nancy Love. *What kind of pilot is named Love?* She dives back into the lagoon and swims for shore.

s i x

GIRLS! WHY WASTE A GOOD MAN ON A TYPEWRITER?

N ancy Love—twenty-eight years old, graduate of Milton Academy and Vassar College, silver medal finisher in the Detroit Air Races of 1936, and test pilot for the Gwinn Aircar Company—slips her fingers under her robin's-egg-blue headscarf and scratches her scalp. She twists unconsciously back and forth in her apricot housecoat, looking more like a grade-schooler than a licensed pilot with 1,200 hours and the co-owner of an aviation company. By way of the kitchen window, the Atlantic overcast sky shines on a letter fresh out of her Royal typewriter. She carefully pinches its corners, as if her nails are still wet, while her wide set blue eyes flick across the page as she reads aloud.

"... and that highly experienced women pilots could transport every type of airplane in military use. Every day, this is met with, 'sounds like men's work.' But this is only true in the small head of a small-minded man, a man insecure in his skin, unable to think in the present tense. If a woman can imagine a thing, it is therefore not a man's thing. As it is true in reverse, so is it self-evident. The uneven field of intelligence is the problem, not gender.

A woman's skills are equally hers. The next time your capable wife bumps into a stubborn man, she should ask him, 'What are you afraid of, sir, my abilities or yours? Are you so weak in your stance that my success reveals your false bravado?' The world is wide enough for both sexes to contribute to any effort, especially in wartime.

Mr. President, I am at your service.

Sincerely,
Nancy Harkness Love

Inter City Aviation."

"You can't send that letter," her husband says, sitting in his undershirt, one hand poised on *The Washington Post*, the other inching an empty coffee cup toward her. His eyes hold fast above his reading glasses.

"And why not?" Her head tilts as she throws a hip.

"Everything was great until the second sentence. Because, dear, you've just insulted the most powerful man in the Western world with logic he cannot refute at a moment when he feels the least sure of himself. You may indeed be able to 'think of a self-evident thing,' but you also know your poor timing is self-evident."

"So there is 'good timing' in war?" she says with a little too much force.

"Are you really that nervous about your meeting today?"

"Shouldn't I be? You know how stubborn military men are. And why are they stubborn, Bob? They already have all the power. There's always a new rule or surprise they like to spring on you."

"They don't like change," he says, nudging the cup.

"You mean they fear losing control of every little thing! Too bad!" She actually stomps her feet, instantly regretting it.

"Hey, I agree with you. A good idea has no gender. But I'm *used* to you flying all over hill and yon'. They are not. But why don't you let me come with you?"

"The logic of my idea is irrefutable. My pilots are already proving it. I can handle it." She exhales loudly and swipes his cup from his fingertips.

He mumbles, "Maybe a little sugar, then?"

That afternoon at Anacostia, District of Columbia, Nancy Love—from Boston, Massachusetts—is offered a seat between Colonel Tunner and Lieutenant General George, head of Air Transport Command. It is an unremarkable room of light gray walls and a few framed portraits of presidents and admirals—reluctant of imagination, strong on functionality. It is the exact type of room in which her husband spends twelve hours a day.

"Do you know why you're here?" Colonel Tunner inquires.

"Sir, I'm hopeful it is in response to my many requests for petty cash, fuel exempt coupons, and train passes for my pilots. They are all going broke from paying their own way, buying and repairing their own cold-weather clothing, and feeding themselves to and from your planes."

"Mrs. Love," George begins, "with all due respect to you and your capable husband, the women of your auxiliary are not an official part of the USAAF."

"And if this truly makes sense to you, shall I have my girls turn their PT-19s around and head back to New Castle and Long Beach? I'll have them return the two hundred and fifty planes they've delivered without a hitch to your airfields."

"We cannot, at this time, make you military," Colonel Tunner declares.

She looks at them for a long moment, wondering who is the good cop. "Can't, sir? Or *won't?*"

"Mrs. Love," the general says calmly, "General Arnold has agreed to Jackie's request to halt all women's auxiliary ferry activities until she returns from England."

Nancy shoots out of her chair. "What?"

Both men rise. "I… we… were assuming you and Ms. Cochran were on the same page," he stammers.

"No, we aren't," she mutters, gripping her skirt, "through our final assessment of the training phase… details." Her eyes dart to each of them. "Yes, sir, we—we are on the same page," she finally sputters weakly. Her face flushes. She wonders how old she will be when she can finally act as confident as she feels.

The two officers turn to each other and excuse themselves from the cramped meeting room. They stand on the other side of the half-glass door. She hears a cigar being clipped—and every word.

"This is in General Arnold's hands."

"And I'm not sure I want to know what Ms. Cochran has in her hands," says Tunner.

"Well, we're not touching this again until we have to."

"If loss estimates bear out, we'll be seeing Mrs. Love and Jackie real soon."

"If the gals would just drop the military status demand, maybe we could get them a paycheck."

Nancy pulls the scarf out of her purse and mumbles, "No kidding?" She plucks out her flight log, writing the date and "East Boston Field" onto the page for her return flight. She imagines Jackie Cochran, the most famous American aviatrix in America, holding court under thunderous four-engine Lancaster bombers in Berkshire, England. The women's auxiliary flyers of the RAF will be just sideways with enthusiasm for their Yankee superstar until they realize every conversation must retroject onto Jackie and her personal accomplishments. They won't know what hit them.

Nancy pulls away from the guard shack at the Naval Air Station in a '40 Dodge Sedan used by VIP visitors to and from civil fields. Her thoughts drift through a slow collage of pilots' faces as if they are on billboards along the road. Her girls, her pilots, the WAFS, are a kaleidoscope of personalities, shapes, and sizes. She admires their toughness and feels both sorry for and proud of their choice to do such hard work. She marvels at how divergent the public's perception of a ferry pilot's life is.

Civilians think us frivolous, perhaps even glamorous. To them, it is unreasonable that we should demand pay and military status for doing a job no more difficult than a Sears, Roebuck, and Co. catalog model. But the military? Especially these two men, pilots themselves, know better. They know. What am I going to tell my girls?

Driving over the Anacostia and Potomac Rivers, she flips a stick of Beeman's between her teeth and thinks, *Stopped by the very war brass who need me, and thwarted by Jackie.* Chewing her gum too hard, she readies her Fairchild for a sunset commute back to Boston. She runs up the engine, spits the Beeman's out the window, and presses her knuckles into her jawbone. She grudgingly admits Jackie has the ball—playing the control game to *win* the control game. Of this puzzle, Nancy has the logical piece: Offer Air Transport Command a steady supply of prequalified pilots. Jackie, however, has the winning piece: The women of the Royal Air Force have been a success story for two years. At the front, no less! Their iron-clad template—train a large force of *military* women to ferry all planes between factories and air bases. And Jackie is now the American expert. Later, Nancy Love's flying women, the WAFS, will be known and appreciated as "the originals." But, for now, they are just fucked.

She rushes up to two thousand feet, just shy of the gray ceiling, and points her propeller north. The imminent debate with Jackie is already writing itself in her head. Nancy will argue, "Do not force a Women's Ferry Command onto the AAF; they will double clutch and throw you out. The Women's Army Corps is our way in. Colonel Hobby holds the key." But Jackie will shoot back, "The AAF deserves its own organization of women pilots, and we have a three-star general on our side." She imagines Jackie applying her very own Wings to Beauty lipstick to her thin lips and adding, "I will personally command the transport pilots. I will not give our girls to Hobby."

Nancy will counter, "But Oveta Hobby knows nothing about aviation! Her hands are full with the WACs. Instead, she can help us quickly organize into the shape of military expectation, then oversee us in title only."

"The women ferry pilots," Jackie spits back, "will be under my command alone, or not at all!"

And there it is. In spite of all the crow Nancy has eaten over the years—forced upon her by small-minded men with large egos—even her own gender cannot turn away from the magnetic influence of power, or the fear of having none. She is convinced the two forces display the same contrail.

Three hours later, she lands at East Boston Field with eleven photons of light guiding her into her hangar. Fifteen of her company's twenty-two planes—

Ryans, Fairchilds, and Fleets—sleep within. A few of her employees are still working, and she quickly ingests summaries of the day's training and commercial activities, says her goodnights, and walks to her car. Rain comes down in large drops, noisy drops like hard-shelled beetles let out of a bag all at once. *There it is*, she thinks, *the first luck I've had all day.*

The stubby street lamps in this old neighborhood are more decorative than helpful, yet they shimmer appealingly on the soaked streets. Her porch light is on, and she parks her '42 Streamliner behind Bob's Mercury. Before she gets out, she notices two shadows standing on the opposite side of the street—two silhouettes, to be more precise. They are clearly women with long coats, hairdos, and purses slung on their arms, yet not one umbrella between them. They seem to be frozen, each with what she guesses is a magazine above her head. Nancy circles to the passenger side and plucks out her umbrella, purse, and briefcase. When she closes the door, the two figures are gone. Halfway up the front steps, she turns.

The two figures are standing in front of the Mercury, the porch light failing to reveal any details.

"Good evening," Nancy says. "Can I help you?"

"Good evening, Mrs. Love," the taller one replies. "We are so sorry to intrude like this. My name is Cornelia, and this is Naomi. We want to fly for you."

"Ha!" Nancy convulses, her purse falling to the crook of her elbow. "I'm afraid I've got nothing but bad news for you. Where are you staying?"

"Uh, we don't know yet," Cornelia says. "We've been here all day, hoping you would show."

"Your planning skills are suspect," Nancy remarks.

"There's no doubt." Cornelia smiles.

Nancy shakes out her umbrella. "Well, girls, let's make your day better than mine."

They gather in the kitchen because they need both hot coffee and tea, and there is minestrone soup to reheat. They pull chairs out of the dining room and into a small canary yellow kitchen that seems to belong to another season.

"Before I catch you up on the fate of the WAFS," Nancy starts, "tell me, when was the moment you knew you were meant to fly?"

Cornelia and Naomi glance at each other, confusion overtaking their faces. And yet, their shoulders relax a little, as if they'd expected a fight over their logbooks or proof they weren't crazy. Naomi nods to Cornelia—she should go first. A copper kettle perched on the O'Keefe and Merritt whistles like a train's send-off.

"Well, Mrs. Love, for me, it happened in two parts," says the slim, brown-eyed, brown-haired Southerner. "And it was because of my father. Though, not in the usual way…"

*

Cornelia, at eight years of age, waited in her shiny sky blue dress in front of the white-columned colonial estate next to her father, dressed in his usual dark wool suit and brown tie. She carefully hid her left hand behind that dress as a long, sleek automobile pulled up. The Negro driver, Epperson, took Father's suitcase and helped Cornelia into the back. She stood up on the seat to better see out the front windshield of the Rickenbacker Sedan.

At Blackwood Field airstrip, a Ford Tri-Motor passenger aeroplane boarded a dozen travelers. Cornelia stood at a low wooden rail, watching two families send their wool-suited fathers away. Three boys, all under ten years of age, played with scrap-wood planes. A smoke-belching CCC bus screeched to a stop behind them, spinning Cornelia around as Father bent toward her. "Epperson will drive you back," he said. "Listen to your mother while I'm gone and don't play with your brother's toys. I'll return in one week's time."

Cornelia compared the bus and the aeroplane and asked, "Father, why don't you ride the aeroplane?" She extended both arms to hug him and suddenly jerked her left hand back, almost forgetting her secret. "Doesn't the aeroplane go faster? High and fast?"

"When flying is as safe as a bus," he said, straightening tall and glancing over at the Tri-Motor. "And that day will never come." He patted her head.

"Okay, Father," she replied with an oversized smile.

The bus departed, a cone of dust chasing after it.

Cornelia ran back to the rail and the magnificent aeroplane. Though it wasn't graceful or sleek, the bulldog stance of its main gear and large propellers shoved into the nose and under the wings gave the impression of sturdiness and strength, but certainly not grace. She wondered how it could fly, why it looked nothing like a bird. Suddenly, two pilots with starched white shirt collars, dark blue ties, dark wool pants, shiny black shoes, and epaulets on their shoulders strolled around the plane. Flat-topped, navy-blue hats clarified their station. They were lean, confident, and conversed easily, seemingly without care. She wondered if they knew their job was too dangerous for her father. They disappeared into the fuselage. Then, surprisingly, one of the pilots poked his head out of the side door and pointed his smile right at her. His eyes and teeth seemed to twinkle.

She turned around to see who was behind her; only the stinky boys, who played on without even noticing. Then, the pilot waved. Her breath caught. She raised her hand to wave back, but the glamorous man ducked away. The stinky boys flew their planes past Cornelia's face, then turned and offered their tongues. Cornelia smiled and revealed her hidden treasure, a finely detailed World War I fighter. But not just any biplane—this was the famous Spad XIII of the Ace of Ace's Eddie Rickenbacker, captain of The Hat in the Ring squadron, complete with miniature fuselage art of Uncle Sam's top hat in the middle of the red ring. No self-respecting future-ace-of-a-boy could mistake that plane for anything else.

The Tri-Motor blared to life. All heads turned, fidgeting ceased, and eyes fixed on the belching exhaust, spinning blades, and tossed leaves. The plane waddled a 180-degree turn and went straight to full power with a fantastic, concussive rumbling and humming. Up the dirt runway it went, lifting, straining, barely visible through its roiling brown plume. The magic plane disappeared, and the boys turned to Cornelia, soundlessly floating toward her. She lifted the toy plane just a little higher, her tongue sliding out of her mouth, and there was nothing the boys could do.

"Little Sister," Epperson called, his smile thinly veiled as he gestured toward the car. Her best "fighter aeroplane" sound burst forth. Teasing the boys, she slowly backed away. She discovered it was impossible to project a raspberry while smiling.

*

Nancy stands stock-still, mid-ladle over the pan of soup, her head inclining back and forth a little. She resumes filling the bowl, enjoying this young woman's voice as it meanders like rubber silk, from Southern drawl to the clipped patois of Kate Hepburn.

"A rare victory over boys," Nancy says. "And at such a tender age. So, Ms. South, was it the Ford Tri-Motor?"

"No, ma'am," Cornelia says. "It was the pilot. So sure of himself, or maybe his uniform, which seemed to belong to the flying machine he commanded. I had never imagined such a wonderful person. I didn't know it was possible. But…" she pauses, retracing, reconstructing. "I didn't know how to connect it to me. Not until…"

*

By her tenth birthday, Cornelia was as tall as her brothers, Ronald and Donald. By age thirteen, she was completely out of sorts. She vexed against reason in the repetition of school, chores, what was women's work, and what was men's. In church, she kept a running count of inconsistencies in the sermons and scriptures, creating a snaking numerical column in her sketchbook. "Hypocrisy" became her new favorite word. She adored writing poetry and began a series of fantasies about being the lost granddaughter of Elizabeth Barrett Browning. That is, until the day she discovered the exploits of Amelia Earhart, an aviatrix—*the* aviatrix. The word alone was enough to ignite a lighthouse beam in her soul, burning toward a gunpowder future charged to blow the tiny furniture right out of her dollhouse.

The following weekend at the polo grounds, this new future was cured cement when a barnstorming squadron demonstrated wing walking and a midair machine-to-machine transfer of an aviator. From that day forth, she was smitten with aviation and the glamorous adventure that came with it. Any man who tried to explain why her desire to fly was foolish was instantly demoted to stooge. "That's his frog to fry!" she would exclaim.

By age sixteen, Cornelia's idea of the modern woman was like undeveloped silver nitrate film, all potential and highly combustible. She couldn't help comparing this incandescent idea to her own stone-colored mother, the gray society ladies, and the beige church women. The future woman *was* the new Wild West. "Don't bring a knife to a gunfight and don't ride the bus when you can fly!" she would exclaim, rejoicing in the sparkling reality that A.E. actually did that. But Amelia Earhart was so far away and so unapproved by her father. What's a Southern girl to do?

*

Naomi, quietly sipping her soup, nods her head vigorously. Her long black hair doesn't completely hide her indigenous American features. Nancy sits on the countertop, lightly banging her bare heels against the cupboard, and says, "How did your father feel about your interest?"

"He did not approve," Cornelia grumbles. "So much so that one day I heard him talking to my brothers from just outside the withdrawing room. They were joining a local flying club, then going into the Army Air Corps. My father's voice rose to a pitch, admonishing against this. He drew up a letter making them promise they would not fly—ever. He wanted them to sign it. I couldn't believe it. I was so frightened for them."

"Did they sign the letter?" Naomi asks.

"They did. I was shocked. Then, it occurred to me he might ask me to do the same. I ran out of the house holding my breath."

"But did he ask you?" Nancy inquires.

"I held my breath for years. Until the day he died."

Nancy takes Cornelia's bowl, dumps the soup back into the pan, and ignites the flame.

"Why didn't he stop you?" Naomi asks.

"My only conclusion is he knew he couldn't."

"Saved himself some grief," Nancy adds and pads over to the dining room to switch out Bob's raincoats hanging above the radiator. "Fathers and daughters," she mumbles to herself. "Naomi?"

"Yes, ma'am?" Naomi starts, as if she's surprised to hear her name.

"Airship or pilot?"

"Oh, yes, ma'am. Airship."

*

Nascha Tachii'ni—everyone called her Owl, not because they thought her wise, but because she stared at you unblinkingly while delivering allegorical counsel, cautionary similes, or bad news. Owl pushed the windblown hair from her face and tracked the noisy, featherless bird circling wide around her home in the Checkerboard area of the Navajo Nation. It finally landed at the abandoned farm half a mile up the road. She ran to see it. The flying machine was the answer to her unspeakable dreams—the confirmation that her own spirit was not *yíní 'áhodildin* (mentally deficient). For the next two months after school, she ran to see the plane. She could outrun any boy, save her two older brothers.

One miraculous day, those brothers—able tractor mechanics—were asked by slender and black-mustachioed Mr. Selfridge to help fix the biplane. He described how he flew the plane for an American oil company/Navajo land liaison office.

"This is my sister, Owl Nascha Tachii'ni," her brother said. "She's eight."

Mr. Selfridge, his hands in the engine of the plane, didn't even look up. "Welcome to Selfridge's flying garage, Naomi."

The Stinson SM-2 Junior was equipped with a camera for aerial surveying, and on one mystifying day, the plane came to the Owl. It was towed to her home and stayed parked in her yard for a full week while her brothers constructed mounts and linkages with which to control a camera's shutter from the cockpit. Owl was spellbound. She drew pictures of the aeroplane at school; she daydreamed of silkworm clouds, and she slept under the Stinson's wings at night. She asked her teacher to bring her books about aviation. Owl read everything and forgot nothing. Her brothers became the aeroplane's unofficial pit crew. Selfridge Flying Garage quietly absorbed Naomi the Owl into its weekly operations. Her first ride came that year. By eleven, she was copiloting, and she soloed at thirteen.

Owl rarely blinks; this creates an intensity she's often teased about. She doesn't mind. She observes the lines of tension between men and women of the reservation as keenly as if there were physical strings attached to them. She perceives the colors of the strings represent different emotions. This is also true of woman-to-woman tensions; the colors are dyed from the secondary or tertiary palette, as primary colors are only for the men. Thus detected, she can step easily around, over, or weave through these strings, avoid or manipulate the tension lines, and create a desired result. Her desire is to fly. Much noise is made about this. She discerns, dodges, manipulates, forgets nothing, frowns, but doesn't blink.

*

Nancy pulls the whistling kettle from the stovetop and refills Naomi's cup. "If it weren't hard enough," Nancy says. "But an SM-2 is a stable ship." She offers wine, but since they are all pilots who might fly tomorrow, no one accepts. "I'm sorry you both missed out with the WAFS," Nancy adds. "Though we've just hit our stride, it could be so much better. We're in a holding pattern for now."

"Mrs. Love, you are proving the impossible," Cornelia says.

"Mrs. Love," Naomi adds, "we just wish there was a way we could help."

"I know this, and please, call me Nancy. Yours is the one unanimous sentiment among all the girl fliers I've met. We want to make practical our profession. Prove we are not just carelessly smitten with flying, but worthy of it."

"Yes, ma'am," they concur simultaneously.

"And if we can do so while serving our country's needs?"

"The perfect dream," Naomi breathes.

Nancy looks at Naomi and smiles for the first time today.

*

Dearest Lewis,

You are forgiven, my love.

A bag of your letters arrived today. I read them without breath. I may have "prayed" to Mars a few times for your life. I'm sure I'm not the only wife to suffer the delays of V-mail. I have been absent a way to picture your daily activities until now. Your squadron mates sound swell. I can't imagine your life with all the death around you. The sinking of the USS (REDACTED)… Thank goodness you and Wiley are good swimmers.

A double batch of loweezies will meet you on your new ship as soon as you can send her name. I'll write again soon from a foreign land called Texas.

Broken- and mending-heart kisses,
Twy

Dear Wiley,

Thank you for your letter. You have no idea the intensity of my relief that you and Lewis are alive. You are a clever fellow. Who knew someday we would be grateful for the natural encryption of Boontling?

I'm glad you and Lewis are taking the bahl chapport to the Japs. I'm sure there is no other place you would want to be. Yet, I am so fearful for you both. Are you getting along okay? Every day, I think of you and what you did for me. Because of you, my nightmares recede. Take care of yourself and bossy-pants. Everyone says this will be over by Christmas.

P.S. Kiss Llewellyn hard on the mouth for me.
P.P.S. While you're in the South Pacific, keep an eye out for Amelia.

Love,
Twy

*

One last bus ride separates Twyla from Avenger Field, home of her best dream or her second-worst fear. In San Francisco, she had stepped off the Lurline steamer and self-flagellated for an hour over whether she should detour to Anderson Valley to see the Tuttles and Gerald Haliday. In the end, she took a taxi to the train station in Oakland. Destination Central Texas would require no less than three trains and seven buses, all the while collecting sneers, head shakes, catcalls, and general disapproval from the perfect American citizenry.

Lying in the final dilapidated and smoke-soaked motel bed of her sojourn, she tracks a variety of local sounds: a two-thousand-part harmony of crickets swells upward. Men's voices intrude, stalling them out in an instant. The chorus tentatively comes back to life, yet just as suddenly stops when footfalls crunch the driest dirt she's ever walked upon. Late-arriving trucks excite her already jumpy heart. People seem to come and go all night. She longs for the islands and the interstice of perfection she and Lewis held before the world changed.

She floats in and out of light sleep and unexpectedly finds herself staring at Castor's face. He is saturated in red half-light, sweaty, and breathing hard. Italian words tumble out of him as he climaxes and rolls off her. She wakes, glistening in her own sweat. A few deep breaths, and she is calm. She hates Italians, hates Italian words. She knows, intellectually, the country of Italy would claim no part in this, but she doesn't care about that. This is her first nightmare since Pearl Harbor. She writes a letter to Lewis.

Do you know, every single time I look up into the night sky, especially when I gaze upon the Milky Way, I just know the party is on. Yet, no one here is even talking about it. Why isn't our national effort toward the exploration of our planetary neighborhood instead of political fights and war? Don't you just think that at the center of our galaxy, right downtown at the soda fountains and colossal galactic libraries, they are laughing at us? Their magazines and books tell about backwood village planets like ours, and they can only shake their heads in pity.

She turns Castor's face over like he's a paper photograph and replaces it with Lewis making love to her. She wonders again if she ever could have enjoyed intimacy with Lewis if Wiley hadn't killed Castor. In her mind, they were two separate baskets crowded with two distinct burdens. Castor hurt her, lied to her, seemed to want and resent her in the space of two breaths. And against this, she froze herself into a solid block. Yet, in Lewis's basket, she feels warm and safe.

But what if Castor could still get to her; would she be so open to Lewis? Was it the sequence of events that made the difference? Lewis and Wiley had acted. The boys promised they would shoulder this problem, and they had. If she could only talk to Wiley, to thank him again and again. Wiley stood against her impossible monster and, with his bare hands, ended it. Ended all of it; gave her and Lewis a chance. At first, she was shocked by the idea of Castor's death, didn't believe there could be an end to his influence, an end to his appearance in her waking nightmare. But it had happened. Wiley did that for her.

I love you, too, Wiley.

*

Excerpt from "A Family History" by Elizabeth Haliday

WILEY H. FELTON, whom you've met in previous pages, is not a Haliday or a Campbell, nor even a Tuttle. Yet, he was, and is, considered family.

Wiley grew up without bio parents. He worked for his Uncle Gordon since he was three. All he knew was work at the general store, the hotel, and every single person in Anderson Valley. He managed to get through eight primary grades when his aunt passed away. Gordon was a wreck for months, long enough to leave Wiley in charge of the whole enterprise and put an end to his formal schooling.

Lewis and Wiley didn't become instant friends, as they both had much to prove. But it was Wiley's humor that eventually won Lewis over. That day in seventh grade, Wiley satirized a newspaper headline about a new scientific discovery that there were actually people dumber than dirt.

"Lewis hooted so hard, he couldn't breathe," Wiley recalled with a chuckle. "I suspect he'd never dipped into humor that far down the well."

They were bonded into the valley's version of Mutt and Jeff, inseparable and almost always laughing at something. Wiley confided, "I've met a lot of despicable people, despicable men, liars, cheaters, vain and selfish and small-minded. I don't like most men. Since a pink age, I've been afraid I am one of them. I always wanted to be an honorable man—someone you could count on. Llewellyn and Twyla gave me that chance."

*

Standing on the side of a flat road in gathering Central Texas heat, Twyla isn't sure what she's looking at, isn't sure she slept one minute last night. Across the road, the telephone poles have four lines strung at their tops and run all the way to the horizon. They droop in the usual manner and glow bright white as the sun gets behind them. Or are they electrical lines? She isn't sure how one tells the difference. The trees along this road arc right over the poles and shade the asphalt, except for one tree-sized empty space and a strange-looking bird perched stock-still on the wire. The bird is thick and dark with a long tail. From this side of the road, she can't make out what type of bird, as it doesn't move, doesn't exhibit that twitchy look-about most birds have.

She drags her suitcase across the asphalt. The bird on the wire slowly resolves into a tree limb, cut square on both ends and speared by the telephone line. She scans the space between the trees and finds a stump half-hidden in dry grass. *There you are… were*, she thinks and stares back up at the suspended limb. She is surprisingly drawn to this hovering remnant and simultaneously curious about her own curiosity. She finds no ready answer. This tree's future was cut short, its past nearly invisible. What dangles on the line is all that's left of what was once flourishing overstory. Save for the lazy, or cautious, lineman, there would be no record of her life as she transmuted the sun and soil, stretched out her arms, braved the wind, and cooled the road. Did this tree know her success would be met with such anonymous violence? *One could disappear just like that*, Twyla thinks. *If Lewis doesn't come back, are Wiley and I the remnant? If both boys die in battle, am I the severed limb?*

A rumbling noise pulls her back onto her blistered feet. A bus approaches and squeaks to a stop in front of her. The door smacks open. The glistening bus driver drags a handkerchief across his brow and says, "Lemme guess, miss— Avenger Field?"

She canopies her eyes from the low sun. "Yes, sir. Why, how did you know?"

His head tilts. "Yes'm, c'mon."

She grabs her suitcase and climbs aboard. Four women are spread across the seats, sleeping soundly in a variety of intimate geometry with suitcases and coats. The driver closes the door and says, "Welcome to Sweetwater."

seven

MARS

he Nolan County bus tapers away, dissolving in a beige cloud above a ruler-straight road pointing directly at the Texas horizon. Twyla hobbles asymmetrically under the weight of her overstuffed suitcase and beneath a sign stretched high above the road, spelling out, AVIATION ENTERPRISES, LTD. Within these large letters is a cartoon gremlin known as Fifinella, the Walt Disney–designed mascot of the WASPs, Women Air Force Service Pilots.

Her arm sweats and itches under a folded wool coat. Her persimmon curls have gleefully escaped her rosemary headscarf as she grunts and shambles over the dirt landscape into a sparse compound. She tilts an ear toward a raspy round-engine on low approach and tracks the stubby plane through the whitewashed structures ahead.

A bell rings.

Turning down a long, low barracks row, she imagines they look just like the chicken houses in Petaluma when viewed from five hundred feet. She spots the bell rigged on a pole above a hastily formed cement wishing well. A startled young man in a khaki shirt and trousers standing below it stares at her through a curl of cigarette smoke. She drops the suitcase, but there's no slowing the sweat spreading under her blue floral, calf-length dress. Her makeup smears across her cheeks; her lipstick has reached her chin. *No way there are women out here. Can a human get any farther from Hawaii?* The young man points the cigarette to his right. She hefts her luggage and runs.

Atop a small podium adorned with a scooped banner of stars and stripes, a striking woman in a white silk blouse, navy blue skirt, and military style cap with thick blonde waves dangling below stares out like a war bond poster. She is a pleasant, somewhat athletic-looking woman of thirty-eight years. She is a household name, a rock star of the early twentieth century, a decade before the birth of rock music and fifty years ahead of her time. She is speed, courage, and futuristic sex appeal packaged so insistently, she will never be an admiral's wife. World-renowned aviatrix Jacquelyn (Jackie) Cochran, multiple air race winner, speed champion, and self-made businesswoman from Backwood-Butt-Scratch, Florida, holds the gaze of thirty pilot-hopefuls. Out behind them all, a dozen primary trainer aircraft spread across the flight apron, now joined by the ridiculous hubbub of the taxiing BT-13 Vultee, the stubby round-engine airplane known as the "Vibrator."

Twyla pushes her way through the crowd, her eyes locked on the little podium, on the first famous person she's ever seen. She stops between a tall brunette, a raven-haired woman of Twyla's exact height, and a curly-headed girl of short stature. Surrounding her are dozens more women of various ages and builds, all anxious and fidgety. *But why are they all dressed in coveralls and boots? How late am I? Why did I have to fall asleep on the bus?*

The curly one points at Twyla's chin. That's when she notices everyone is staring at her. She sets down her luggage, pulls a handkerchief from her purse, and says, "Sorry I'm late."

"Right on time," Curly replies while giving her a sideways glance.

The late afternoon sun saturates the flyers in the trichromatic half-light of expectation. A breeze kicks up, charging the air with electricity. Jackie smiles at the flyers with perfect poise and perfect lipstick. They gawk at their blazing hero, every one of them wanting to *be* her.

"Ladies, pilots, WASP hopefuls, welcome to Avenger Field—by way of a few adventures, no doubt." Ironic chuckles and bobbing heads loosen the women just a little. "Chance has turned her gaze upon us," Jackie continues. "Prove yourself in this program, and you get to ring the graduation bell." All heads pivot to look for the bell, though they can't see it from here. "Afterward, for the rest of your life, you will wear this pin on your lapel." She touches the silver propeller-shaped pin on her jacket. They all lean forward like synchronized sunflowers in the breeze, breathless. "You are here because you are experienced pilots, and your Army Air Corps needs you. This war needs you. Every airplane a woman can transport from factories to aerodromes here in the States saves a man to do the real work at the front. I am committed to this program above all else. It is our war effort. But make no mistake, girls, this is a dangerous business. Listen smart to your instructors. There is much to learn, and your hard work will be rewarded with the hot advanced trainer, the AT-6 Texan."

"Oohs" and "ahhs" tumble about as each woman imagines driving 650 horsepower gear up. Just like the men. "Thank you for doing your part for the war effort. Smooth flying, pilots," Jackie finishes.

"Thank you, ma'am!" hollers the tall brunette next to Twyla in an appealing Southern accent. She turns to the women around her, adding, "For whom the bell tolls, girls? It tolls for we belles."

The bell rings for each branch of the military—its curved peal quick to disappear across the desert prairie. As Jackie shakes hands with the field staff, Twyla absorbs the new faces around her. No one else moves in Jackie's presence, save for Curly, bouncing up and down and panting like a dog. "How many flying records does Jackie have?" Curly asks.

Raven Hair, just on the other side of her, says, "All of them. Detroit airshow in 1937, three-kilometer course. First woman to average three hundred miles per hour."

"Yes, ma'am. That's newspaper true," the tall brunette adds.

The pilot hopefuls begin to fidget in their "one-size-fits-all" olive drab jumpsuits, yards of extra fabric turning them into Vaudeville mechanics. They track Jackie and a half-dozen officers meandering away from the recruits.

Tall Brunette adds a stick of gum to her mouth, then reaches behind Twyla and says, "Becca?"

Curly turns. "Affirmative and thank you, Pilot Cornelia." She plucks out several sticks of Beeman's, offering them to Twyla and the other girls near her.

"How 'bout you, Owl?"

"No, thank you," says Raven Hair.

Twyla looks at their faces again and back to the real-life Jackie Cochran and those dozen military planes parked on the apron. *Just for me.* She pinches herself in the side until the pain verifies her consciousness. *The perfect dream really does exist*, she muses and says, "Becca, Owl, Cornelia, I'm Twyla."

"Pleasure to meet you, Twyla," they all say at once.

Cornelia snaps her gum, pirouettes, and says, "Mister, there's nothin' quite like a finely tailored suit to best express the geometric splendor of a woman's edges."

They giggle at the bag suit.

"Toto, we ain't in Kansas no more," Becca adds.

Owl leans close to Becca and says, "Please don't mention the flying monkeys; I won't sleep."

"Oookay," Becca says with a roll of her eyes and grabs at her britches. "Hey, I think I have this figured out." Pulling her pants up to her knees, Becca jumps in place, crosses her feet, and spins around backward, her boots still facing forward. Laughter floats like dandelion seeds.

"Walt the mechanic would do it that way," Twyla says.

"Gasoline Alley!" Becca shouts.

"Wrong, skeezix! Harold Lloyd, y'all," Cornelia puts in.

"Stan Laurel," Owl offers, and this is agreed to be correct.

"Do you think they'll make us jump with a parachute?" Twyla blurts, ruining the merriment.

"Oh, hmmm, maybe," Becca says. "But who cares? Jackie's backing us. Everything's bird."

"If they turn us into honest-to-goodness military pilots, I'll jump from a plane," Cornelia says heartily.

"Not me," Twyla says a little too quickly, then decides to shut up.

The new friends imagine jumping *out* of an airplane. Becca snaps them back. "Hey, you've buttered your bread, now sleep in it!"

"Thank you, Gracie," Owl mumbles.

"Howdy, girlies," says a black-haired man in snug officer's khakis. Three similarly dressed male pilots with helmets and goggles in hand are right on his heels.

"Howdy to you," Cornelia replies.

Twyla steps back, almost pushed by the force of their confidence.

"You must be the replacements?" Snug says. The women glance at each other. "The previous class is all gone. Yes, they were fine girls."

"Indeed," Becca says. "So are we. We're the next class. I'm Rebecca Lawrence, this is Cornelia South, this here's Nascha the Owl, a.k.a Naomi of the Navajo Nation shuffleboard area—"

"Checkerboard," Naomi corrects.

"We grew up practically neighbors and didn't even know. And Twyla's our ginger from Mysteryville," Becca concludes, pleased with her command.

"Whoa, Seabiscuit," Snug wedges in. "No point do-si-do'n names."

"Why's that?" Cornelia asks.

"Oh, well," he says, glancing at his trio, "the previous class of girls was a good-looking bunch, but they washed out. Every one. They were okay in fixed-gear primes with an instructor in the seat, but as soon as they went solo in advanced machines with RG, they fell apart. Too much to handle." Cornelia looks to *her* trio, and they stare back. "It's okay," he says. "Y'all aren't built for the military planes. But, boy howdy, do you look good in bathing suits painted on the sides."

A man's voice behind them startles Twyla, "All right, fellas, you know the rules."

"Wilco," Snug replies with a half-hearted salute. He winks to his clique and saunters away.

Twyla swivels to her new mates. "Is that true? They all washed out?"

"Five out of thirty," Naomi says.

Cornelia rolls up her sleeves, "Don't listen to that peacock." But they can't help watching the men swagger a beeline for another group of women.

"Good morning, 'pilot-hopeful' ladies," says a short, stocky officer with close-cropped russet hair and a mouth so fast, his little mustache has to cling for dear life. He squares up on them. "Please try to arrange yourself into two rows of five." He says *try* as if it might be beyond them.

"Gravity," Naomi mutters. Twyla considers Naomi as the girls shift about.

"Listen carefully," he continues, "there are three things necessary to fly. Three. I'll give you the first one…"

"Wings," Naomi whispers.

The lieutenant points with a magically appearing riding crop to a plane on the flight line. Twyla and Naomi glance about for his horse, then stare at each other.

Becca blurts, "Wings. You need wings."

The lieutenant's invisible charger hits a rut and throws a shoe. "Yes. That… yes, an airplane is the first thing needed. And if you justifiably are who the jingling brass *say* you are, then you, the pilot, will be the second thing needed." He lines up on Rebecca. "If you talk less and pay attention…" he steps to Cornelia and lifts his sunglasses, scanning her from top to bottom, "and you *will* wash out or die if you don't, then you will exceed all expectations and learn the third thing needed to fly. By the by, I'm—"

*

"Lieutenant Hicks!" Cornelia trumpets twenty-four hours later as thirty girls march in parade through the barracks and out past the flight line of PT-19s and BT-13 trainer aircraft. "…was out in the back forty instructin' a mule on the nuancee'z of stubbornness when the Western Union arrived, spelling out just how many more flight hours we dames have than he does."

They reach the middle of a sandy, heat-baked parade ground, their manes and mops bound in white hair scarves, sleeves and cuffs rolled up. A blonde section leader, already sunburned, marches up front. "Hup, hup, hup, har!" The four new friends tramp shoulder-to-shoulder, bringing up the rear. Naomi says, "But the wind blew the Western Union off the porch, so Hicks never saw it."

Cornelia makes a mustache out of her finger and, in a low register, rumbles, "That'll double-clutch yer Studebaker!"

They laugh quietly as Becca grabs Cornelia's finger and puts it under her own nose, "You girlies…" Becca stomps the accelerator, ramping up to Hicks's speed, "will endure a hundred and fifty hours of flight training, twenty hours of LINK training, five hours a week of calisthenics, and a hundred and eighty hours of instruction in airframes, engines, navigation, ATC procedures, and meteorology! On weekends, you will practice military posturing, scratching, and spitting, after which you will all wash out!"

*

Journal, Sweetwater, 1943

Lewis is still in the PTO with Wiley, now flying from the Enterprise—*"The Big E" or the "Betty Eubanks," as we call her in Boont'eez. Reread his dozen letters, including his account of the sinking of the* Lexington*! I've now got a better mental newsreel of what he's been through—by way of Boont, card game, and baseball metaphor encryption. Boontling was easy loweezy, but I had to enlist help from my new friends to decipher the rest. Especially the baseball gobbledygook—like trying to read Polish!*

Out here in the middle of nowhere, there is a nearly constant thrumming, buzzing, and barking of airplanes. We do jumping jacks and study maps on walls or on children's desktops stolen from a local school—or "requisitioned for the war." There's perpetual note-taking and pencil-sharpening and diagrams of aircraft engines on the chalkboards and in our thick books. We even study whilst sunning ourselves between the barracks. The men drink Coca-Colas and watch us like we are on display in the world's driest fishbowl. Corny calls herself Pencil-Cola Dirt Floor-ida. Somehow, she got us all into the same billet! We honestly try to study our equations and military procedures, but all we can talk about is the AT-6 that came in last night. We're already sick of the Vultee and PT-19. None of us have ever been pulled by 650 retractable gear horses before.

Though we have different backgrounds, education, and political views, we're all MAD for flying!

The patch of dirt between the barracks and classrooms creates a rough "quad" to gather in between instruction. For weeks now, the men naturally congregate on the perimeter at this time of day to watch girls sunbathe in t-shirts, shorts, and even swimsuits.

Twyla sits in a folding chair wearing her bag suit uniform zipped all the way up, her books in her lap. She chews on the magical properties of Bernoulli's principle and fails. *Why would a faster-flowing liquid be under less pressure? Why would air flowing across the top of a curved airplane wing create lift? It has farther to go—it would fall behind. The invisible world!* And her mind is suddenly up at eight thousand feet in an autogyro with Amelia. Aboard the obnoxiously loud and spindly open-cockpit helicopter plane, she hugs her hero around the waist. She thinks, *The poor woman feels so skinny and frail.* Amelia turns her head and shouts, "Next, I'm going to set the cross-country record in this thing!"

A round engine blasts to life, snapping Twyla out of her trance. *Let's see the great Bernoulli Brothers explain the autogyro! But how do you properly respect something you don't understand?*

Across the fishbowl, she finds Hicks wedged like a keystone in an archway of nine male instructors.

Naomi sits reverse straddle on her dirt scaffolding, her chin on the chair's back and her jumper peeled to the waist. Becca has tipped her chair forward and lies on her stomach, her face pressed into the diagonal chair back in a most uncomfortable angle. Her aquamarine bathing-suited body splays over her coveralls. Cornelia lies on a towel, face down in shorts, her long, pink legs extending across the sand and into her immense boots.

Hicks jabs a pinch of tobacco into his lip, handing the pouch to the man next to him. His voice transmits clear as a desert bell, "Anything with tits or tires, you know there's trouble down the road." Sniggers in the affirmative and the clinking of Cokes follow.

Twyla shares a glance with Cornelia, who says, "Oh, the country club life. If only they would let us pay for housing and food and clothing and transportation."

"Wait, but I *do* pay for all that," Becca chirps.

"And what did Nancy Love tell us?" Naomi prompts. Blank stares. "Patience."

Eyes roll. Twyla throws a pencil, spearing Becca in the curls at the back of her head. "Hey, what the—?"

"Bec, how do you memorize the technical stuff?"

Becca extracts the pencil and turns her fierce, chair-embossed face to Twyla, rubbing her head. "Ever forget the words to a jump rope song?" She flings the pencil back at Twyla, who catches it.

"Hmmm," Twyla intones and notices Hicks looking square at her, nodding. *What does he want?* She nods back. He spits and jerks his head sideways. *Oh. Time to fly!*

They traverse the flight line between BT-13 and PT-19 training planes meant for beginners. Twyla stutter-steps, expecting to stop at each of them, as she has for the last several weeks. Suddenly, they turn straight for the advanced trainer, the AT-6 "Texan." *Jiminy!*

After an exhilarating takeoff, the powerful engine heaving her against the seat, she finds herself flying just above stall speed at ninety knots, slouching through the air at five thousand feet. Hicks sits behind her, his sighs of impatience adding to the white noise flooding her ears.

"Nice and slow," he says. "We build up to a proper speed in due time. Speed takes real skill and training. Most of you gals aren't used to using a radio in flight; we'll get to all that. For now, you only need to know one word: mayday. If you're in trouble, real trouble, call 'mayday' on the radio three times. Not once or twice, depending on your emotional needs, but three times in a row. Report your position and altitude. Got that? All right. Warhawk protocol, top to bottom!" he yells—unnecessarily, as the interphone mic is inches from his mouth.

"Sir?" she says.

"Jesus Howard Christ! Smaller words, it is. Now let's pretend, in spite of everything, you pass this program—you don't get killed, you don't wash out. Pretend you start ferrying planes out of the Republic, and you just kicked the tires on a P-40 Warhawk. Now what?"

"Oh, sorry, sir!" She squares her shoulders, and Lewis's face comes to mind. His years of instruction combine with Becca's skip rope song advice. She adjusts her helmet, takes an extra deep breath, recites the first line sotto voce, then lets it fly. *"Willa Brown brought her wings to town, and Warhawk was her name.*

"Mix at idle. Cut off throttle. One-inch is the game;
center tank, cold air carb, batt' and generator same.
Still on the ground, Brown brings it 'round.
Guns off, fuel pump. Circuit breakers fold;
fuel pressure, prime engine, three strokes cold.
Click off fuel pump, mix controls;
if magneto checks, hit breaks and hold.

Strike the Hawk.
Feed auto-rich;
twelve-hundred Rs will make her itch.
Twist fuel on; oil to eighty;
Temp to rise; climb to forty.
Lever open, cowl flaps shortly.
Knurled mixture levers creep, so
a keen eye keep and go.
Willa's bird is ready for the show;
rotate elevator tabs T-O!"

"Are you singing? Knock it off!" he howls. "There's no singing in the air corps!"

Three dozen miles pass silently beneath them, now at 150 miles per hour. Twyla can feel his irritation. She wonders if the silent treatment is a military thing, too. She imagines him as a six-year-old pouting above his Sunday shoes.

"Girl pilots," Hicks grumbles. "A plane is not flown with feelings; it is flown with aeronautical precision and concentration."

Twyla observes her squinty, confused face reflecting in the canopy glass.

"Manifold pressure after takeoff?" he jabs.

"Thirty-five inches," she replies without hesitation.

"Under what circumstance do you go to manual boost?"

"If auto fails. But sir, that's only the case with a two-speed supercharger."

"That's right. You're paying attention. Why do we start with fuel switched to fuselage tank? You wouldn't know, so I'll tell ya—"

I know this! "Because," she interrupts, "the fuselage tank is positioned aft of the fighter's center of gravity. We want to burn through that gas first so we don't have three hundred pounds of fuel sloshing around behind the wings, making combat maneuvers impossible." *Oooops!*

"And why in Jesus Pete would a broad know that?!" He falls silent again. "Take us back." She dips a wing, revealing wild horses crossing the switchback of a dry creek. He says, "You may continue, but slow the hell down. I can't hear that fast!"

Cornelia, Naomi, and Becca are alternating between Miss Mary Mack and Che-fou-mi when the Texan sets down like butter frosting on a cupcake. The canopy slides back, and the two pilots climb out of the noble taildragger. Hicks's mustache is full throttle, though he doesn't look any of them in the eyes. "And none of you trim better get me killed. I have important work, on *real* fighter planes, after this little summer job is over. With all the new Army procedures you have rattling around in your little heads, I can't emphasize enough that you remember to put your landing gear down before recovery. You gals fly fixed-gear, so it's not your fault it don't come natural. Hell, none of it should! On occasion, a malfunction will occur, which doesn't allow both wheels to lock all the way down. After a dogfight perhaps, but for you dames, there is no excuse! These airplanes are Army Air Corps property!"

The pilots stare at Twyla for any indication of what the hell happened. When Twyla rolls her eyes, they nearly lose their shit right in front of him.

"By the by," Hicks continues while accelerating away, "girls are never allowed to fly in formation or engage in aerobatics. Ever! Ms. South, you're up after I have lunch."

"What did you do, missy?" Cornelia accuses.

Twyla's shoulders nearly touch her ears as she says, "But I can't think of the last time I flew so well. Didn't miss a trick. The Texan is a honey of a ship."

"You selfish twat," Becca groans. "We have to follow that!"

"Dog barks because dogs bark," Naomi adds. "Even when nothing is wrong."

They convulse with laughter. Cornelia has so perfectly pictured Hicks on all fours, she folds to the ground, dying for a breath, tears popping from her eyes.

"Twat!" she gasps. Laughter flares anew. They pull Cornelia to her feet.

"But what questions did he ask?" Naomi presses.

"Yeah, what's the big deal?" Becca inquires. "Did he want you to do something advanced?"

"At first, he had me do a couple of turns," Twyla answers, "one without rudder to a tight diameter, then rudder only to check my side slip control…" She raises her hands in demonstration. They are now shoulder to shoulder, their hands flying in formation, "stall, then a dead-engine two-turn spin and recovery."

There's a flash of silver from the runway as a glossy twin-engine Spartan Executive flying-silk-bed lands without so much as a tire screech. The troupe suddenly twitch like yard cats on a blue jay. Jackie Cochran and the easy-smiling General of All Allied Air Forces climb out of the Spartan in a parade of dust devils.

The pilots purr. "Holy smokes, that's General Arnold," Cornelia breathes. They watch two flight officers greet the big bosses.

"General Arnold is here?" Becca says without moving her mouth.

"Jackie's back," Twyla sighs.

"How many aviation records?"

"All of them… still," Naomi says. "Brooklyn to Miami in four hours, twelve minutes—beating Howard Hughes by eight minutes."

"That's newspaper true," Cornelia adds.

Twyla looks at her crew. *How lucky are we?* When she turns back, the two superstars are much closer, walking toward them. Jackie gestures with her hands toward the girls: *two planes turning*. As the general strolls past, he nods and winks at Twyla. Twyla shyly returns a smile. Cornelia catches this and, as soon as the coast is clear, hoots, "Whoa! I do declare." Twyla flushes and elbows her. They both laugh. Even Naomi's face is checked surprise.

"What's that?" Becca jumps in. "No jive, I missed it. What happened?"

"I don't know. Honestly," Twyla says.

"Broads, dames, ships' ballast, and—oh, yeah—pilots, attende!" Cornelia commands. Finger becomes mustache. "Dear emptyheaded, purposeless carbon-based water buckets, AAF regulations clearly state that *you* are irregular, requiring regulations relegated to reciprocal and restricted response, retroactively. Reserved respectability and reversed reality are rewarded. Righteous and riotous regards, your royal and round Rear Admiral Harry Floppybottom Hicks!"

*

At 0700 the next morning, the girls, decked out in their oversized zoot suits and hairdo rags, stand with fifteen pilot hopefuls on an empty dirt field—all with rolled-up pant legs and sleeves. One girl accelerates into a fabric-flapping sprint, throws herself onto the ground, and tumbles head over heels into a pile at the feet of a skinny, sunburned instructor who can't be more than nineteen years old. He shouts, "Did you see that, pilots? Betty broke her wrist when she bailed out of her plane because she stuck her hand out to slow her roll. Now she can't fly or even rescue herself! Do *not* use your hands and elbows when you fall! Run and roll! Run and roll!" he yells.

"Poor Betty," Cornelia whispers. "But she can still go to the ball. I plan on breaking my head so, come pumpkin time, I'm not scrubbing the bathroom floor."

"Pumpkin time?" Twyla asks, betraying her lack of fairytale knowledge.

"Yeah. Ya know, midnight?"

"Oh, right," she lies and changes the subject. "Cornelia, where's your family from?"

Cornelia's eyes crinkle at the corners, her face turning childlike. "My daddy's farm, the Southland Farm. Ten miles north of Nashville."

"But that makes you a… I've never met a Southern belle before," Twyla says.

Cornelia tells of riding with her father to the bus stop at the county airport, about the handsome pilots of the Ford Tri-Motor, and the toy plane she hid behind her dress, teasing the boys. How her father had forbidden her brothers from flying. And then, near the end of his life, he climbed into his daughter's plane and they flew the length of Kentucky Lake.

The "Dirtwater Superettes," as her squad is labeled today, are transfixed.

"Next pilot!" Instructor interrupts. Becca runs and throws herself down into a tumbling, somersaulting cloud. "Pilot, twist to your back first!" he shouts. "Forward tumbles will only get you hurt or killed and will tangle you in your own parachute. Next up!"

"I'm never jumping from a plane," Twyla assures herself. She runs. It feels good to run, her joints loosening inside her whipping and snapping jumpsuit. She throws herself onto the ground, all hands, knees, and elbows, and skids to a stop, coughing and spitting. "Ouch."

The instructor's face turns red. "*No! No!*"

Naomi runs up right behind in a graceful rounded-back rotation, rolling right over her head and onto her feet.

"Good!" Instructor calls but stops short of acknowledging Naomi as the perfect example. "Everyone, again!"

At the back of the line, Becca says, "My old bruises are complaining to my new bruises they ain't got room. I don't wanna be the tumbling twats no more."

"Then, finally," Cornelia continues, shaking dirt from her hair like a wet dog, "when I was a teenager, I realized the incongruity of my father. He owned a Rickenbacker-built automobile. Eddie 'Ace of Aces' Rickenbacker! But my father hated airplanes so much."

"Pardon me," Twyla says, "but what business was your father in?"

"Insurance," Cornelia says.

"A worthy irony, yes?" Naomi offers.

Becca shakes her head. "No flow, clogged fuel line; I'm stallin' out."

"I remember this," Naomi continues. "The Rickenbacker Automobile Company didn't last long because Eddie was too far ahead of his time."

"Mmm, thematic probability 'round here," Cornelia quips.

"Eddie was the first to install four-wheel brakes on his cars," Naomi goes on. "He also built them lower to the ground. Safest cars on the road."

"Forcing the other auto companies to retool," Cornelia adds. "And while they did, they slandered Eddie's company until it sank."

Twyla's lips bunch to the side. "Our own war hero?" She attempts to animate the photographs in her memory of the great man and his famous fighter plane in France in 1918. He was credited with twenty-six kills. Before the war, he was a famous American automobile racer. Lewis often spoke of Eddie's flying instincts and mechanical skills, born out of his days behind the wheel and under the hood. They kept him alive and ahead of the steep learning curve in history's first aerial war.

"Next pilot!"

They shove Twyla forward. "I'm doin' a Beachey 'Dip of Death' and breaking my neck this time," she mutters.

"Naw!" Cornelia interjects. "Just tumble like a Vaudevillian. They did three shows a day on a hard stage floor."

"Yeah! Like Harpo," Naomi adds.

And this Twyla can picture, thanks to Lewis insisting she see Marx Brothers movies. She runs and does a perfect dust-clouded Harpo, cutting off the instructor mid-complaint. Naomi, Rebecca, and Cornelia run flip-flappy, drop to their backs, roll over their heads, and come up in a cloud of belly laughs.

*

Moonrise accompanies an enthusiastic cricket symphony carried on a faint breeze of magnolia blossoms, though Twyla hasn't seen any. There's also a bit of what Naomi counts as blooming prickly pear cactus. Twyla sits on the barracks doorway—no porch, just a stingy concrete slab. She slides a hardcover under her ass and ponders an illustration in her navigation book, captioned: *Celestial readings from an open bomber top-hatch using a bubble sextant and a height-reduction equation.*

She squints at this, looks up at Mars as it grows pale with the moonrise, wonders how Martian cactus will smell, and turns back to the long, open room. Cornelia flies a model airplane on a low pass over Becca, who lies on her cot, staring at a letter. In the foreground, Naomi reads a military history book.

"But if we *do* graduate from Not-a-Drop-of-Sweetwater training," Becca inserts, "I mean, if we actually make it through, do we get a certificate or something? How do they notify us?"

"There's a graduation ceremony," Naomi pipes up without raising her eyes. "The day before, you'll return from your studies and find an invitation to graduation on your pillow."

"But what if there's nothing on your pillow?"

Even the crickets heard this question and shut the hell up. Twyla's jaw clenches. She wonders how they all can be so qualified, so eager to do their part, and still be rejected?

Becca's face turns sour. She raises a booted foot against this disagreeable subject. "When does that *Look* magazine photographer get here? We pinup gals get invited to all the functions."

The crickets crank back up as Cornelia snorts her model plane on a strafing run down the wall shelving.

"My brothers are Code Talkers in the Pacific," Naomi says, unbidden. The crickets are aghast.

"Negative, flight command." Cornelia spits and sputters as she pulls her plane straight up. "Static on all bands," the toy stalls out, tail slides, and flips into an inverted spin. "Mayday, mayday, mayday! The Owl has spoken unprompted! Flat spin, unrecoverable, no map for this terrain."

"Did the crickets just stop?" Becca inquires.

Naomi takes the teasing with a shrug of her shoulders while Cornelia's model lands on her head. Naomi goes cross-eyed.

"Against the Japanese," Naomi begins, snatching the toy. "Marines use the Navajo language for their coded communications between the islands… in the PTO." Becca slides closer, and Twyla scoots indoors. "It's a nearly extinct language."

"What a clever idea," Twyla says, padding up the aisle and adding this to her scrapbook of evidence vis-à-vis her own lack of cleverness.

Cornelia grabs the model. "But how did your brothers… I mean, they were able to get into the military?"

"Yes, a long shot, I know," Naomi says with a slight pause. "After Pearl, they tried to join up and were turned away. Then, out of the blue, they were needed. No matter what happens now, they're carving a new legend." Glances exchange, no one interrupts. "We worked a farm, and when my brothers got old enough to fix the tractor and our neighbor's biplane, my family took over his land surveying business."

Twyla recoils as sharp images of Papa and Tommy charge at her from across the room. She stomps them out before they can resolve. She hopes it isn't the word "farm" causing this intrusion and rubs her scarred eyebrow.

Becca asks, "What's a Navajo code word?"

Twyla is grateful for this.

"Well, you just take a word—for example, *na'asts'oosi* is 'mouse'—but it could mean anything in the cipher. *Na'asts'oosi* could stand for 'troop ship' or 'battalion' or 'carrier'—anything when you construct the rules of your encryption."

"Hicks," Becca adds. "What would it be for our *charismatique* instructor, Monsieur Hicks?"

A none-to-fore seen dimple appears on Naomi's cheek. "*Awee'telii*."

"*Aaahweee telleee*," they repeat like an amateur trio of drunks.

"Baby donkey."

They fall about the bed, laughter bouncing off the stark walls. Naomi is pleased. Cornelia lands her model on Twyla.

"What about you, Apple Pie? Your father fly?"

"In France," she says and catches her reflection in the window across the room, but before she can stop it, Hawkeye's face replaces hers. He turns profile and pulls on his flying cap, then looks right at her, young and intense. "Hey, hummingbird," he says, "I need to tell you something."

With a quick shake of her head, she looks away. "Hey Bec, what did you say about hot water?"

"Oh, yes," Becca says, enthusiastic for the setup. "I often put boiling water in the freezer. Then, when I really need boiling water, I simply defrost it."

"Thank you, Gracie," Naomi mumbles.

"Twyylaa?" an accusatory tone from Cornelia.

Becca squints. "Lafeet Escargots?"

"Lafayette Escadrille in the Great War," Naomi corrects.

"American volunteer," Twyla mumbles.

"Mmm, he died?" Cornelia queries.

Twyla's back straightens, but she keeps her head down. "Um, no. Armistice."

"So, he made it?"

"Well, yes… He had many assisted victories and four confirmed kills when it ended."

"But that's good, right?" Becca adds.

The girls are patient with Rebecca, except Cornelia, who says, "You're right off the cob, aren't ya?"

Naomi closes her book, adding, "By the end of the war, every pilot wanted one thing."

"*Five* kills," Cornelia finishes impatiently.

"Uh-huh. Five is nice," Becca says.

"Right," Naomi confirms, "Five kills makes you an ace."

"Ooooh," Becca finally lands on it. "Five. Sorry! I never knew."

Twyla nods. "Papa wanted to teach my brother, Tommy, to fly, but he had bad lungs or something," she trails off. "And I was a girl. So…"

A shared experience so obvious, no one responds.

"But my grandma," Twyla continues, "used to say if there was ever another war, Papa would find a way to return and set things right."

Cornelia's eyes cross, and she asks, "But your father *is* dead?"

"He is now. I got his old flight bag. It used to be filled with German knives, belt buckles, and some medals. Even had a pistol."

"Then your father was… I mean… where's your brother?" Becca stammers.

Twyla pulls off her boots. "He's, uh. He's—"

"How 'bout your mother?" Cornelia persists.

"Well, ummm… there's correspondence between my father and mother somewhere. I just haven't found it yet." She glances at her bag; a small brass iron-cross medal is pinned on as the zipper pull. It gleams at her.

Cornelia rubs her temples. "That's a poorly shuffled deck."

"Then your whole family is, uhh…"

"Her spirit guides," offers Naomi. Twyla glances at her. A smile grows between them.

"Becca, your turn," Cornelia announces.

"Hmm? Little ol' me?" Becca says in theatrical wonder. "Well, if you insist." She herds them roughly onto Naomi's bed.

"Hey! Watch the goods!" Cornelia protests.

Having thus arranged her playhouse patrons, Becca plucks a towel from a chair back and makes a curtain in front of herself. "Once upon a time, there was a girl," she begins, "from a foreign yet bewitching land known as 'The Albuquerque.'" She lowers the towel and smiles like an ad for lemonade. The entire auditorium giggles. "At a tender age, she was teased for buffing her nails all the livelong day, slouching at the table, and pretending to be splayfooted. She was the first teenager in the high desert to own sunglasses; she traded and sometimes 'liberated' turquoise and tortoiseshell hair combs from undeserving women. Rebecca Elena Lawrence was adorable, wily, and cunning—but more than that, she was clever."

Cornelia snorts and says into her invisible headphones, "Master Sergeant, we have a superfluous set of matching redundancies."

Becca holds up her hand. "The house asks that you please control your outbursts during the performance."

"Safety protocol," Corny quips.

Bec plows on, "One day, Ms. Lawrence was at the Bernalillo County fair when her father introduced her to powered flight. He was on his last thirty-two minutes of sobriety and bought her a ticket to ride in a barnstormer's plane named Almost Dizzy. Her soul cried out! And for the first time in her long, twelve-year life, she saw her future—and it was in an aeroplane. This was quite contrary to her parents' idea of her future in the typing pool or beauty counter at Neusteter's department store. The following year, a bona fide miracle befell her when her very own uncle purchased a Curtiss Jenny, certifying her vision."

"My father had one!" Twyla blurts.

"One more outburst, young lady, and the usher will throw you out into the snow on your bony arse." She gestures to her right, steps over to a tall, invisible man, introduces herself, and shakes his hand. Then, she glances over and points to the "trouble section." In defense, the girls pose as a trinity of purity. Becca looks doubtful, but as she pivots away from the usher, she yips and jerks her hips, as if pinched on the ass. She whips around and points a finger at "him."

The girls erupt in laughter. She ignores this, straightens her invisible tie and coat, and dusts off her dignity. She continues, with occasional glances of disgust/flirtation at the offending man. "As I was saying, legend has it, Rebecca's screams of joy startled every human in her twenty-eight-unit apartment. At first chance, she painted a red heart wearing sunglasses onto the aircraft and christened her 'Ruby Swirl.' Then one day, her father's brother, sturdy and *sometimes* sober Uncahol Glenn, offers her a chance to fly—at a price. Having no money, Becca trades the only thing she possesses for flight instruction." The theater patrons are horrified and brace themselves. "Hair combs," Becca says, generating shallow nods of universal understanding. Awkward relief passes between the bunkmates. "Nope, that's incorrect," Becca reverses. "It was the dirty thing."

"What's that?" Cornelia protests.

"Oh, nausea!" Twyla moans.

"Aw, don't pop your hydraulic lines," Becca says, then slings a coy smile at the "usher" and continues. "In spite of Rebecca Elena's imploring, her mother divorces her father over this. She was a saint, Mother Lawrence. Though many a congregant would witness her running stop signs in her Dodge-dash to church. To make matters worse, Rebecca flies herself, via her uncle's wings of freedom, to uncomfortable holidays with her dispirited mother, who for a time, moved to

Colorado. Once there, our fly girl would collect a trophy case of unintended slaps in the face. Thusly, this natural-born aviatrix built up many flight hours and collected stories of death-defying moments among the deserts, mountains, and extreme weather of New Mexico and Colorado." She sidesteps toward the "usher," batting her eyes. "And finally, ladies, Rebecca Lawrence's idols are Pancho Barnes, Jackie Cochran, and Katharine Hepburn."

Cornelia and Twyla nod their heads heartily.

"Kate in *Little Women*, *Spitfire*, or *Morning Glory*, holding her own against Adolphe Menjou and Douglas Fairbanks, Jr.! Ladies! Tarts! Trollops and tramps!"

Cornelia whistles. "You aren't wrong, you diminutive desert flower."

Becca raises her chin, apparently content with her story, and says, "Thank you for attending this presentation of Heroines of the Air. Oh, and two bits to the usher on your way out. But watch your six."

A standing ovation replete with whistling and hooting fills the billet. Becca takes a bow and acknowledges her costars and the orchestra, then pulls a pretend coin from her pocket and hands it to the "usher" with her thanks. Cornelia approaches her with a massive bouquet of invisible flowers.

"That's a performance that can only be followed by a movie," Naomi says. "Sand farmers, follow me."

*

The plywood floor of the Quonset hut is the only thing separating the girls' feet from the desert floor, and its curved tin roof is no help in a sneaking operation. However, thanks to a bustling apron and the constant overflight of howling planes, the squad is successful in reaching the door to an inner classroom. They nudge it open a few inches and push their faces in, one above the other, like the Marx Brothers sisters—rear ends sticking out into the hall.

The sprocket whine of a film projector accompanies the flickering light bouncing off a portable screen, where aerial gun camera footage of German and British fighters pulse. Two men in semidarkness drink grape Nehi from bottles. A black-haired man of perhaps thirty years stands stock-still in his short-sleeve khakis, arms folded, rocking slightly in his polished black shoes. Next to him, a skinny blond boy, likewise dressed, slumps in a folding chair angled sideways to the screen. Oblivious to his own huge and bobbing Adam's apple, he says, "It's just bug spraying with machine guns."

"It's way more than that," Black Hair says. "It's outmaneuvering your enemy. Cuban eights, Immelmanns, barrel rolls, loops… It's about getting from one trick to another before he does. See that RAF chap there?"

A Hawker Hurricane makes wild turns, tracers biting in as smoke pumps out of the engine. "He's a dead Limey now because he blew the transitions that woulda got him two moves ahead of that Nazi. He fucked the dog. You must fly flawless aerobatics and make precise guesses."

"Like chess?" Adam's Apple says.

"High-stakes chess, sport."

"But the Russians are good at chess, and the Nazis have half their country."

"That's because the Rooskies are too busy eating their own children to build a decent fighter."

"So why the hell is Uncle Sam giving them our aeroplanes?"

"That's one item I agree with Roosevelt and Churchill on. Send the Reds planes and guns, but keep our boys the hell out of Russia."

Cornelia turns, frowns, and whispers, "Johnny Appleseed and Headwind Edwin are ruining the movie."

They slowly back away and close the door.

Dear Ladybird,

You must be on cloud nine!

I'm proud of you for getting in with the ATC. Our new kites are great. My squad is great, the rookies are taigey! Tell General Chaos to fix that. Send pictures of your girlfriends. Big hit with the boys.

Happy birthday, Ms. Bloom. I miss you.

Doc's Friend Walt
Doc and Betty Sequoia Eubanks say bilch!

P.S. How do you like the T-6? RT and 650 horses!

Twyla kisses Lewis's letter and tucks it inside her jumpsuit. She sits on her meteorology book in the dirt, watching Hicks introduce his mustache to a group of new woman flyers. Her mind wanders aboard a skyrocket propelling her at an unimaginable speed deep into the Pacific. Just before the rocket bursts into fireworks, she jumps off and lands on a sandy beach under a cloudless azure dome.

From her new vantage point, knee-deep at the shore break, she watches Lewis pull his feet under him, cross-legged, and snap the sand off a letter. Clad only in undershorts, the sun bakes his shoulders and feet. Two of his equally naked squadron buddies zoom out of nowhere and crash into him; sand sprays in all directions. He crawls back to his letter, flattening it across his thigh. He is tackled again, but Lewis now wrestles with them, each using the Army hand-to-hand combat training they learned back in the States. Wiley appears and picks the tormentors off of Lewis like fleas, tossing them away. They are young, handsome, sunburned, and seemingly carefree.

Naomi shuffles up next to her with fifty pounds of books. Twyla's attention is drawn to the apron, where a pilot stands next to a Vultee, buckling a parachute pack. Twyla frowns.

Naomi says, "In the Great War, the war to end all wars, even if the parachute was available, pilot honor left no room in the cockpit for it. Pilots sat only inches behind the engine and propeller, breathed in smoke, oil, and fire while they fought. I honestly don't understand why the designers didn't stick with the pusher style of aeroplane. The Wright brothers got it right from the very start; it would've solved so many nasty problems. Boys are always in a rush to trouble…"

Twyla recalls Lewis standing up on the seat of his bicycle and crashing it into Wiley, who would extend it into a stage-worthy knockabout death throe. She says, "You ever think how amazingly lucky the timing of… I mean, being born just a whisker after powered flight was invented?"

"Most days, yes," Naomi says. "It alarms me how close I came to being born a few decades earlier as well, when my path would've been cut with obsidian and this current path couldn't be imagined."

"Exactly." Twyla shivers. "I'm afraid of who I would've had to be."

Naomi writes on a page titled *LINK TRAINER LOG* and adds, "The converse is true; what if we were born a hundred years later?"

"Mmm, I guess that depends on how this war turns out," Twyla says and pulls Lewis's letter back out of her pocket. She twists around to look between the barracks; perhaps three hundred yards away, she can just catch a slice of the graduation bell.

e i g h t

Raw Sex

2 July 1937

Dear Ms. Earhart,

Happy Independence Day to you, wherever you are around the world. My name is Twyla Campbell. I am learning to fly from my best friend Lewis. You are the bravest person I know. Your flying records of speed, endurance, and altitude are a marvel to consider. Please allow me some questions. Do you keep your hair short because of your flying cap? How do you urinate during a long flight?

*

15 Aug 1943

"My friend Mabel, she just graduated with the previous class of WASPs. She got assigned to Camp Davis over in the Carolinas. She's towing targets for anti-aircraft gunner practice. Can you believe that? I never thought of how those artillery boys learned to shoot down planes. Rumor has it, the pilot known as Sexy Mexy is in my class now, but no one knows what she looks like."

(Overheard in the LINK trainer queue)

Moments before sunrise, Twyla sneaks out to the flight line. The night seems to peel away before her eyes, its dark skin exposing pastel fruit. A speculative breeze from the east warms and nudges its way along the prairie. At the end of the apron hunkers a gray hulk, the

P-47 Thunderbolt fighter, affectionately known as "The Jug," and for good reason. *Or the barrel end of a baseball bat*, she reflects and glances around the parking lot of aircraft, which appear monochromatic and soft under the extending blue sky.

Seeing no one, she tightens the do-rag holding her bedhead together and climbs up into the slugger's ample bucket. She's never been in a single-engine plane so stout with such a massive propeller and so high off the ground. It has an enormous Wasp R-2800 engine, the first to reach four hundred miles per hour at level flight in the Navy's Corsair airframe. There seems to be twice the amount of standard instrument gauges plugged into the dash panel. Everything in the spacious cockpit is thick, heavy, and painted in a color Corny calls "lizard green."

Faint, high-performance engines pierce the breeze, sounding like two aircraft in formation. One has a fairly high-pitched whine, while the other, a throatier growl. No. A single plane. The whining is its propeller tips at supersonic speed, while the growl is the engine itself. Twyla's brain assigns it to twelve thousand feet over Abilene. Her fingers move slowly around the control stick, eyes sweeping across the instruments again and flicking out over the flight line. She squares her eyes on the gun's targeting mechanism framing a pink-tipped cloud and a black speck, perhaps a hawk or airplane miles away. It plunges through the device.

"Say your prayers, Hirohito." She squeezes the gun trigger and shakes the stick of her budding fantasy. "Adieu and adios, Adolf." She banks hard left, then reverses; the ailerons and rudder swish softly around her.

A voice cracks from below, "Hey, missy, you better be cleanin' the windows!"

Twyla bolts out of the seat. "Yessir! I mean, no, sir. I'm just, uh… reviewing for an upcoming test is all." She scrambles out of the seat, jumps off the wing, and lands with a grunt in front of a crop-cut master sergeant.

"Rrriiight," he says through a sneer. "A Thunderbolt? The day me 'n Rosebud'r sledding in hell." He looks her up and down. "The P-47's a man's ship. The 'P' doesn't stand for pussy. You ain't got the man muscle. Go play with your toy birds." He kicks a wheel chock and eyeballs her until she walks away.

"Hey, Boondoggle!" comes Cornelia's voice as she jogs up to Twyla.

"Jiminy, Corny!" Twyla yips, startled. "And it's Boonville, by the way, not… Where'd you come from?"

Corny's finger jabs toward the runway. A P-51B Mustang banks steeply on a short approach, its mirror finish reflecting the new sun's spectacular grace. "Look… at… that," Corny says in a half-whisper.

The engine I heard a minute ago, Twyla recalls. "What's that doing here?"

Cornelia monotones like an automaton, "A raptor flew into a large sheet of molten mirror metal, drop-forged in a giant sculptor's hands, tumbled through a wind tunnel, then cooled, hardened, and was carefully buffed into that."

"Becca calls it the 'Cadillac of the Skies,'" Twyla replies.

"Sure, with six fifty-caliber guns, a two-speed supercharger, and a Packard-Merlin engine that'll whip that pony up to 440 miles per hour."

The advanced pursuit fighter hovers in front of them, touches down on its main gear, and eases onto its tail wheel. Its sound is nothing short of a hot-tempered purr.

"The first time my Lewis heard that new Rolls-Royce engine, he called it the 'speed-tuned harmonics of an unapologetic owner of the quivering middle-distance.'"

"I don't know what that means," Corny offers, "but… exactly."

The sleek fighter turns and taxis toward them. The sun sparkles dazzlingly from the spinner hub of the propeller to its tail, giving way to the stretched-mirror reflection of desert colors in the shape of its muscular, raw sex. The Mustang saunters into the flight line. A funnel of "growling pops" envelops the girls as the overtuned horsepower stacked inside twelve huge cylinders gathers toward its tie-down.

"Coconuts…" Twyla stammers. "That… that…"

"Uh-huh."

The propeller twitches to a stop, the canopy opens, and the helmet comes off. The handsome pilot with perfect teeth and gosh-darn dimples offers an honest smile and a wave.

Golly jeepers.

That night, the girls stand shoulder to shoulder staring at Esther, whom they would later know as the high school winner of Sweetwater's August Scrap-Metal-Drive-for-the-War contest. But for now, Esther sleeps on her elbows in the cramped ticket box of the Texas movie theater. The marquee boldly displays the movie title: AIR FORCE.

Ed Herlihy's famous newsreel voice perforates the lobby, pressing down on poor Esther's eyes. An old man in a red vest takes their tickets and punches a hole in each one. They enter the theater, and Bec says, "Hey, I'll take those." She grabs their ticket stubs. "I like to keep 'em. Hey, Twyla, what's the name of the hole they punch in these?"

"Stuff it, Bec," Corny groans.

"But it has a name, right, Twy?"

"It does. I just can't remember it," Twyla agrees.

The gilded and velvet-draped theater is sparsely attended by senior citizens. In the front row, Cornelia and Becca take turns with a bottle of Mr. Boston Five Star Brandy. Naomi and Twyla frown up at the screen, at the Russian infantry, artillery, tanks, and planes flying over a column of German prisoners marching through the frozen tundra.

"No nation in the world thought the Russians could win back Stalingrad. Not with the massive army sent against them. Herr Hitler himself can't believe it, as every man or boy of fighting ability from many occupied countries is conscripted into serving the Führer's front of terror," booms Ed Herlihy. *"But the Yanks have something in store for Mr. Hitler…"*

Anti-aircraft guns, tanks, and planes cross dissolve into an American flag snapping in the wind as a fighter plane zooms past. *"This is the newest weapon hot off the assembly line at North American…"*

Four sparkling silver fighters catch up to a B-17 Flying Fortress.

"Yes," the girls purr in unison.

"Yes, the P-51 Mustang—hot pursuit and long-range escort fighter, all-in-one combination punch… Go ahead, bomber jockeys. Go deep into the Rhineland, deep into the Ruhr, deeper still. We'll be right here with you."

They gaze in wonder.

"Jiminy."

After the movie, an elderly couple offers them a lift back to the airfield. In the bed of a decomposing '37 GMC truck, they share the brandy while the wind bestows all of them with crazy hair.

"I saw the Mary Ann over Honolulu," Twyla blurts.

"What's this?" Becca asks.

"The B-17 from the movie. She—the Mary Ann—flew right over me and Butch after we ditched on the beach during the Pearl ambush. I always wondered what happened to that plane and crew."

"Corpus Christi," Cornelia utters. "Not one of them boys could imagine the welcoming party waiting for them when they took off from Cali."

Becca clutches Cornelia's thumb as if it were a microphone and says, "Meet world-famous Lieutenant Richard 'Dick' Hicks working his magic with the poor, troubled girls of Avenger Field. Without daring American airmen like him, these frail nymphs would quickly lose their homing beacon, their way of life, and their minds! Girls! They laughed at Joan of Arc, but she went right ahead and built it!"

"Wait for it," Naomi says. Three ticks later, Cornelia spews brandy. "Thank you, Gracie," Naomi whispers.

Horse laughs bounce out of the truck, spinning into the night air. Twyla leans into Cornelia and says, "It's Boonville. I'm from Boonville."

"Roger that, ginger snap!" she says. "It's just my accent."

At 0200 hours, an unyielding cricket chorus curtainwall's their billet. Naomi rubs her temples, and Rebecca holds a bucket under her own chin. Twyla sits on the end of her bed while Cornelia secures the last drop of brandy. Twyla falls back onto her pillow and says, "In four hours, when the sun gets up, you're really going to hate yourself."

"Who's waiting?" Cornelia grunts. "Men. Those men. Those lucky men don't know what they have."

Twyla rubs her eyes.

Becca sets down her bucket. "Hey, congrats, you study machines! The tests are all done… you earned this drunken stupor! Flash your hash, you'll be fit as Fifinella."

"Oh, nausea!"

"Some men know," Twyla retorts. "Lewis knows."

Cornelia flings the empty across the room in a beautiful arc that crashes into a metal can, waking everything in Central Texas, plus the other pilots in the barracks. Voices launch like mortar fire from the far end, "Shut the hell up!"

Becca ignores this. "How handsome was that P-51 driver? I wouldn't mind a sheet metal courtship with that cowboy. Though probably dumb as a jar lid. I wonder if he likes it rough."

"What?" and "Pardon me, madam?" protest Twyla and Naomi.

"I'm just thinking it seems like they all like it that way."

"And how on all three sides of flat Earth do you know that?" Cornelia asks.

"I've met a few," Becca murmurs like an innocent schoolgirl.

"The 51 pilot was very handsome… almost as handsome as my Lewis."

"I've seen you write letters to him," Becca adds. "Why does he spell it like a last name?"

"Oh," Twyla tucks a folded letter under her pillow. "He says spelling it L-o-u-i-s looks too much like a girl's name."

"Louis Armstrong doesn't care," Becca says.

"Pops? Satchmo?" Corny offers. "Ambassador Satch? Are you sure he doesn't care?"

"What's Lewis short for?"

"Llewellyn. By god, don't ever call him that!"

"Handsome men," Becca drawls, "make a girl tingle on the ground floor of her Bloomingdales."

Giggles percolate about.

"What?" Becca protests. "That's a strong itch to scratch sometimes. And damn if it ain't made worse when you fire up the Vultee Vibrator. The pulsation of that poorly balanced tractor engine through the seat? Better than riding a horse, huh girls?"

Naomi and Twyla's heads incline, minds comparing—they flush. Though Cornelia's in a mood, she can't help but smile.

Becca wiggles her hips and says, "Don't you sometimes want to just slouch low in your cockpit against the control stick and—"

"Becca!" Twyla declares, genuinely embarrassed.

"Yessir," Corny cuts in. "My knees run into the instrument panel before I can make meaningful contact. My legs are too long!"

Cackles and hoots make their faces hurt.

"Don't it explain why Amelia drove an autogyro across the whole country?" Becca asserts. This bubbles them up again.

After catching her breath, Twyla adds, "Doesn't sound like you're a churchgoer?"

"I like church," Becca says. "Plenty of handsome men there, too."

Cornelia kicks off her boots. "Church, the perfect place for men to tell us the rules of the world, the way it is, and what it all means. They might as well describe the surface of Mars. Religions and superstitions that tell you *the way* it is. Lazy, intolerant ignorance. No one knows. That's the game here on Mother Earth. They're just guessing to control everything and everyone. They're guessing out of fear. Freud is guessing, Carl Jung, every minister, politician, businessman—"

"Carl who?" Becca wedges in.

"Luckily for you, it's very simple to be happy," Naomi says. "Unlucky for you, it is very difficult to be simple… Becca notwithstanding."

Twyla stifles a laugh.

Cornelia doesn't hear this because her throttle is already set to emergency war power. She takes a deep breath. "Every man in a uniform of 'knowledge,' is guessing. Ignorance begets fear, begets control, begets insecure guessing, begets more fear peddling to maintain control. Something isn't actually true just because you fear it not being true. Where the Golden Rule ends, fiction begins."

"You're not afraid of going straight to hell?" Twyla asks.

"I'm not superstitious. I believe in gravity, Bernoulli, and internal combustion. What if one day we find out women rule the red planet? That we're in charge! Then who knew anything… ever? Men write books to explain their own inadequacies, telling the world their weaknesses; their lack of imagination is their own fear masquerading as a universal truth. A collective nod of fedoras, and away they go! Our military is exactly this. They'll let any man in any plane. God forbid they consider the best of us!"

"But we're here. We're flying…" Twyla says.

Naomi cuts in, "My grandmother said a woman before her time is happy until she realizes it."

Cornelia unbuttons her shirt and steps on the toes of her socks, stretching them out ten-year-old-brat style, and adds, "We're every bit as good as the men."

Becca turns to Naomi. "What did you say?"

Naomi doesn't repeat it.

Twyla unconsciously turns her back to them as she undresses. "You mean fight, Cornelia South?"

"Yes."

"Enemy bullets specifically trying like hell to kill you in your airplane?"

Cornelia doesn't move, doesn't breathe. Despite the heat, Twyla pulls on her pajamas and begins to fold her clothes. "You don't know what you're talking about."

"Girls ain't built for fighting," Becca chirps, gathering her toiletries.

"How can you say that?" Cornelia fires back. "This can't be the limit of your imagination."

"Well… yes!" Becca admits.

"'Cause I've been there!" Twyla says.

"Exactly! What if you coulda shot back?"

"What?"

Cornelia stands up on her bed, a blaze in her eyes. "Yeah, what if you could've given what you got, stood your ground, fed the Japs nine yards of their own medicine?"

"From a Taylorcraft?" Twyla mumbles.

"'Cause even Jackie said so!" Becca shouts in her confounding inability to read the room.

"Hearsay!" Cornelia spits through her teeth. "Third person, assembly line truth for the sake of comfort! How do you *know*? Reb? Naomi? Twyla? How do you know what you're capable of? How do you really know who you are?"

Babushka's face is looking down at Twyla, waiting for her to answer the mourning dove. She ignores her and turns back to Corny. "You mean a war is the only way to answer this?"

Becca is flustered. "Didn't you hear Jackie? Men start wars—all wars. We don't start 'em because we ain't fighters. We reason through things before it gets that bad. Think about that. No, we aren't meant for it, and there's your answer."

Like a record needle jumping out of its groove, this stops them all, while they wonder who Becca is.

"But this is incomplete," comes Naomi's soothing voice. "Men write history, almost always leaving out the backstory. As when the North Fork council chief's wife is jealous of the South Fork's camp across the river—its larger shade trees, deeper bathing pool. She charges her man to fix it. He sends a boy to tell the South Fork council chief he wants to take over his summer grounds. The boy is sent back with the answer: 'Absolutely not.' The North Fork council chief, understanding this is correct, claims, 'I tried.' His wife disagrees and argues he has done nothing, that he never does, and she never gets what she wants. Perhaps she has staged this bit of theater in front of the whole council, even enlisting the council wives. The North Fork chief must send the boy back for another try. At this point, the boy is detained or worse, for he has disrespected the South Fork chief, who doesn't entertain the same question twice. Back across the river, the chief's wife has dug in on the matter. She can't turn back now. You know where this goes."

A muddy silence follows.

"Thank you, Pocahontas," floats a voice from the dark end of the barracks. "Now shut the hell up!"

Glossy silver light easily reaches under the T-6 and finds Twyla leaning against the main gear wheel. She imagines a multi-masted schooner pulling the harvest moon out of the black prairie hills.

"You look pale… paler," Naomi greets her, ducking under the downward-angled propeller blade.

"I'm not drunk," Twyla says, "I just have red hair."

"Right. I keep forgetting."

"I thought I could walk off my sour stomach."

Naomi offers the moon a rather convincing wolf howl. Twyla chuckles. "So that's the call of the nearly extinct Wolf-Owl? You're never short of surprises."

"My oldest brother could do it much better."

"My brother liked to sleep with dead crickets." Twyla scans the dark apron full of planes. "I thought with the WASPs, I had captured the moon."

"And then Cornelia rolled out Mars," Naomi says, leaning on the propeller.

"Do you think women should fight in this war?"

"I suspect they already do. But it won't happen here unless the war comes here. Conventions of that nature change only when an enemy invades your homeland."

Twyla nods then catches the Owl staring at her. "Pearl? That's what you want to know about, right?"

Owl doesn't blink.

Twyla considers. "I'll trade you for your surname."

"Good trade."

Twyla takes a deep breath, steeling herself. "Okay, it was bad. Never felt that kind of angry, fearful chaos. Like a nightmare in the day, a beautiful, Hawaiian day. Don't stand in the path of Death, for he is impersonal, empirical, and… he just don't care."

"You're describing my grandfather's world," Naomi mutters.

"Oh, Jiminy." Twyla flushes.

"Go on."

"Well, the Navy was caught flat-footed—no, worse… asleep. Many men died. I was piloting a check flight with a small company I was hoping to work for. The Japs fired on us at close range. I landed on a beach and ran. Those poor men… the smell. Those minutes seemed like hours. I got lucky. It's just, if Cornelia had been there, actually there, she might feel different. Fear… it's overwhelming. I wonder if it doesn't take a lot of training to fight through it, to fight back."

"For those not accustomed."

They watch the moon for a moment. Naomi's face is always untroubled, as if she is perpetually wading in the shallow end of a pleasant pool. Twyla puzzles on her for a half-minute and concedes that she, conversely, feels she is always dog-paddling in the deep end. "However," Twyla continues, "two good things happened: Lewis and Wiley weren't hurt, and I met an amazing lady named Doris McCuskey."

"The spirits can be generous as well. And who is Wiley?"

"My good friend. He's like the brother I never really had."

"But you had a brother?"

"Tommy was, in fact, my cousin. I didn't know this until… he was all I ever knew of a sibling. Though, in retrospect, he never felt quite… I don't want to sound mean, but with Tommy, something was incomplete. Have you ever suspected you were missing a family member? A sister?"

"Hmm, I always felt I was missing a baby brother. Thank you for telling me about that day. Tachii'ni is my clan name," Naomi says.

"Tak'ii'nee," Twyla attempts, mangling it.

"It translates, 'Red Running into the Water.'"

"Jiminy."

Naomi smiles. "Are you glad you asked?"

Twyla shivers in the warm air and blurts, "Middle name?"

"More of a nickname: Mexy."

"Ha! Mexy. Right. Okay. Well, big day tomorrow." She jerks around to stare at her again. "Wait! Sexy Mexy?"

Naomi grabs Twyla's hand and yanks her to her feet.

Twyla stares hard. "No, that… that can't be you."

Naomi gathers her hair into a tail. "It can't?"

They turn their backs to the moon, and Twyla's head lists. "Well, I'll be dipped in apple shine. I'll never drink again."

"But you didn't drink tonight."

"Oh… right."

Back in their barracks, Twyla folds her sad pillow and jams it under her head while a thousand Jiminys comfort her. She thinks the whole day was a reminder of how behind the times she is. Her mind diffuses, and Lewis is suddenly kissing her knee, making her memory self laugh at her tickle spot. She imagines him atop his aircraft carrier in the radiating South Pacific, windblown, deeply tanned, and happy. The old man at twenty-seven, wisecracking at some sapling for being too slow at connecting his drop tanks, or just cuffing Wiley while he loads bullets by the quarter-ton.

Stay safe, my loves.

Finally, she admits to herself that all the hubbub of this day was to avoid thinking about tomorrow. After almost two months of military training, testing, and endless attempts to disqualify the female pilots, the girls were an inch from being invited into America's most exclusive women's club.

"Annie Oakleys!" she blurts and claps her hand over her mouth. *That's it! Holes punched in movie tickets are called Annie Oakleys.*

The girls meander away from the mess, hauling dark bags under their eyes. The new sun mocks them as it casts carbon blue shadows of their stilt legs across the baked ground. Becca breaks the silence. "You trim think the Army uses powdered eggs and milk as a way to thin the herd?" For weeks, they have posited dozens of theories on *what is military food?* No one answers. The unstated agreement to avoid this day's possibilities barely holds their collective dread at bay. The angle of approach to their billet seems to slow and bow off target.

"Have you noticed," Naomi finally says, "the closer you get to losing something, the more you want it?"

Cornelia throws her hands up. "Why the blue blazes are we so nervous? We have more flight hours than every man here!"

"Just not the Army way," Naomi says.

Cornelia stops them twenty feet from their barracks door and puts out a fist. They quickly form a circle and count aloud, "Chi… fou… mi!" their hands turning into gestures of rock, paper, and scissors. Becca quickly loses, grumbles at this inevitability, shuffles forward, and opens the door.

"Real quick, Bec, please," Twyla pipes.

"Yeah, and don't make any faces," Cornelia adds. "Just a thumbs up or down as you see each bed."

Becca offers her tongue against this insult and steps halfway into the barracks. The fearless flying sisters turn away—the end of the perfect dream is too much to take.

If no WASP graduation invitation is found on her pillow, it spells doom; the pilot is cut, and her military flying career ends before it even starts. Right here, right now. It's the tide rolling up on Tiger Lily, up to their chins in a robust wave of scarcity. Scarcity of new planes, new opportunities, new ways to be seen by others, to see themselves…

They are a moment from losing their chance at meaning in a man's world, a chance at validation for all the years of sneaking, begging, and heartache. Now, there is but one thought, *Ring that goddamned graduation bell, get thrown into the wishing well, and show every doubting man he's wrong!*

Chi-fou-mi had determined the order in which the beds were to be viewed. The plan was this: Becca would enter the barracks and check her own pillow first. Upon seeing the blazing white envelope, she would yip, jump, and pee herself, laugh, recover her breath, and present her thumbs up in the doorway. Hoots and cheers would ring out. Becca would then turn and disappear, headed for Corny's bed. Meanwhile, Cornelia, unable to stand her own skin, would shoot away toward the latrine, rounding the building in an off-camber dust cloud like a Warner Brothers cartoon character.

Twyla would follow after Cornelia, but she wouldn't run. She would try to hold onto the perfect desert dream under Jackie's protection, where the sweet song is positive and hopeful. Because, if the dream dies, the song will turn into a black noise the shape and depth of her bedroom at her Aunt Edna's ranch. Naomi would tug at Twyla's sleeve, and they would walk hand-in-hand, staging themselves at Corny's cartoon corner. Becca would suddenly appear in the doorway and fire off a single shot of thumbs up. Naomi and Twyla would mirror this and hold steady as Corny, stumbling out of the latrine, would wipe the vomit from her mouth, spot them, drop onto the dirt, flop to her back, and yell, "Baby!" Corny would later describe how precisely one million raucous, dirty, scratching, beating, ripping teardowns of herself would flash through her mind, then *poof* disappear. "Uuuuuuugh!" she'd bellow from her gut. "Maybe I'm not crazy-a-little!"

Twyla would be next, and though her hands cover her face, she would spy a vignetted view of Becca's boot-adorned Irish jig, note she's surprisingly agile and graceful, then her shadowed ass would again disappear into their billet. Twyla would muse, *My dream blooms or is stomped out right now. I wish I were strong.* Becca would emerge with a thumbs up. *Wait. What? Her thumb is up!* Twyla would lose all strength in her legs. A sudden longing for Lewis would overpower her, and she would sob into her hands, followed by two gasps and a dusty throat swallow. Here, she'd catch sight of Naomi's face, whip back to Becca reemerging with a preposterous smile, half-hidden behind her fist, yet raising the fourth and final thumb. They *all* made it!

Twyla would spin back to Naomi, who would somehow stand perfectly still, eyes closed, as a flipbook of photographs would pass through her mind, her hidden dimple reappearing at the realization she has a sparkling new story to tell her family. A welded door of immigrant-American steel had unlocked with a reverberating *clonk* and swung wide onto a new frontier, welcoming her over its threshold and into a modern legend.

But none of this happened.

Instead, Hicks's voice comes like a punch to the forehead: "Hey, you four will do. Git to the flight line at once!" He's standing with two instructors ten yards behind the ladies, his riding crop in hand. "Final check ride for you gals. The Army Air Corps way!"

Becca skids into the barracks doorway as Cornelia says, "Sir, are we sandbaggin'?"

"No, ma'am," Hicks shoots back, "you each get a bird.

n i n e

Gravity

This surprise task was at once aggravating and exciting. They would drop two aircraft at a field called Morning Star Ranch for unspecified radio modifications, after which some other pilots would transfer them over to Grand Prairie and the North American aircraft plant. They would double up for the return and presumably pick up where they left off.

No better distraction for a fretting pilot than to go on a hop, Twyla muses in her cockpit.

"Two thousand feet, ladies." Cornelia's voice is a warping hiss over the radio. "Tighten up now, RAF finger-four. The radio is never for chatter. Except for us. Becca?"

The four craft squeeze close together. This in itself is a highlight of satisfaction for these experienced pilots. Cornelia takes the lead finger, with Becca to port and Twyla and Naomi to starboard. They can't help but smile at each other through the sun-streaked canopies of the AT-6s, except Twyla, who flies her frown in the office of her Vultee Vibrator.

"Don't start! Don't start!" Becca squelches back.

"Becca?" Corny says.

"But I didn't get three steps into the room. You know? The beds are at the far end!"

Twyla cuts in, unable to hide her panic. "You didn't see *any* of our pillows?"

"No! No! No! How could I?"

"Hicks!" Cornelia shakes her goggled head. "All right, pilots, this is our day, maybe our last, but it's still ours. Six hundred horsepower and unflappable. I tell ya, when this whole mess is over, I'm gonna Southern charm Uncle Sam outta one of these babies."

Twyla cuts in, "I'm quite sure I have only forty-nine tired horses, so don't get too itchy, y'all."

"You can fly a kitchen table as long as the motor is strong enough," Becca offers.

"Thanks, Beachey," Naomi replies.

"Is it just me, or did *you all* get the distinct impression that Hicks and a few of the other clip-on ties wanted us gone for the day?" Cornelia asks.

Becca clicks, "They gotta top off the fountain, shine the bell, and rake the lawns for our party tomorrow."

"Roger, lawn party," Corny answers. "A few more hours of high anxiety don't bother them a wit."

Naomi chirps in, "My mother said to me, not a few times, 'If I throw a rock high into the air and ask gravity to ignore it just this once, just for me, then I am acting crazy, as gravity cannot help its nature.' To which I argued back, 'But isn't that exactly what birds ask gravity to do?'"

"See that?" Becca says. "Affirmative and correct. Very good, Naomi."

"My mother replied, 'Not only are birds not shaped like rocks, they have wings; nature has seen to that.'"

"Way to miss it by a country mile, Bec," Cornelia chuckles, letting off her mic switch mid-giggle.

"The Owl also paints petroglyphs over the radio," Twyla adds, making bug eyes at Naomi. She's surprised to see the Owl's shoulders jerking, her head bobbing. After a few seconds, Naomi looks back at Twyla, gestures at her instrument panel, and raises her thumb.

"Now listen up, you bird-shaped rocks," Cornelia says, "at Morning Star Ranch, we'll leave one T-6 and the Vultee behind for some other poor bastard to ferry eastward, but not before we triple-check their condition with a ground crew witness. Does that sound right?"

"Roger Wilco," Naomi and Twyla click back.

"Handsome ground crew?" Rebecca asks rhetorically.

"After which," Corny continues, "we'll sandbag it back full throttle in time to unfold chairs and ice the Coca-Colas. Just five more screw-up-free hours, and back where I come from, some of them masters-of-knowledge will have to find a new dog to kick."

Becca hoots. Naomi says, "Ladybirds, how are your instruments behaving? Anything unusual?"

The radio crackles, and a male voice breaks into the flock's world: "Howdy, girls. Thought I might find you at two hundred megahertz. How's the barnstormin'?" A P-40 Warhawk single-engine fighter slips into the group only one hundred feet from Naomi.

"Good morning, Warhawk," Cornelia says. "We're on a cross-country out of Avenger Field. Please give us some room."

Twyla can easily see the Warhawk pilot scanning the formation, his five o'clock shadow resembling a test pilot's full-face helmet.

"Aw, hey girls, don't worry—there's plenty of room out here."

The Warhawk jerks violently, port wing down. Twyla flinches in her seat. *He's going to crash into Naomi!*

"Hey, look out!" Becca yells.

But the Warhawk snaps level ten yards from the formation.

"Good ailerons," he squawks, moving flatly, tauntingly away.

"Hey, pal!" Cornelia barks. "Your Warhawk's a dandy, but your flying stinks."

Twyla catches Naomi twitching frantically in her cockpit. She does a quick sweep of her own instruments while keeping an eye on their guest.

He says, "AAF Rule Three: You're not cleared to fly formation… direct violation. Rule Two, do not needlessly endanger Uncle Sam's property. And Rule One, don't flinch." His wings torque in a flashing twist, and he's abruptly five feet from Naomi's wing.

"Jesus Pete! You horse's ass!" Corny shrieks.

"Oh, that's jake, but there's always room for improvement." He slips away again.

"Twyla?" Naomi clicks over the mic, "point, please."

"What?" Twyla returns. "I mean, I'm sorry. Repeat, please."

"Take point," Naomi repeats, then says, "Corny, how do you turn a mule?"

Twyla squints harder in hopes of sudden smarts. *Point? Turn a mule? Damn it! They have a plan. Compass point? Direction? Lead?*

Naomi repeats herself once more. "Twyla, point."

"Yes, sir," Twyla blurts, deciding to go with lead.

Although they're only flying at 140 knots—a little over 160 miles per hour—Twyla shoves the goatlike BT-13 full throttle, coaxing it past Naomi and pulling straight away.

"Roger Wilco," Cornelia replies, and she cuts down and away.

As their formation breaks up, Naomi stays steady on. From three hundred feet away, Warhawk says, "Not bad… but I do like it tight." His self-satisfaction is loud and clear. He banks steeply and comes level inside Naomi's starboard wing—mere feet below it.

"Oooh, ain't it nifty?" He twists about in his bucket. "Hey, where did the rest of—"

Cornelia zooms up from below, tucking her starboard wing just under the Warhawk's port wing. Bec slides in behind him, and Twyla slams the breaks and shuts the front door, creating a neat diamond-formation trap.

"Hey, whoa! Easy, girls!"

Twyla feels the hair on her neck extend. She has a sudden urge to get her friends home. Down below, a cattle fence runs to the horizon, a dark speck at its end. She clicks her radio mic, "Pilots, left turn on my mark. Mark." She turns slow at first, allowing them a moment to synchronize with her moves. The girls easily maintain a matching turn. The Warhawk, wedged inside this flying cage, is forced to carefully flow with them. "Reverse direction on my mark… Mark." Twyla nearly knife-edges the goat in a steep turn. She grunts with the blood-draining load.

"Son of a bitch! Look out!" he shouts.

They turn 360 degrees, losing 1,000 feet of altitude in the process. Warhawk's head swivels about. "Y'all back the fuck off. None of you job-stealers are supposed to fly formation!" Becca raises her plane just enough to remind the ass where she is. "Whoa! Let me out right now, and I might not report—"

"WASPs, dive on my mark… Mark." The group noses down, the P-40 tightly in their grasp. They level at two hundred feet.

"Hellfire! I'm serious, girlies!" he yells.

Twyla realigns them with the smudge at the end of the running fence. "WASPs, to the deck." She's shaking now, throat is cracker dry.

The five tightly grouped planes swoop low in the flat blatting and buzz of round engines and propeller tips, tracing just fifteen feet above the cattle fence line, less so for Twyla's permanently extended wheels. *Now what*? she muses, the distant smudge becoming clearer, as does an idea. *Twyla, not a good idea.*

"When you apologize, we will let you go," Naomi says calmly.

"I have a right to be here! You don't! Now get lost!" Warhawk roars.

"You came into our airspace," Cornelia adds. "You *will* apologize."

"Apologize and skedaddle!" Becca commands, trying to sound in charge.

"Fuck that! Girls have no business in the military!"

"You're trapped, you ignorant pig farmer!" Cornelia scoffs.

"No, I'm not! I can play all the livelong day!"

Two miles down the fence line, a thirty-foot windmill water pump looks like a tall, determined woman spinning her sun hat to beat the devil. Twyla's heart thumps, adrenaline prickling at the imminence of her plan. "No, you can't," Twyla interjects. She wheels around and watches Warhawk's goggled head ping-pong back and forth.

"Oh, yes, I can! You broads have gone too far! All you tomboy trim can take a flying—!" He sees it. "Aww, shit!"

"Bec, encourage the lost soul, will ya?" Cornelia says.

Becca pulls up and over, showing off her propeller a mere six feet from his windscreen. He shrinks in his seat. Twyla pivots, whipping her eyes from the water pump to Warhawk. His static-laced voice cracks, "Nuts!"

Becca settles back into the rear position. The windmill is now only seconds away.

"How 'bout that?" Cornelia adds.

Twyla is concentrating so hard, she can barely breathe. She has leaped right out of the apple tree with no idea what's below in the dark. *Pitchforks? Tractor parts? Angry Papa? What is happening?* "What am I doing?" her face utters. "WASPs, break just before impact."

"You can't do this!" Warhawk shouts.

Cornelia clicks back, "Roger that."

"Loud and clear," Bec shoots.

"No fucking hell!" he screams.

"Becca," Twyla says, "I know you can't see, so break on my mark."

"Wilco, red leader!" Bec replies.

"Five seconds," Twyla says in someone else's calm voice. "Four… three…" The windmill leans toward them, no way out. "Two—"

Garbled and shrill, his voice blasts in their ears, mangled but unmistakable, "Fuck it! I'm sorry!"

"Break!"

They perform an ass-crushing, high-gravity diamond split. Warhawk is sprung, but the windmill lady lunges.

"Ooohhh fuuuuuuuuck!" The P-40's propeller crashes into the top of the windmill. The bone-dry paddle blades explode into a trillion splinters as the fighter shoots vertical. He climbs in silence for an interval, no doubt checking for damage or leaking fluids. His voice comes in hot: "Hellfire, you're done!" he screams. "All you fucking cunts! Done! No more flying whores! The whole program is finished!" He arcs up and around, hightailing it for Avenger Field.

Twyla feels ill. *What did I do?* They turn and form loosely.

"Gravity," Naomi says.

Twyla compulsively checks her compass as if she's suddenly on the wrong course. The pilots nod to each other.

"Hey, pilots," Naomi says, "do you mind if we take this up a few thousand feet?"

"Of course," Cornelia answers.

They ascend above two thousand feet.

"My bird is ill… don't know if—" Smoke puffs from Naomi's exhaust manifolds, and her engine slackens and tugs, her ship falling behind.

"Naomi?" Twyla prompts.

"She's cutting out!" Naomi clicks.

"Mayday, mayday, mayday!" Twyla calls. "WASP emergency, twenty-four hundred feet at a hundred and seventy—"

Naomi's plane stalls and drops like a shot duck.

Twyla bangs her head against the Perspex as she tries to track Naomi. *NO! NO! Not this!* Her heart claws up her throat as black shapes invade her vision.

"I got her back!" Naomi shouts.

"What?

"Loss of power," Rebecca calmly cuts in. Her plane lags and sinks just as Naomi rises.

"Becca?" Cornelia prods.

"Faltering RPM."

"Let's get you some altitude."

"Switching tanks!" Becca says.

"Climb, Bec."

"Better."

"Good."

Becca grunts, "Nope, not better. Can't raise the RPM."

"Switch again!" Corny yells.

"I know. I did."

"Altitude, Bec!" Twyla twists around to see her. "Remember, no low, slow and pull! Becca! No low, slow and pull!"

Becca's Texan sags nose up, the wings tip over, and the whole thing plummets toward the desert floor. Their minds play out Becca's crash in a quarter second, making the next four seconds a lifetime of horrific anticipation.

Rebecca's voice says, "Engine—" and she slams into the ground.

"Becca!"

"Becca!"

"No, Becca!"

The three planes diverge. Naomi and Cornelia turn to starboard. Twyla arcs to port.

"Don't scatter!" Cornelia warns.

"No! Becca!" Twyla cries from her guts, staring down at a plume of dust and smoke. The plane has been torn in half, a wing dismembered. They circle around, forming back into a loose group. Twyla can't breathe. *No! No! So sudden! Too sudden! My dream? Our dream is dead! Becca is surely dead. No! Shut up, Twyla!*

"Naomi," Cornelia's calm voice starts, "if your plane is willing, we're going straight to ten thousand and on to Morning Star; it's closer than turning back. Twyla, stay a while longer, just in case. Do *not* try to land. I know the fence road is smooth enough, but it's not wide enough. Twyla? Twyla?"

But Twyla can't stop the nauseating, plummeting, overwhelming images swirling through the blackness assaulting her vision and the torsional ringing in her ears, with Becca's voice embedded in the shattering of their dream—their disassembling dream. *What just happened? Becca? We've lost everything we've worked for—selfish! Becca is surely dead! Dead! No! This can't be! This was no one's plan. Fuuuuuuuuck!*

"Twyla?"

"Yes, Cornelia,"

"Meet us there."

"Yes, Cornelia." Her eyes are locked on the aircraft of her two friends, waiting for them to fall from the sky, too. But they glide away smoothly. She circles around.

The desert prairie is so void of color—empty of life. The shadow of her plane slides over no flowers, no stream or shade trees, not even an irrigation ditch. Instead, her cross-shaped shadow surges over sand, scrubby bushes, and tumbleweeds. *This is no place to...* She rewinds the film of the last hour, replaying frames of Becca in her cockpit and the banter-filled anticipation of a wondrous future following tomorrow's graduation. Men *and* women would at once look at them with new eyes. *You fly for the Army? Wow, I didn't know women did that. You're a regular Amelia. Do you know Jackie Cochran? Hey, pilot, why don't you come work for us at Republic... North American, Lockheed, Bell...*

Now that's a war effort!

All of it. Gone.

She widens her arc and directs her shadow to cross right over the wreckage. *Becca, I'm here with you.*

The radio crackles. "Twyla?"

"Yes, Cornelia. Corny, how—"

"I know. I know. See you at Morning Star."

Naomi cuts in, "Power hesitation again. Think there is a line clog or bad fuel."

"Keep switching tanks. Does your bird have outer wing bladders?"

The last thing Twyla hears through bending static is Naomi's thin voice, "Not sure I'll make it..."

t e n

Sugar & The Two-Headed Civilian

But she does make it. They rendezvous with Hicks at Morning Star Ranch and leave Naomi's ill bird behind. Twyla flies back with Cornelia, Naomi with Hicks.

Back at Avenger Field, standing in the dirt, Naomi speaks softly through quivering mortification of sabotage and dark near-future scenarios. Twyla feels her own determination dissolving, perhaps that of the whole program. Naomi's near demise leaves her no direction to turn. So much uncertainty, but many decisions must be made quickly, all while holding the death of an intimate friend at arm's length. Privacy's release is many hours, if not days, away.

*

They raised modest funds from women, and even a few men, before taking the train to Flagstaff. Mrs. Lawrence was the only family to receive them. They swallowed hard against the bile and exhaustion so Rebecca would be remembered for her sacrifice in a dangerous job for the war effort. Their visit was cut short by a telegram requesting the three pilots return immediately to Avenger Field. They left Becca's mother with a pantry full of food. During this time, the owner of the shattered windmill transported Rebecca's body to the coroner in Sweetwater.

On the train to and from Flagstaff, they speculated about what the Warhawk pilot had reported. Did he blame them for Becca's death? Did he accuse them of reckless flying and murder—after attempting to kill *him*? Oddly, Cornelia argued Warhawk was in their airspace as a witness. But she wouldn't, or couldn't, bring herself to clarify her supposition. No offer to cover travel or burial expenses was forthcoming from the U.S. Army Air Corps. Many arguments were sparked, but one thing they all agreed on: Everything was lost.

*

After forty-eight hours without sleep, Cornelia, Naomi, and Twyla stand in the dirt, shielding their eyes from the sun ricocheting off Jackie's tin Quonset hut forty yards away. Miniature tornados of dust juke between the buildings. The women kick small stones around and bite on nubby fingernails. A dozen staff members and four brass hats come and go. The wind kicks up. They chew raw the insides of their mouths. Twyla feels conquered by Avenger Field, and there is nothing sweet about Sweetwater.

Abruptly, Hicks walks out of the hut, angling for the flight line. The girls run after him, and Cornelia calls out, "Lieutenant Hicks?" He doesn't respond, doesn't slow, but they catch him. "Why did you assign that cross-country flight?" His eyes flick back at them. "Give your boys a chance for one more sucker punch? We successfully completed the course. All of it! Was that the problem?"

A white-hot steam boils in Twyla's stomach. She blurts, "You killed Rebecca!"

He stops and barks, "I had nothing to do with it! In spite of excellent training by *me*, you were caught showing off. Did I not explicitly tell you never to fly in formation? When you drop the sewing scissors, don't try to catch them!"

"What does that mean?" Twyla splutters.

"You've lost; don't make it worse," Naomi murmurs.

He accelerates away, shouting, "You fucked the dog!"

The pilots pull up short, grief-stricken and angry.

"Ladies?" A clerk stands at the entrance of Jackie's hut, shading his eyes and jerking his head toward the door.

Inside, the rebels stand at attention, listening to voices and watching cigar smoke curl out of the loose hinges of Jackie's closed office door. Fine dust and cigarette ash coat everything, rendering desks, cabinets, and floors a monochrome gray.

Twyla, hands clasped behind her, makes a small pile of sand on the sill with her fingertips. She wishes the smoke were thicker so she could hide behind it. *Ruined the dreams of my new friends. Becca dead! Ring that stupid bell!* Her eyes follow a curl of smoke taking the shape of a horse's jawline. If she could just bury her face in Maggie's mane, nudge her forward, and not look up until she was far away…

Jackie's voice snaps her back onto her sore feet.

"The double standard you flash in front of us at the least provocation is entirely unnecessary." A chair squeaks, and the wind shoves and sucks at Jackie's door, opening it several inches—enough for Twyla to see her and

Nancy Love seated behind her desk. In the foreground, a man's uniformed shoulder leans forward. The eyes of the two great aviatrixes meet Twyla's stare.

"That's correct," Uniform says. "*We* aren't trying to prove anything here. You are!"

Jackie stubs out a cigarette and says, "And the minute your boys screw up or hide criminal behavior behind their 'war effort,' you just sweep it under the 'learning curve' rug and march on."

"We have to move forward; there's a war on!" he says as if it's news.

"And why is it, if we're on the same side, you treat us like the enemy? How does that make sense when we want the same thing?"

"I'm not condoning this behavior," he says. "I can't be everywhere at once. Boys will be—"

"No!" Nancy jumps to her feet. "You don't get to use that here." Now, Jackie rises. "Not here. Not with a pilot's life. Colonel Tunner is your boss, too. He backs this program because it is necessary and it works."

"Nancy," Jackie says softly in an effort to de-escalate.

But Mrs. Love has diving speed. "Help us win this. Or you can tell us right now, in no uncertain terms, how *our* women successfully delivering planes to *our* men have anything to do with how you feel!"

Jackie's expression approves of this point.

"Everybody but you seems to know war is a man's business," he growls, stubbing out his cigar.

Nancy steps around the desk, focused and intense. "It most certainly is. Men start wars, make a big mess of everyone's lives, and we're left behind to clean it up. Not this time! Y'all have finally outdone yourselves. A four-front war means there aren't enough cavemen to spread around. Seems everyone but *you* knows that!"

Twyla flinches as Jackie's door whips wide open, and Uniform, a lanky ATC officer with a peeling, sunburned nose, walks out of the room, not missing a chance to give the women a sneer.

"Coyote," Naomi whispers.

The two bosses begin a spitting exchange. Nancy shoots out of the office, then skids to a stop in front of the pilots, surprise on her face, as if she's forgotten why they are here. She pulls her suit jacket down, smiles, starts to say something, closes her mouth, and looks at each of them in turn. "Pilots," she says, "I'm sorry about this. About Rebecca." She walks out. All eyes fall on Jackie's back framed in the doorway, staring out her window.

Standing before Jackie, the girls steal glances at each other. Twyla's brain calculates this moment as her third lowest of all time. *Won't she let us explain what happened?* "A serious situation," Jackie begins. "Will one of you volunteer?" She turns and looks at each of them.

A collective gulp, and somehow, the floor lowers. *I'll take responsibility and my lumps,* Twyla decides and steps forward.

A sharply folded letter lies on Jackie's desk, and she slides it toward Twyla, saying, "Not long ago, I sent a copy of this letter to the First Lady. Please read it." Twyla hesitates. "Go ahead."

She glances at the bottom of the page. *The First Lady? How much trouble are we in? Sabotage? Are we now being accused of sabotage?* She looks at Jackie, who responds with pursed lips. Twyla reads.

Dear Mrs. Roosevelt,

The so-called Negro question was recently laid on my doorstep in a very direct way. Several Negro girls applied for pilot training.

I interviewed these particular applicants in proper order without prejudice or preference, hardly knowing what I could do at this stage of my program if any one of them had passed the preliminaries. Fortunately, for the formative stages of the work, none met all the specifications. Finally, one, a New Jersey school teacher who was a pilot and a fine physical specimen, made application for acceptance as a student at Sweetwater. I asked her to my New York apartment for breakfast.

Naomi and Cornelia are rail-spiked to the floor. Even the prairie wind is staying away from this hut.

There, I told her about the manifold troubles I was having getting this program started and ended by stating I had no prejudice whatsoever with respect to the color or race of my candidates. However, with over 130 air bases scattered around this country needing our planes, the many necessary overnights in lodges, motels, and inns are simply not available to Negros. These and other complications she had brought up for decision might, for one reason or another, prove to be the straw that would break the camel's back.

This fine young woman recognized the force and honesty of my arguments. She stated that, first of all, the women pilots' program should be stabilized and strengthened, and she withdrew her application. I appreciate her understanding, and I respect her as a person.

Mrs. President, I just wanted you to know.

Most respectfully,
Jaqueline Cochran

Twyla sets down the letter and steps back into the line of shame. She desperately wants to rub her exhausted eyes.

Jackie's voice emits from her sun-flared silhouette, "Each trainer, fighter, and bomber a woman can move frees a man to fight. This is the most we can do for this war. God only knows what the future holds for women flyers. But in *this* war, it is our most direct link to victory. We have an important role in the Army Air Corps, and as I've said, it will always be dangerous. Right now, it is also fragile."

Out that damn window, a flatbed trailer hauling Naomi's T-6 diesels by. Twyla side-eyes Naomi, who has not missed this. Naomi's face begins to change, transforming from grief to anger. She bites her lip, holding it back.

Jackie steps around the desk. "I'm sorry about Rebecca. I'll be at her service. We will all miss her." To Naomi, she says, "Now, about that Warhawk driver. How do you say 'jackass' in your home?"

There is the slightest nod from Naomi. Cornelia says, "We know that one." Twyla half-exhales. After a few moments, they realize they have been dismissed, that Jackie will handle—or has already handled—the Warhawk pilot. Twyla glances at her friends—*Am I getting this right?* Jackie holds fast. Startlingly, they are compelled to rearrange, reshuffle, and reorganize their futures. They stagger out, each in her own spinning cockpit.

"Naomi, stay a minute more," Jackie says, only half-closing the door.

"Yes, ma'am?"

Twyla's brain feels hot. *But this can't be all of it? This job is dangerous, Becca is gone, we nearly killed a man… Flying is dangerous, nothing has changed. Are you in? Are you out?* Twyla presses her knuckles into her eyes. *Dead or not, the war effort does not stop because it's dangerous.* She drags herself through the smoke of the outer office and into air so clean and new, she becomes lightheaded. *Another near-future without a shape. Naomi will explain.* She U-turns, heading back through the smoke, stopping just outside Jackie's open door, and is ignored.

"The letter—" Jackie says, but Naomi jumps in.

"Yes, ma'am. I understand it was for me."

"Mmm, not entirely. When I was growing up, we had nothing. Dirt poor, as they say. My best friend, who had even less, would hear me complain about something I didn't have and say, 'Jackie, someone's always got more, and someone's always got less.' I couldn't argue that, and I learned not to complain. At least, not out loud."

"Ma'am, if I may? I'm very aware of how lucky—"

"Sugar was found in your fuel."

"Ma'am?"

"Someone sabotaged your plane. You were fortunate to make it to Morning Star."

Twyla steps back a little. Jackie turns away from Naomi, shaking her head, tamping down a budding anger. "Apparently, they didn't put enough in your tank to do the job."

Naomi nods. "And Rebecca?"

Jackie lifts her chin ever so slightly, then shifts her eyes out the window, hauling in a breath. "This program skates on the thinnest slip of ice."

"Yes, ma'am," Naomi responds.

Jackie circles her desk and offers her hand.

"Fly. Fly in their faces. Keep flying and keep a sharp eye; triple-check your machine. Change comes stubbornly to most men, impossibly to military men. Keep flying. This is how we turn a mule."

*

In their billet, the girls take in the perfectly made beds, letters of invitation to graduation on all four pillows. They don't dare look at each other. No one has a tear to spare. Next to Twyla's pillow rests a small parcel wrapped in newsprint and tied with a string—from Edna Gultch. She tosses it into the nearest can.

They send a letter to Rebecca's mother, each adding a personal poem.

Altostratus, Cumulonimbus, rain confetti thick
Becca soars forever now
chamois-soft touch on the stick.
– Twyla

Why does man claim only one color is true
When both appear at sunrise
Clouds of pink, sky of blue
Becca turns among them now
Flygirl, do we miss you.
– Naomi

Rebecca, the cloud collecta
Righteous hair comb protecta
Theater usher rejecta
My friend
Perpetual troposphere inspecta
– Cornelia

Journal,

Goddamned cautionary tale right in the middle of a glorious dream. I want to go home to Lewis and think about it slowly, or not at all. I need Lewis. Need him home. I saw her die. Can't undo it.

What is the point of flying and death? Why must the two collaborate? Flying is a poem of personal, physical exaltation. Not a means to end one's life. It is a celebration. That is all.

Death and Mars. It's Mount Hamilton all over again.

*

The Central Texas wind whips up a show at sunrise, a single churning thunderhead at thirty thousand feet rapidly saturating in pink, as if to say, *Okay, ladies, you took your lumps, done what you came for. Now scram!*

Twyla stares out the window nearest her bed. A few dust devils dart, tilt, and climb to several hundred feet. Without fail, they find bits of white paper to fling aloft. She glances back toward Rebecca's bed. The new girl is in it. Her friends sleep yet, so Twyla writes a letter.

Sept. 43

Dear sunburned island native darling,

I miss you all the way to the moon and back... or the Kwajalein Atoll, whichever is furthest...

Sixteen graduates of the Women's Air Force Service Pilot's training program gather on the apron among the airplanes. Smiles and laughter come easy to most; shoulders lower, addresses are exchanged, and rabbits' feet are rubbed for assignments to come. Twyla, Cornelia, and Naomi squint and posture at each other in their best military pilot mimicry; whoever loses their martial scowl first does ten push-ups. Twyla lasts all of eight seconds. The three pals drop to the warming concrete. Inseparable.

… I made it, my sweet love! Cornelia and Naomi also. I am happy, sad, and greatly confused by the events of this past week. I suspect this is what is meant by "one must soldier on."

Fit, polished, and shining, the pilots stand together in front of a T-6. They wear sharp, Jaqueline Cochran–designed, Santiago-blue uniforms and smile for a deeply hungover photographer, who wrestles with his fifteen-pound Graflex Speed camera, frowns at them, and flashes a picture.

… How can two events, one of such brightness and one so unfair, happen together? I go to sleep tonight as a two-headed civilian. One head, ecstatic as the day you found me at Edna's prison—joy I haven't felt since we flew over the Golden Gate Bridge together. The other head, in mourning for my friend.

Patriotic bunting decorates a small stage and podium. Hicks stands with three of his instructor buddies while two privates hold firm the blowing flags of the U.S. and Texas, respectively. General Arnold and Jackie conspire.

… I wake tomorrow as a military pilot. Twyla Campbell-Haliday, flying the best planes America has for the war effort! No dream more perfect than that! Well, not officially military… yet.

General Arnold looks square at Twyla, smiles, and shakes his fist as if to say, *Go get 'em!* She spins to catch whomever he's looking at, realizes it's her again, and smiles back.

… Often, I turn to talk to Becca and remember once more she is gone. Can't help but feel it's my fault. When you're king of the land, will you fix everything? The Owl would say your family are those who fight alongside you. I'm so glad you and Wiley have each other. My darling Lewis, come back to me. And I promise to be here.

110 octane kisses.

Alice in Befuddledland

Coca-Colas and smuggled rum find their way into tin cups. The friends huddle together while waiting in line to pull the graduation bell's rope.

"Now, we're all clear about what that third thing needed to fly is, right?" Cornelia asks rhetorically.

"But we're not going to give Hicks that satisfaction," Twyla adds. They yell in unison, "No way, José!" raise their cups, and sing a new marching song.

"The best WASP pilot from sea to shining sea.
We punch a hole in the sky all the way to Winnetka.
Women in the seat, we fly so neat.
You'll never see a pilot so bird as Rebecca!"

Jackie mingles, offering congratulations. The three amigos raise their mugs in appreciation for Jackie, who pulls Twyla close. "Your father would be very proud, Ms. Campbell-Haliday. As I'm sure your husband is. I know the general feels a personal satisfaction in helping the daughter of his friend."

"General Arnold knew my father?" Twyla asks.

"I assumed you knew. The general and your father were among the first flyers. The general holds Military Aviator Certificate No. 2, with your father right behind. They were personally instructed by Orville Wright."

Twyla hides her ignorance with a swig of mostly rum. *That explains the general's attention,* she muses. Jackie smiles and half-turns to the other pilots.

"Oh," Twyla blurts. "So, I mean… it was the general who vouched for me?"

"Not at all. You were recommended by one of the charter members of our flying club," Jackie explains. "More precisely, that is why we gave your application a closer look."

"The Ninety-Nines found me?"

"Doris McCuskey."

"Oh, my! Doris." Violent, tropical memories from a century ago—or just three months.

Jackie smiles at the crew. "Good luck, pilots. Now let's show the world what American girls can do in war."

"Yes, ma'am! Thank you, Ms. Cochran!" they chime like third-rate Andrews Sisters.

Twyla raises her mug in honor of Rebecca. "Becca would say, 'Never place a period where God has placed a comma.'"

"Newspaper true!" Cornelia shouts.

Naomi says, "Say good night, Gracie."

A single voice begins another song, which becomes an instant chorus. Hats are launched into the sky. They spin upward like startled birds, arcing toward towering, dark clouds

e l e v e n

Moose Balls and Marina

"Wooo-hooooo!" Twyla whoops in the cockpit of the Bell Aircraft Corporation's P-39 Airacorbra fighter. Neither the vapors spiraling off her wingtips nor the South Dakota ethers care one particle about this little bird hauling ass above this seamless expanse. She's disappointed to be too far north to see Mount Rushmore but eager to see Yellowstone.

She slips a freshly stamped letter into her snowsuit, re-grabs the stick, and pulls up sharply, prop-crawling toward the king daddy of grow lights. No other airplane she's flown sounds like this one. Its mid-engine is shoehorned just behind her, growling a bone-penetrating bassline, while in front of her, the propeller tips sing out a fibrous alto tenor. She extracts the two coveted letters saved just for this high-altitude private library. She hesitates and recalls the letter she'd sent to Lewis weeks ago.

Translated from Boontling encryption:

Dearest Dear,

Please write more often. Newsreels of the PTO make me nuts.

I can't help but look for your face on every man pulled from a burning plane or hoisted around on a stretcher; makes my stomach hurt. I know I'm just a girl with a girl brain, but I aced transition training into the 39. I love tricycle landing gear and hate Buffalo, NY. Does that mean I'm complicated?

This baby is sweet but feels loose of her wind tunnel sometimes, like she's got a shallow draft when you lean into her. Anyway, I seem to recall a certain braggart boasting he would always fly better planes than his wife, who is currently north of three hundred miles per hour with a thirty-seven-millimeter nose cannon pointed toward the Rockies!

1,200 horsepower kisses!

Mrs. Skeezix misses Skeezix

She tucks her map into her thigh pocket, checks compass against watch, throttles back to two hundred miles per hour, trims her ship to rail perfection, and opens the first letter.

Dear Tricycle Driver,

Don't watch newsreels, except when they show us creaming the Japs! Boast again when your nose cannon is loaded! Avoid evasive maneuvers in your "shallow drafter." Your peashooter wants to tumble tits over toenails when it ain't loaded with bullets. Navy calls the P-39 the P-400—we call it a P-40 with a Zero on its tail.

No end to hair-raising sorties here. Wiley says I'll be promoted soon. Nips are insane. You would not believe what we've seen from the "Sequoia-sized Betty Eubanks." Kawasaki and Mitsubishi kites are agile. Juke them out of ammo, and they will try to ram you! There is nowhere to land if you're in trouble. I'm not sure which is worse, getting lost at sea or fire in my "office." Still, better than dying like a meat stick down on the sand with those senseless creatures. Wish I was back on the Gathering Place with you. I would speak nothing of this personally and with emphasis. I miss your freckled face.

Real R & R in a couple months. I need to see you. I think squadron commander wings would look good on me, get me off the firing range.

2,000 horsepower-supercharged-reduction-gear kisses!

Walt (not Skeezix) and Doc sends his love.

P.S. I know you like the Airacobra and Mustang. What if you went to work for Bell or North American? They could use actual pilots on the factory floor—someone to argue for more armor plate and better visibility. Sound swell?

Dearest Apple Farmer,

I hang on to every word of your letters to Llewellyn. Please know I look out for him best I can. As you might imagine, Lewy is an accomplished airman, an impatient teacher to the newbies, but a natural flight leader. You know I can't share details of his work. Let's just say he sleeps little, and the strain is great, but there is nowhere he would rather be than with his squadmates making hell for the Empire of the Sun. He and I miss you terribly. We talk about your flying success and are both proud of you. We want you to stop flying. Please stop flying. Be there for Lew when he gets back. He will need us both.

Love,
Wy (like Twy without the "T")

P.S. Lew's Hellcat is named Boonville Redhead. She has taken down four enemy kites. You know what comes next… right?

The Midwestern prairie stretches to infinity. Twyla flies perplexed. *Factory job? Stop flying? Really, boys, how could I?* She levels off at ten thousand feet and, for the umpteenth time, tries to scratch her head through her helmet. The mid-engine fighter keeps her backside warm, but her fingers and toes are always cold. *Thank the crickets this ain't no P-38 Lightning—no warmth at all! Although, damn those futurists at Lockheed! That's a fast bird! Now, why would Lew suggest I stop flying? Is it the Airacobra? The center of gravity problem? What has he seen?*

Could she meet Lewis in Honolulu? For sure, she would kiss him and never let go. If she did let go, he would bounce off everything in the Moana Hotel—physically and mentally. Admiral Nimitz this, MacArthur that! Who should get credit for killing Yamamoto? *Stop flying? No.* She shoves this away. Inevitably, she's making love with him. A hot afternoon followed by a hot bath, the smell of his skin, his attentive strength… *Twyla, why do you do that to yourself? Nincompoop!*

The American Rocky Mountains dominate her field of view while she lands at ninety miles per hour, Great Falls Montana ground speed, and guides her fighter toward the fuel service apron. Her ass hurts, back hurts, legs went to sleep hours ago… It'll be murder standing up. The automobile-like visibility of the Airacobra during taxi means she can navigate unfamiliar airfields and make it to the latrine that much faster. A burly avgas operator services a P-40 Warhawk while staring directly at her. She pulls her helmet off, rubs her head, stands awkwardly on her port wing, and does some careful stretches. Burly man loses interest.

She shouts, "Hello! I could use some—"

"Get in line," he grunts. That's when she realizes the ten P-40s parked in a haphazard stagger, steam rising from nose cowlings, represent the "line."

She hops off the wing, hearing Cornelia's voice, *Dick in the diaper, you know there's trouble ahead.* She hobble-hops toward the latrine, cursing the electric needles in her feet and Corny, for good measure.

Four hundred and twenty-eight nautical miles later: "Beat that, you flying hairdo rags!" she exclaims to Corny, Naomi, and Becca as her wheels screech upon the runway at Edmonton, Alberta, Canada. *Did it!* Her first aircraft, delivered on schedule for Lend Lease with Premier Stalin. On to Russia this flying gun will go. She hopes it will knock down some bad guys and end the war sooner. Next up, figure a way back to Buffalo for another Bell bird.

Inside the great room of the Alaskan Wing Air Transport Command office, ill-yellow sodium-vapor lamps coat desktops of unfiled folders towering a yard tall. Thick smoke reveals thin shafts of daylight stabbing through window slats, while exactly a dozen prairie war staff strike typewriters, puff cigarettes, and shout into telephones. On the radio, Glenn Miller's brass section slings "The Jumpin' Jive" but is no match against the percussive rap of keys and blatting round engines out on the apron.

A redhead typist who could be Twyla's twin sister, a cigarette teetering on her lips, gestures for Twyla's paperwork while maintaining one hundred words per minute on her Royal Standard. Twyla stares, mesmerized by her aspect, rubs the smoke from her eyes, and proffers the transfer form. "How do you do?" Twyla says. "I made it. This is my first ferry mission." The young woman snatches the form, stamps it, plucks a pencil from her ear, ticks at a dozen tiny boxes, and slams it on top of a tilting stack, hardly missing a stroke. Twyla waits expectantly, hoping for something like, "Atta girl, pilot! We appreciate your skill and sacrifice!" Instead, she feels the violent concentration of everyone in the room. She thinks, *And this is their war effort. Is this what Lewis really wants for me?* Suddenly, her twin stamps a new form and smacks it down in front of Twyla. Her peashooter is going to Fairbanks. Scribbled next to the box labeled "pilot": T. Campbell. *No foolin'?* She hadn't heard of any WASPs flying to Alaska. *Thank you, General Chaos, sir!*

Back on the flight line, all the 40s are gone, replaced by a dozen Airacobras and two Kingcobras. Several male pilots speed walk past her in the universal body language of bursting bladders. She wonders how all these planes got here so fast and is unexpectedly struck by how glad she is they are here. All these planes are bound for a pilot who desperately needs them; pilots just like Lewis, stymied of their next missions without them. And nowhere more so than the teetering Eastern Front, where Luftwaffe squadrons have been chewing up Red Army pilots. She's seen the newsreels. *The poor Russians are getting blistered.*

Between Edmonton and Fort St. John, she designs no fewer than six improvements to "The Campbell Pilotess 200" bladder relief bottle. Folding funnel meets glass bottle. *Collapsible glass bottle? Need better container material*, she thinks. *And sew a bigger relief flap into crotch of snowsuit.* "Amelia's Range Extender," she says aloud. *That's a better name for it.* "For your cross-country pilot wife…" she arranges her voice Ed Herlihy style. "Yes, folks, you heard it here first on GAB radio. Gasoline Alley Broadcasting and Campbell Flying Unmentionables present ARE—the Amelia's Range Extender. If Amelia would've used it, so should you. Because let's face it, fine folks—if you're going to fly cross-country, you A-R-E going to pee while flying. Amelia's Range Extender is Ninety-Nines approved. Look it up in your Sears, Roebuck, and Company catalog." Her chuckle is cut short by the sight of a massive thunderhead to the west. She muses, *One proper hailstone, and I'm dead.*

Exhausted by the Rockies rollercoaster, she discards three bladder-relief designs as too embarrassing to transport on the tarmac. She thinks she's identified the Liard River and realizes she has run out of Rockies. *I am honest to goodness north.* At Watson Lake, she executes twenty minutes of sinew-stretching calisthenics. She soars over foothills brushed with trees, scribbled with streams, and blotted with blue lakes. She targets impressive herds of caribou along a silver river. She wonders what Lewis is doing at that exact moment—*It's still morning deep in the Pacific. Solomon Islands? Philippines?*

Iwo Jima? Where the crickets are the Solomons? Breakfast before sunrise? All their sorties are over water. Do they take food with them on lunchtime missions?

After a freezing night on a broken cot at Snag, Yukon Territory, she flies half-lidded, peering down on little elongated black and brown dots from six thousand feet.

Bear? Bear herd. Bison? Bears don't wander in herds. Moose. Bull Moose? Moose herds? It's hard to tell. As smooth as the P-39 flies, she still exerts a constant high rotary vibration, making everything a little fuzzy.

Less than five hundred miles to Fairbanks. "Almost, Twyla!" she yips. Abruptly, smoke obliterates her vision. Heat presses in, and she can't read the instrument panel. *What language is that?* She can't breathe, and the fire is making an odd racket. She rolls down her window and opens the door into the slipstream. She grabs for the rip cord. *Wait! I need more altitude! But it's fire! Can't wait! No! It's jump, then rip cord, stupid! Dead in seconds!*

She awakens. Javelins of adrenaline prick her torso. *Shit! Twyla!* "I'm awake now!" she yelps. "I'm awake now. Altitude! Airspeed! Mountain elevation! Oil temp! Uuuugh!"

The western sky is a fading cobalt blue above an amber-edged, jagged horizon. Dozens of fighters and Skytrain transports fill the apron before the large, open, and brightly lit hangar at Ladd Field, Fairbanks. Pulling into the fourth row of planes, Twyla shuts down her engine and pops her canopy door, her breath vaporizes, the sharp air a welcome slap to the face.

"Moose balls! That is preposterously far!" She pulls out her father's flight bag, sets it on the wing root, unbuckles her chute, and climbs down. She notices a figure silhouetted in the mouth of the huge, steam-obscured hangar. She inspects the peashooter, her eyes wandering to the hangar. The bulky and apparently hairy silhouette is now pressing through the second row of planes, something sharp in its hand. Twyla checks the nose gear, glances over her shoulder—nobody there. Back to the other side, and she is startled to see the mysterious creature working a screwdriver on her plane.

The first aid kit hatch opens. It bends down, pulls a pair of sparkling, emerald-green heels from a small bag, carefully inserts them into the compartment, screws it shut, and mumbles, *"Bud' ya proklyata, yesli vernus' s pustymi rukami."*

"Eto horoshaia idea," Twyla's mouth blurts ahead of her brain.

The furry creature flinches, its covered head twisting. It straightens and pulls back its hood, revealing a beautiful, dark-haired young woman with a bandaged forehead, who says in Russian, "How do you like the tricycle gear? But you must urinate, no?"

"Uh, please slow, please," Twyla struggles. "Am little… am I little… I am little…"

"Rust?" the woman prompts in English.

Twyla nods vigorously and tries her Russian again, "Many, very much years."

"Tricycle gear?" The woman kicks the nose wheel.

"Oh, wheel! Easy drive. Yes, it cheating, feelings," Twyla stammers.

"Good." She stands motionless and seems to regard Twyla earnestly. "How do you know my language?"

"Babushka."

"Is this why you are here… in Alaska?"

"I don't know. No," Twyla says. She puts this young woman in her late twenties at most, despite the dark rings under her eyes.

The woman extends her hand stiffly. She says slowly, "Marina Khomyakova. I am a pilot for army fighter group five-eighty-six."

"Oh," Twyla says, taking her hand. "I clever. Marina, very good, meet… Twyla Campbell… Haliday… me. Please meet you. I are ferry pilot, Bell aircraft. You fly plane to bases?"

Marina puts a hand to her bandage and says, "It is my job this week."

Twyla notes this wording. "Oh, what you last week… do?"

Marina gestures to the planes. "I fly a fighter." Marina stares back confidently, unblinking.

Twyla is disappointed at how much she's lost of the language. "Me comrade, Cornelia, say women pilots am America best pilots. Sisters."

"Yes, sisters," Marina agrees and tosses her flight bag onto the Airacobra's wing.

Twyla bounces in place. "Yes, big urinate." They walk at a clip toward the office, passing three identical C-47 Skytrain transports.

"How many flight hours?" Marina asks.

"I got a bunch of… bananas." Twyla gives up, too tired to think of the Russian words for numbers. "You?"

Marina pulls out her logbook. "Just today, I passed fifteen hundred."

"Wow, that are big."

"Which planes are you rated for?" Marina asks.

"I am good light, two motors, and the Airacobra, and the Warhawk, and me finish class instruct… teach a Thunder—"

"Thunderbolt? You can fly everything!"

"Oh, big bombers, not… of course. And the pursuit five, one, Mustang. No yet."

Marina's eyebrows arch. "This is good. Have you seen the Knife… Messerschmitt Me one-oh-nine? Very fast, high-altitude fighter. Lavochkin is good, MiG also, but soon, we will have the Yak-3. America sends many P-40s to my country, out of date now; not in the same class with Yak or Me. The Airacobra has a good nose cannon." She pulls her jacket sleeve back to check her watch. "You like it?"

Twyla scowls. Instead of admitting she knows nothing of the quality of its nose cannon and that it's against the rules for ferry pilots to fly with ammunition, she says, "Yes," and is startled by Marina's watch. "Your watch is big beauty."

"Thank you. A present from the King of England. At the front, we are very busy."

"The King of—?"

"England. George the Sixth. He is very happy with us." Marina points to a C-47 with a red star on the tail. "If you get on that one, you could come see my squadron. They fly skillfully. But do not come. Soso would get mad. Of course, you are not married?"

"I am."

They march past the steamy maw of the giant hangar and into a Quonset hut slouching at the foot of a long multistory building under emergency construction. A short, round Army clerk rises from behind a filing cabinet and says, "Comrade Pilot, why are you still here? Stranger pilot, welcome to EON."

"EON?" Twyla bites.

"Elbow of Nowhere. On a good day, that is." He back slants his hat.

"And on a bad day?" She immediately regrets asking.

"Entrails of Nowhere, of course."

"Of course." And because he is so pleased with himself, she offers a smile. "Well, I think it's beautiful here."

"Soon you won't," he says.

She adds the date and time to her paperwork and drops it on an in tray. The clerk glances at it, turns, and adds numbers to a giant chalkboard grid on the wall. Marina updates her departure time in the big logbook.

"I'm Twyla Campbell-Haliday, sir. This is my first delivery."

The clerk tips his hat toward her. "Congratulations. The odds were against you. They call me Bibs 'round here. All of 'em. Army folks, moose, the long-tooth snark, and the wily beaver." His eyes suddenly seem too close together and his nose is bulbous—like a clown.

Twyla shakes his hand. "Nice to meet you, Mr. Bibs. I'll be right back." She runs to the latrine.

"And I'll be right here," he says.

The flyers hike back out to the flight line in the extended twilight. They track two pilots preflighting a Skytrain—Twyla's bus back to the States.

"Ms. Khomyakova, do you go asleep flying?"

Marina stops, locks eyes with her, and slowly shakes her head. Twyla wonders, *Did I insult her?* A few seconds pass, then an ironic laugh ratchets out of Marina, followed by a spellbindingly beautiful smile. Twyla flushes and turns away. Marina puts hands to hips, widens her stance, and says, "I feel shame every time I do. It is impossible to avoid. Call me Marina."

"I much glad hear this, Marina," Twyla stammers.

"When will your president open a second front?"

"Oh, uh… I not know what he think—"

"American forces could chute down through the Baltic, drop a hammer on Fritz, pulling their attention north. Just this one disruption would allow us to—"

"I not know."

Marina touches her bandage, winces, and says, "Americans do one thing well—test everyone's patience. But this one thing, *patience*, is the lesson of my entire life."

"I sorry."

"After the Fascists invaded my country, all of us pilots wanted to go to the front. To show we could defend the Motherland."

"I know this feel."

"It is simple, no?"

Twyla nods *yes*, mumbling, "Poor mailmen… so many buses."

Marina pulls toilet paper from her pocket, dividing it between her flight suit and her bag resting on the Airacobra's wing, "The history against you, against women, is considerable," Marina says. "So, if you want something, you must push back, concentrate with all your strength. This is what I did, and I was forced to be patient. How do I, Marina Khomyakova, from—butt-itch backyard village—how you say… get to the front?"

"Close enough."

"One must go directly to the mouth of the river."

*

Aero club cadet Marina Khomyakova sat in moldy darkness at the Soviet Air Defense Forces Committee, Moscow PVO. She folded her dirty gray overcoat across her lap and adjusted her bright red beret. Her leg bounced and fingers tap-tapped the arm of a chair designed with obvious contempt for the human form. She peered back up the long, dark hallway to the watchful, disapproving secretary, who long since overran her official party uniform. Marina wondered anew how anyone carries extra fat when there is rarely enough food. A large poster hung behind the secretary, displaying soldiers, tanks, and aeroplanes along with the words, *THE MOTHERLAND IS CALLING! WHAT HAVE YOU DONE FOR THE WAR?*

On the secretary's desk stood a calendar turned to 22 October 1941. A reference to the *League of the Three Emperors* in bold type—a reminder to all visitors that the League was founded nearly seventy years ago on the agreement that Austria-Hungary, Germany, and Russia would stick together against any trouble from the Balkans or the West. Marina always appreciated unintended irony; better yet, if it were official. Still, she was nervous, unable to keep her thoughts straight. She scolded herself to be calm and focus on her agenda. *You will wait as long as it takes to meet Commander Raskova. Concentrate now! Why are all government offices so dark and stuffy? This cannot be an architect's aspiration… Thank Rusalki of the Forest they sealed in the cigarette and pipe smoke!* She giggled at her joke.

Directly across from her, a three-meter-high, full metric ton door swung open. Through it stepped Major General Mikhail Gromadin and Marina Raskova.

Marina Khomyakova's brain spasmed. *My hero is truly here! Look at her! She has pulled her hair back tight; her uniform is spotless, perfectly pressed. Her face is stern, yet pleasant, and concentrating. See that, Marina? Concentrate!*

The general and the legendary first Hero of the Soviet floated past and through another twelve-foot door obviously designed to withstand a Medieval siege. Marina couldn't breathe, couldn't feel her body. *No! I am not the type to cottonmouth when seeing a living hero in person. How many arguments with my friends about this? My composure is made of granite? Wait! I didn't stand at attention! When Major General… and… and… Oh god! I didn't stand!* Her stomach soured and lurched. Spinning right, she saw nothing but an empty corridor. She dashed headlong up the hall toward the surly receptionist, skidded twenty feet across the black marble floor, squeaked to a stop at the waste can, and vomited. She wiped her mouth on her sleeve and dry heaved two more times. She glanced at Surly, who had given way surprisingly fast. Marina raised a finger, *just a second*, then nodded *all was fine*. She hugged the can, her face pointed proudly at Surly. The *clip-clop* of shoes bounced off the dark fortress walls. She spun around. In all the centuries of the Empire, all trillion acres of the Soviet Union, the stratospheric Marina Raskova walked directly toward her. *Again!*

Throttle down, you backward peasant! she admonished herself. *Quiet the blowing wind in your ears. Are you the ass-end of a cart horse? No! You are the smartest girl from your village. You have perfect eyesight. Top gymnast of all your girlfriends with the best marks in glider training. You will tell Hero Raskova what an inspiration she is to you and everyone you know, that you, Marina Khomyakova, are also meant to fly for the Motherland to help defeat the evil Fascist invaders. The two Marinas—not Catherine's army! Not the Tamanskaya! Not ten thousand T-34 tanks… the two Marinas! Imagine that!*

As the two radiating supernovae marched by, Marina's stomach flopped again. Her face, now a surrealist painter's caricature, wretched stridently into the can. Commander Raskova and the general stopped and stared at her. She was actually meeting the great aviatrix. She set the bucket down too hard; it reverberated brightly off the stone floor, echoing to this day. She saluted with her left hand and wiped her mouth with her right. A long moment later, she corrected her hands and presented her most winning smile.

*

Twyla clamps her mouth with her hand, laughter leaking around her fingers. Marina says with a fox's squint, "Patience! You see? But I must save my stories of triumph for the next time."

"Patience," Twyla confirms.

"I had to wait four more days to see the great aviator. We knew she was putting together an all-female—"

"Oh!" Twyla blurts. "She's your Nancy Love, or… the Jackie Cochran of your country!"

"She changed our lives," Marina says. "She is dead now."

"Oh."

"But she is a hero. My hero," she says with a sorrowful smile. "Time to fly."

Elongated twilight lies gently over one dozen ferry pilots fanning out to their planes. Twyla assists Marina with her parachute pack and says, "My husband go the Pacific. Fly at his number two ship. The first one sink. In letters, he fly the… boat, *Enterprise*."

"I don't like to fly over water. But he is alive?" Marina asks, holding her gaze.

"Well, yes."

"Does he love you?"

"He want I stop flying."

Marina nods and says, "So, this is what you have."

This reminds Twyla of her lost Babushka, who often reasoned this way. Perhaps next delivery, she will ask more. For now, she says, "This Cobra's prop pitch… more slow to change."

Marina nods again. "Your Russian is already improving."

"You are generous. Also, mind her tork-witch at takeoff. She dig straight away… tugs all up power band."

"Tork-witch?"

"Yes, um, twist? Roll? When you press it?"

"Ah, thank you. This is usual." Marina nods and smiles like a Sochi sunrise.

My dearest, bravest,

The Alaskan Territory is breathtaking, so thick with bugs I'm afraid they will stall out my engine. Then it got cold. Can't wait to train in 51s in warm California. Sexy Mexy should be there already. This has become my dream plane. It's so fast and beautiful, I can't stand it. Met a Russian transport pilot named Marina. She talks too fast. She ferries near the battlefront with Jerry shooting at her. No, thank you!

That's four successful deliveries to Fairbanks. Damn the weather! But I haven't seen Marina since. Why are Americans so skittish and stuffy about women?

I only need two things in this life: you and the WASPs. Watch your six o'clock and stay out of the big pool.

Smashed bug kisses,

Twyla

P.S. Marina said male pilots show off too much and get killed. Don't do that. Marina also said "Privet." And I'm still ignoring your Rosie the Riveter suggestion as island-fever homesickness. I love you, too.

Spring rain pelts three transport aircraft idling outside Ladd Field's flight office. Four corrugated Quonset huts protest the plain's wind and rain with an arrhythmic performance of howls, squeaks, and clangs. Tonight, the frontier military office decor of gray desks, black chairs, and gray walls is molested by a yellow party dress bouncing to and fro. Twyla is a high-wattage electric light as she sways to the rattling windows, snaps her suitcase shut, and flops her completed form onto the tray. Bibs slants his hat, sets a large envelope next to her, and says, "Mademoiselle, please escort these exciting frontier reports back to Buffalo."

"It's *madam*, Bibs. And why can't we just fly the planes all the way to Russia? Has Marina been back?"

Bibs un-slants his hat and says, "Uncle Joseph won't let any Yanks in his country, save for an occasional technical expert. Rooskies are a particularly paranoid people, dreadful at paperwork and time schedules. But damn, the vodka!" He re-slants his hat.

"They're our allies. That doesn't make sense. I like Marina so much."

"The two Marinas, Gram Gram!" Twyletchka yipped.

"That's right, Wheels!" Gram hollered over the kitchen counter as she squeezed Sebastopol honey on a pile of peanut butter. She stirred it together with a fork, grabbed a brick of graham crackers, and angled to the living room.

"Gram, you and your friends vomit a lot," her granddaughter said, rolling up next to the coffee table and gazing at the boxed puzzle on her lap. "I'm going to start in the middle of this bad boy."

Gram Gram hobbled in. "Hell, you are!" She stared at the photo on the one-thousand-piece puzzle box—an Austrian village with dumpling clouds reflected in a meandering river surrounded by a trillion cobblestones. "Shit!" Gram said and set down the snack. "Ya see my large-of-brain, suspect-of-smarts bird, the trick is to frame it in first. Start with the outside pieces. Chaos, true, but with a guiding edge." Gram grunted all the way down onto the couch, smiling through worry.

"Mmm, that could make sense," Little Twyla agreed.

"Sweetness, I'm not sure I can carve the next bit of my story in a straight line." She scooped some peanut butter out with a cracker and handed it to her granddaughter. "So, I'm going to tell this next passage in a different way as not to get too melancholy."

"So, you're gonna start in the middle of this bad boy?"

Gram laughed and said, "Smartass! Yes, I am. Then jump around a bit. Is that okay?"

Little Twyla looked up from the puzzle. "I think my Gram Gram would say to me, 'Too much story about your story; git on with it!'"

"Right you are."

t w e l v e

Southern Charm

The hammered, copper moon slips behind bald cypress trees dripping Spanish moss and fizzles out his last oxidized gasp. Behind Cornelia, the new sun dazzles on the Atlantic horizon, illuminating Camp Davis, North Carolina. Marinating in aviation fuel, swamp gas, and phantom chiggers, she stands on the flight line next to a man-child mechanic with knee-buckling halitosis and watches him fill a tin mug with water from one of the carburetors of a well-worn A-24 Banshee. Her grandfather's heated face comes to mind because he had a saying she could really use right now. Instead, she says, "How come you boys don't fill the tanks at the end of the day?"

"I dunno," Halitosis says.

"You don't know?"

"I dunno."

"Well, that dog won't hunt." She sweeps her hand over the A-24. "And this bird won't fly!" She waits for the merest slip of cognizance. *Bupkis.* "Condensation, man!" she finally says.

He shrugs. Next to them, an A-25, SB2, Helldiver coughs to life; its four massive six-foot propeller blades hack through the black smoke surging from the exhaust pipes. She hopes it will drive away the no-see-ums. "Bikini Bride" is looped in faded paint on the fuselage below a weathered, amateur illustration of a girl in a swimsuit under a palm tree. She presumes this represents Bikini Atoll in the South Pacific.

She turns back to Hal and says, "Well, aren't you going to note this in your log?"

"Sure." He does nothing.

"But Hal, this is the very moment when you promise to fill the tanks at the end of the day."

"I won't be here."

"You won't be… oh, well in that case, when the engines drown on takeoff, we'll just let the lady pilots die. The upside is y'all will have one less POS to neglect!" Her face contorts as she tries to remember, *What the cuss is that phrase of grandfather's?*

A Jeep pierces the cloud of A-25 smoke and grinds to a stop next to Cornelia. Syd, the short and fit flight line commander, is at the wheel. "Pilot, yer bumped up two slots," he says. "Git on up there."

"Yes, sir," Cornelia says, pointing at the landing gear. "But sir, these tires are bald. They'll fail on the next landing, and there's water in the—"

"Huh, well." He jerks a thumb toward the A-25 belching calliope. "Take that son-of-a-bitch!" He pulls the Jeep into a tight U-turn and accelerates back up the line of planes. She watches Syd drive away, hating the very shape of his head. Syd stops three dog-eared dive-bombers away and talks with a mechanic. They turn toward Cornelia. Syd points a finger at her.

"Well, I'll be damned, Hal," she says, staring at Syd. Her grandfather's voice ricochets, "*Your mother is a sunbeam of anger!*" *No, that's not quite right.*

The boy mechanic wobbles, stupefied and impatient for release from this intense woman. She ponders on his behalf. *What to do, check my ass or scratch my watch?* She tries a different approach: "I met Amelia Earhart, Hal. I'm a Ninety-Nines original," she fibs. "I've raced Jaqueline Cochran, and she's my boss."

"Who?"

"*Who*? Hal, that's not possible. You weren't literally born in this swamp?"

"Name's not Hal."

Syd and Jeep return, and he hollers at Cornelia until she climbs all the way into the plane known in the Pacific Theater as the SB2, or the son-of-a-bitch Second Class. She knows with a certainty that Naomi would have a special name reserved especially for Syd.

*

Naomi hustles a P-51 Mustang under waning light toward Athens Field, Georgia at the far end of a 2,200-mile day. A cluster of clouds to the west flows from orange to pink to gray. She chews on a letter from Cornelia describing life at Camp Davis and how the girls aren't allowed in the officers' club but are allowed to fly to other bases if they can find a flyable ship. The girl pilots can also wear the men's dress pinks and greens—shirts and slacks—but no store or restaurant in Wilmington would permit pants-wearing women inside. One of the WASPs was even arrested for impersonating an officer!

Naomi slaps the groggy out of her face and yells above her own engine. "Corny! Twyla! Becca! I present to you, bladder-relief design Number Sixteen. Fit barf bag to snipped talking tube of high-altitude flight mask. Hold in place with inner thighs. Pilot must slouch first. Sorry, Cornelia, knee room is essential." Becca's pleased face suddenly fills her forward screen. She sighs and muses, *I know, Becca, I know.* Then she recalls the drunken photographer at the WASP graduation and wonders what happened to the photograph he took. She mentally scissors out her own photograph of Rebecca and tapes it onto the group photo in her mind, completing the portrait of the Horsepower Housemaids, The Terrible Twats, or The Avenger Field Angels, or... *and Twyla Campbell-Haliday, I will see you in Long Beach, California soon!*

She clicks her mic. "Athens tower, radio check." White noise blips back, followed by a male voice slurring something about a military plane on approach. She tries again. "Athens tower, Alpha Tango Charlie North American 51 on approach. Pattern instructions please, over." The radio clicks, and smeared static is followed by silence. "Athens tower, P-51 circling, request traffic, over." More clicks, and the man says, "Girl pilot, please stay off the radio. We're trying to bring in a P-51 Mustang!"

Naomi scans around her and sees not a soul in this lush, green dusk. She calls again for instructions. This time, there is an instant reply, the man shouting, "Hey, peach pie, get off your daddy's radio set; it's getting dark, and we're trying to make contact with a high-performance warbird!"

She triple-checks her airspace to be sure. *I see.* She clicks on, "Tower, let me clarify for you..." Naomi banks steeply, peeling sharply off her downwind leg. "You are talking to the pilot of the P-51, by authority of ATC and Jaqueline Cochran." She straightens out, hovering over the exact centerline of the runway, and softly touches down.

The radio crackles, thick with southern charm, "Aw, now that's a silk hanky." She grinds her teeth and taxis toward the flight line, toward the rising hazy and grumpy Man in the Moon.

She climbs out of the cockpit, yanks off her helmet, and scratches her head. Her hair shoots out in all directions, supercharged by static electricity in the soggy Georgia twilight.

Hollering male voices rise to meet her, "It's a girl! Look at that!" Somehow, twenty more cadets pile out of the Athens Field ready room, eager to see the hot-rod pursuit plane. They cheer and whistle like she's Lindbergh standing on the wing. She pulls a pre-tied scarf around her head, waves to the boys, and smiles with all her teeth. "Corny, you won't believe this."

*

Cornelia writes on a pad of paper; below it, her map is string-tied to her thigh. She steers her plane-of-many-names up over the North Carolina coastline.

BALD TIRES
WATER IN FUEL TANK
LOW OCTANE FUEL
AIRSPEED INDICATOR FAULT
VENT HANDLE MISSING
MANUAL GEAR HANDLE BROKEN
NO APPARENT MAINTENENCE
EXPENDABLE!

She clicks her radio. "Sears Landing control, this is A-25, target-tow proceeding downrange, estimated turn at eleven thousand feet in four minutes." Distorted pulses return. "Sears Range, slotting into pattern for initial orientation run." She presses her headphones hard onto her ears, listening for the correct number of words and syllables equivalent to, "Roger, A-25, proceed to tracking course. Enter at eleven thousand." Instead, she hears, "Roger, Bikini Bride, begin artillery run. Enter ten thousand, descend all gunnery ranges at five thousand feet per minute. Exit small arms range on the deck. Sears, over."

"Roger, Sears Landing," she says. "Entering gunnery range at—" *Artillery run? Hold on—what?* "Sears Landing, repeat? Sears Landing, I have no target banner operator on board. Sears, please repeat!" Two mic clicks echo in her ears, and she knows control is busy with other air traffic—or ignoring her. *What did he say? Enter ten thousand? Descend five thousand per minute? That's a steep dive in this penny arcade!*

Dammit, Twyla! And she wonders at which end of Timbuktu her letter to Twyla got dumped.

Dear Twyla,

Twyla, come out, come out, wherever you are! I've been flying four-hour solos in a Dauntless at ten thousand feet with no oxygen for fuzz-faced, radar-tracking gunner-noobs back and forth in a seat that wore out during the Battle of Midway! Camp Davis should be renamed Camp Neanderthal. Stevens, our commanding officer, whom I've yet to see acknowledge our existence, suddenly cleared out the storeroom, set up a table and chairs, and put up a poster that read WASPs Nest. We were interviewed by women reporters, then the whole thing disappeared as if it never happened! Men hate us for taking their jobs and ruining their beliefs of what women should be. Strong muscles and weak imagination. Really, God? How can proud ignorance exist as a way of life? Makes me hate humanity whilst admiring the men who created powered flight!

I can't stand myself!

Ginger Snap, don't come here.

Cornelia unbuckles, twists herself around, and threads her long arm between the seat back and rear canopy. Her fingertips can barely touch the banner reel-out handle. Grunting with poor leverage, she unspools what is supposed to be a one-hundred-foot-long cable with a twenty-foot target banner. After only twenty-five feet, the spool jams. She plops back into her bucket and mutters, "Hal, Syd, pals, I'm going to murder you."

She initiates her final turn when an earsplitting *crack* jolts her plane. "Fuck!" She pushes the nose over and is immediately bracketed by detonations. Black puffs of flak explode so closely, she can hear them over her churning engine. Bright yellow-white flashes blink up at her from the shoreline. "You're pullin' my leg!" She grips her stick too tightly, can't figure out why she's side skidding, then realizes her left foot has slipped off her oil-slicked rudder pedal. Booms and blasts puncture her concentration. She steadies her ship and aims for the far end of *Topsail Island? Wrightsville Beach? Just get me past the large guns!* The medium-gun range comes abreast, muzzles blinking and puffing. There are as many bursts ahead of her as behind. "Get it together, you inebriated Everglade swampbillies!"

A concussive shock shoves her ship's nose inland. She pulls her stick right, pushes the right rudder, and straightens out her wings, but her nose wanders westward. *Ailerons it is,* she relents. The oversized rattletrap moans as she wrestles her into a steeper dive. She doesn't know the extent of the damage to her plane or if the target banner is still attached. Bikini Bride plows over the small-arms firing range just one hundred feet off the deck. Though she can't hear these guns, she flinches lower in her seat—at any moment, a few painted bullets will rip her head off. Her RPM begins to fade.

Bikini Bride banks rudderless for the runway on the west side of the marsh. The oil temp rises as its pressure falls. She straightens the plane out on final approach, instantly feeling a crosswind shove. Her engine begins to cough up bad fuel, and she skitters just a few feet above the treetops bordering the alligator bog. *No way I'm making this one.* "Come on, baby, make this one!" Her bald tires slap the tips of bald cypress trees while she begs a little throttle and gets none. The lagoon opens up for three hundred feet, then one final wall of trees before the strip. *Nope on a rope.* The suddenly operational radio squawks, "Bikini Bird, you are clear to land."

"No shit!" She dips the nose, gaining a trickle of airspeed, skims the wheels across the water, and pulls up. "Come on, Wolf Swamp!" She crashes through the final stand of trees and stalls out forty feet above the runway.

The Helldiver drops like a manhole cover. Upon impact, both tires blow, absorbing some of the downforce, but her breath is crushed out of her. The port gear collapses, and the plane bounces up with a twist, shoving her hard into the side of the cockpit and forcing a full right rudder correction, which does nothing. She hits the tarmac again, now on a collision course with an abandoned Dauntless at the edge of the runway. *Really?* she reels, desperately trying to recover her breath. The aircraft's spinning momentum is slowed marginally by the shredding tires, and she braces for another impact. The other landing strut folds, slamming her down onto her belly in a sudden grinding stop on the newly paved runway. Her bent propeller tips kiss the ass of the undeniably daunted A-24 Dauntless.

Her lungs whistle as they fill, her eyes popping wide with sudden success. A turn of her head presents an outstanding view of the cypress she just pruned. The silence is startling and brief, quickly replaced by emergency vehicle sirens.

And now she remembers her grandfather's favorite phrase: *Your mother is incandescent with rage.*

TAILSPINNIPSLIAT

Twyla frowns down at the borrowed dun suitcase on the floor then glares at her giant snowsuit hanging on the coat rack of Bibs's office. She wonders what to do with it. Her case is stuffed full. *Wear it? Probably, unless they've fashioned some heat for me in the jump seat.* She regards herself in the glass door of a gun cabinet turned file storage, her canary yellow swing dress flattering her curves. *But what to do with too much luggage?* Rebecca and Gracie Allen offer guidance: "*I don't see what difference it makes what side your bread is buttered on; I always eat both sides!*"

The wind blows a tall, dark humanoid into the building, and it slogs toward Bibs. Its black oilcloth folds sway under the weight of the deluge from which it emerged. Its drapery arms tip back a dark field hat, exposing an unshaven man with sunken eyes and the green pallor of tempered glass. He flips open a mailbag, casting Alaskan rain in all directions, and thumps a large letter bundle onto the counter, clomping away without pause. Bibs says, "Thanks, Chuck. Stay dry," and begins sorting and tittering. To Twyla, he says, "Ya know, there's scuttlebutt about you gals."

But Twyla is still watching the mailman. "Whoa, Chuck is a jamboree!" she says. "What about the WASPs?"

"The equal military status question," he adds with a know-it-all tilt of his eyebrows. Twyla extracts handkerchiefs from her pockets and holds fast. "Think about it," he continues. "There's no way they can give it to you. They'd have to give it to every woman in every armed forces branch—all the nurses, WAAVs, WACs, SPARs… Box of frowning snakes, eh?"

Twyla pulls on long white gloves, performing several catalog model gestures. "You just want me to stop bouncing around. You can't upset me today. Besides, Jackie's on this, and I think the general's sweet on her. The breeze of attraction can subdue certain protocol. And if you're really in love with someone, you'll board six buses and ride thirty-three hours on an overturned bucket behind a navigator just to be with him for one day."

"No," Bibs snorts, "only *you* would do that. Remember, Bell Aircraft wants you back PFQ," he adds. "That's pretty fucking quick—"

"Yes, I get it! This is birthday jive at my expense. Oh no, not this day, not this dame. I'm gonna see Lewis. Then on to Long Beach to fly 51s. Bell promised me a transfer." She unconsciously flicks through forms atop his in-tray, messing up his neat stacks. "P-51s, Bibs!" she says with a squeak she didn't intend.

He smacks her hand, un-slants his hat, and slides two envelopes toward her. "No touchy my trays, and no jive. But happy birthday."

"Not *my* birthday—Lewis's." She plucks the letters. "Thank you and thank you."

"It's m'pleasure," he says, compressing the phrase with "snarkasm," as he calls it. "Three twin-birds are ready to go, one to Long Beach, one to Long Island, and one to a long ways away. Don't get on that one." His brows arch— *did she catch his superior triplet?*

She did. She skips to the rack and pulls on her overcoat, pokes her miniature journal into her bra, picks up the overstuffed suitcase and Papa's flight bag, and says, "Ain't the rain lovely?"

The door opens, and the wind howls and blows Chuck back into the office, followed by two equally tall men shaking out their hats. Chuck suddenly points to Twyla and grunts, "That's her." He pivots in his puddle and sloshes out the door.

One of the men says, "Mrs. Campbell-Haliday? Mrs. Lewis Haliday?" As he unbuttons his coat, his chaplain's collar seems to glow.

Twyla's suitcase slips from her fingers, tumbling down and down, never hitting the floor, never making a sound.

Blood orange light from the dying sun sparkles on water made from shifting obsidian plates near the Pacific's Marshall Islands. Lewis coughs up blood and seawater. His Mae West has been shot through, and its ragged edge flaps against his bobbing head. Much of Halsey's and Mitscher's fleet are to his back. Kwajalein Atoll and two thousand of his shipmates are only sixty minutes away. He ingests ragged gulps of air through clenched teeth, where his wedding photo is clamped. He pivots to watch a Mitsubishi A6M2 just one hundred feet away with X-212 in gold letters on the tail; it bubbles, flashes, and disappears into the depths.

Lewis shoves the photo under his helmet and blows into the tube attached to a life raft. He coughs out, "Ha! You're dead, too, Katsumoto!" He spits up more blood and tugs on the raft. That's when he sees the bullet holes in the rubber. Sucked under for a long moment, he bobs back up, hacking water and swiveling about, looking for anything to float on. As the sun disappears, the sea turns to black mercury.

He imagines Twyla, Wiley, and his father Gerald learning of his death. This kickstarts his heart with a surge of adrenaline. But his lungs gurgle, and his body spasms as he runs out of oxygen. *Twyla, I'm done*, he thinks. After another coughing spasm, *Sorry, Miss Bloom*. For the first time in Lewis Haliday's life, he relaxes. It is his final effort. The Carpenter Bee of Anderson Valley vanishes into the sea.

No. No. No. No. No.

A clotting hum in her ears. Her head is soaked, makeup streaked. She sits on the cargo hold jump seat, twenty feet behind the pilot's cabin door. She's numb but not cold—not anything. She stares in the direction of the flight deck. Her brain, feeling quite separate from her, thinks, *Door? C-47s don't have cabin doors. Installed against the cold? Don't feel cold.*

The plane moves. The chaplain's voice echoes, "The odds were against him, but he took two of them down before they overwhelmed him. I'm very sorry, Mrs. Haliday. His final encounter was his sixth enemy plane destroyed. You can be proud of…" And Bibs's voice was thin and distant; edging out the chaplain, he had said, "Tough break, Twyla. Go home with Johnson and Jaspersen, they're heading south to…" Apparently, he had pulled on his raincoat and picked up her bags. She vaguely remembers wet hair plastering her face, squeezing her snowsuit as blistering taxi lights stabbed streaks of rain on the soaked apron. Three roaring Skytrains surrounded her. She hadn't heard the engines run up or felt prop wash blow her WASP cap out of her hand, tumbling away into the darkness.

Now, pinned into the jump seat by a force she has never felt—well, almost never—she cannot conceptualize Lewis's death; not just the loss of Lewis, the loss of thought. Since age fourteen, her mind ran in a plaited square dance through Lewis, her curved logic locked arm-in-arm with his right-angle reason without effort. Lewis's voice is in her head just as much as her own. She is a *WE*.

The plane taxis away from the only town in a hundred miles. The air around her shimmers. The hot stink of avgas strikes her in the face. *Burning oil, burning sea.* Though she sits perfectly still, her dark surroundings seem to vibrate such that she can bring nothing into focus. She glances at her hands, two letters crushed in trembling fists. She exhales and feels an invisible marionette's control bar manipulating one of the letters then flicking her Zippo.

Dear pilot Ginger Rogers Snap,

Goddamn it, Twyla! Camp Davis will kill us before the Krauts and Japs—

But that's as far as she can go. *Any other day, Corny. Any other day.*
Twin propellers turn full thrust. Somehow, within the hubbub of wound-up engines, the cleaving gale, and crates of rattling war cargo, Cliff Edwards's glossy voice slips out of the cockpit radio and seeps into her temples.

"… Like a bolt out of the blue
Fate steps on and sees you through
When you wish upon a star
Your dreams come true…"

Twyla's heart disassembles in drops of stone, pressing her hard into the metal seat. *What will keep this airplane aloft? The sky is falling. Lewis, don't go.*

Shock pulls at her like a strong undercurrent. The black wave is on the horizon, rolling toward her—a density of sorrow from which she will never recover. The flight smooths, and moonlight from the tiny hatch window wedges through her sodden eyelashes. *Must've cleared above the weather*, her mind thinks for her. *Marina would have some folksy peasant story about… Why is this plane stuffed full? Cargo doesn't flow this direction. Oh, Lewis. Lewis. I'm not strong enough.*

With hundred-pound arms, she pulls the string-tied parcel out of Papa's bag, the package she had tossed into the can at Avenger Field. The return address reads: Edna Gultch, Philo, California. Loath to open it during her transition training in Buffalo, she opens it now for some reason and pulls out Hawkeye's flying cap and goggles. The Skytrain passes in front of an unreasonably large moon, the red star on its tail more purple on the shadowed side.

Marina Khomyakova presses her face against the Russian-built Skytrain's rear hatch window; moonlight upon it is intermittent through the clouds. Her father's relentless advice comes with strength to her mind, *Work is not a wolf; it won't run into the woods.* The dense patchwork forests of the Central Belarusian front scream by just two hundred feet below. *Where are you, comrades? Where are you?*

A male voice bellows, barely audible above the droning engines and thumping payload. "Look for a triangle fire! A partisan flare! Our delivery marker!"

"I know this, Flight Engineer!" she yells back. She turns to the mountain of weapons, ammunition, fuses, detonators, and food crates, impatient to unload all of it and bolt away. The plane jerks violently. "Oy!" She hits her head against the hatch window and bounces to the floor, head ringing and her nose full of smoke. Someone yells, "Green flare!" She crawls along the floor, grabbing at anything to help her stabilize. Touching her forehead, she finds blood.

"Marina?" comes another voice.

With bent knees and wide strides, she makes her way forward, yelling, "Flight Engineer?" No response. She reaches the cabin. "Commander?"

"Hit by the devil's fighter," the pilot grunts, taking quick glances at her. Brown hair pokes out around goggles and frames his twenty-five-year-old flushed aspect. Next to him, the baby-faced copilot is transfixed.

"Why is our tail gun silent?" the copilot asks.

"Yes, Comrade copilot." She careens toward the tail, yelling, "Flight Engineer?" She weaves among the cargo. The machine guns are wrecked, and holes in the fuselage, where Boris should be standing, suck out smoke fed by a leaking fuel tank that is—

"Fire!"

She leaps toward the rear bulkhead, which pulsates brightly through the black smoke. A body is crumpled on the floor. "Boris? Boris, get up! Fire!" She grabs his face and turns it toward her. His eyes are fixed. She touches his neck— no pulse. Artillery bursts bang away, and she scrambles back to the cabin. "Boris is dead!" she says to her commander. "The tail is on fire, and I don't know where—"

"I'm climbing. Get everything out!" he orders.

The plane is rocked hard and dips in a steep turn, slamming Marina into the bulkhead and onto the floor. She stumbles away as bullets rip into the cockpit right next to the commander. He does not turn to look.

Twyla shivers awake. *Where am I? Corny. Jiminy, it's freezing in here! Oh right, bus back to the States. Gotta see Naomi and Mr. Haliday.* Her brain ticks backward. *Lewis's birthday. Wait. Lewis! Lewis.* And all the broken pieces seem to liquefy via burning, blinding magnesium then form back into place. *Lewis is gone.* Her heart breaks again. *How can this be?*

As she tugs on her snowsuit, she considers, *Maybe they reported the wrong pilot. There are so many stories of the Army informing grieving mothers of their dead sons only to have them walk through the door weeks later! How many clerical errors are possible between the South Pacific and Fairbanks, Alaska?*

She remembers her smoking, speed-typing twin and the towers of forms. *There must be mix-ups all the time.* Her brain flat-out refuses to believe she's lost Lewis; it begins to force a winnowing and rewinding, an undoing of the chaplain's dismaying narration.

Deny it. Revise it. Reverse it.

She glances at her Molly Stark—fogged over. Maybe the pilot can get a message out? *Because it cannot be true.*

Reverse it. Revise it.

She rises, instantly lightheaded and suddenly very cold. She struggles past large crates and knocks on the makeshift cockpit door.

"Jaspersen? Johnson? Hey, in there? You guys forget about—"

The door opens. A surprised pilot bellows, *"Kto ty? Kakogo cherta ty zdes' delayesh'?"*

A pistol is thrust into her face.

Reverse it.

His parachute rises off a Pacific swell near the Marshall Islands, like a pinned bedsheet catching the wind. The stitched silk fills and snaps into a perfect dome, yanking Lewis out of the cascading brine and drying him instantaneously. He ascends into horizontal sunset rays as blood drips upward to the heels of his boots, climbing in rivulets under his pants, across his shins, thighs, and groin, burrowing into his stomach wounds.

He is pulled higher and higher, groaning and coughing blood through his teeth. His eyes flick up to a gaggle of enemy torpedo bombers two miles away while, three hundred yards behind, a parachute slings his Imperial opponent aloft.

Up and up they go.

Below, a dark Pacific wave collapses in a plume of bright foam as Boonville Redhead, his Grumman F6F Hellcat, launches upward, as if spat from the mouth of Ahab's whale. Juddering and skidding, it reels tail first, riding a long smoke trail, curling skyward, and lapping up stretching tongues of flame.

The enemy pilot spasms to life only two hundred yards away. Their parachutes suck violently into their packs, and both men catapult skyward. In seconds, they are rocketing upward at 120 miles per hour. The two fighter planes accelerate in reverse on an intercepting course, spinning like featherless darts, smoke vacuuming into their engines.

Marina reaches the flight deck, staring directly into the commander's bloody lap.

"Commander?"

He looks at her like she's a ghost. "How are you still—? Push everything out!"

"But Commander—?"

"Everything out!"

She turns and stumbles over the plummeting floor, bumping into every hard edge. Something hits her from behind, and she watches the copilot rush toward the tail. *He's going to help me unload? No. Do as he says, Marinetchka!* She pulls open the hatch door to a whooshing wave of burning smoke escaping as fast as it can. *We'll blow up any second!* Although the firelight is helpful, she can't help but notice it is the parachutes on fire.

She grips a ninety-kilo box of rifles, sliding it toward the door. She chucks the rifles out one at a time, shouting, "Flight Engineer! Please help!" Her voice is sucked out the door and chopped to bits by the propellers. She bends deeply, jabs her elbows onto the tops of her knees, leans back, and lifts the box with a teeth-gnashing grunt, tipping the whole thing out. She thrusts her face into the slipstream, watching the weapons tumble into the gloom, and makes a wish: *Please land on five SS officers huddled to congratulate themselves!*

She trips over the flight engineer crumpled next to a box of detonators, moaning. She's ready to slap his face in anger when she sees four… five… six bullet holes in his body. *Marja Morevna!* She draws two monogrammed handkerchiefs from her coveralls, glares at how tiny and thin they are, and stuffs them back into her pocket. She unzips her jumpsuit, pulls off a layer of long underwear, and shoves it into the nastiest-looking wound. "Hold this!" She lurches around the cargo and tugs six fifty-kilo canvas bags of detonators out the hatch. Wheezing, slick with sweat, she pushes equally heavy boxes of ammunition to the door.

The tail fire flourishes as the plane angles into a steep dive. She caroms down to the cabin like a pachinko ball.

"Marina?" the commander chokes out. She pulls herself next to him as he sucks in shallow breaths from a new chest wound. Blood soaks his coat and lap.

"Commander?"

"I need… assistance… pull."

"But you're hurt!"

He indicates the steering yoke. She leans against him and pulls back with him. As he feels her help, he begins to lose strength. "Copilot?" he asks.

"Worthless!"

"Yes, I know. Elevator damage. Tsar's ball." He coughs. "I can't…"

Does she help him or…? "Commander, there are still explosives on board!" She considers this could be her last minute on Earth. Will his face be the last she sees? *No! My husband! My children!* She grabs the wheel with a fiery vigor. Together, they bring the ship level.

"Get it all out. Get it all out," he hisses between rasps. She gently lets go of the yoke and darts back through dense smoke to the remaining three crates—they won't budge a millimeter. Grabbing an ax, she steadies herself over the wooden box, knowing full well she may blow herself up if she mis-strikes and hits the explosives within. She swings down sharply. The box splinters a little, enough to wedge the ax handle into the gash and make a bigger hole, revealing a crate of thirty-six forty-kilo boxes. She hoists them out one at a time, then stacks up two at a time and wills herself to move faster, coughing and panting through the blighted air.

Faces of people she hates float through her memory—mean uncles, boys from her village who touched her without permission, the political police who were always leering, ready to steal anything of value, especially dreams… She tells them off, all of them, in a fantasy death speech, reducing every man to a sobbing child as she dies a hero's death for her fair Motherland. The fantasy has played out before she realizes she's moved ninety boxes.

"Marina!"

Did I hear—? She scrambles back toward the nose, her feet sometimes leaving the floor as the plane dips and dives. She reaches the cockpit in time to hear her commander shout, "Brace!"

R e v i s e

      a n d

              ReverseReverseReverse

Lewis tumbles like a ragdoll, coughing through blazing pain as tears seep from his blurred eyes. The wind howls, and his breath sticks in his destroyed guts. His fighter plane drives straight for and just over his head. He accelerates horizontally and is sucked toward the inverted cockpit of his beloved Hellcat. He hovers there for a brief moment, his hand and foot reaching out to the cockpit edge, dangling upside down over the absurd Pacific infinity. Eyes squinting against the slipstream blast, he settles into his seat, clutching his stomach and convulsing for a breath, pain contorting his face as his goggles settle into place.

Two rocking booms smear together, and the shattered Perspex canopy instantly repairs as the hyper buzz of his plane's emergency war power RPM resumes. His breath and face reform into the sound and shape of intense surprise, and his head flicks starboard as the enemy recedes. *Where the fuck did he come from?* His expression reorders into granite concentration.

With quick twists of Boonville Redhead, and altitude gained, Lewis watches X-212 slide into his gun sight and burst with a wisp of smoke and leaping blaze. Bullets race toward his wing guns, where they are vacuumed up in flaming puffs, the tracer glow dying as they re-enter the gun barrels. A smile forms. He thinks of his enemy, *This shrapnel of Divine Wind is not so divine.*

The Hellcat's considerable speed slows from a five-hundred-mile-per-hour dive into a cruising speed of two-fifty. He flattens out and forms back into a pack with his buddies in a staggered line of four Navy Cats, among a total flight of twelve. A one-hundred-fifty-gallon drop tank comes tumbling up to his ship's belly. His gloved fingers push down the T-handle release. The fighters slide and slide for a perfect hour, eventually reeling toward a massive carrier fifty miles dead-west. Long, bright wake channels are visible through broken clouds like claw scratches on the dark water.

Lewis brags, again, about *his wife* being the first pilot to engage the enemy way back in '41. His buddies tease him about the menacing quality of her "Taylorcraft fighting ship." The planes separate and circle over whitecaps, the gray protective battlements of cruisers and destroyers spreading low diesel clouds on top of the bottomless pewter sea. A smile overtakes Lewis's face.

A crazy smile contorts Marina's face as her ship skims into the ground. There's nothing more she can do, and she is tossed about in a cacophonous tumult, transmitting into and out of her bones. The plane skids and jolts for two hundred meters, screeching, grinding, and rocking into its final resting angle before rapidly filling with smoke.

She staggers to the engineer and grabs him under his armpits. She has no strength left, but that doesn't matter. At the hatch, she lowers him into the waiting arms of the navigator and tail gunner, then turns and runs back to the cockpit.

"Commander!"

But he is making strange sounds as his breath comes in short stabs, his bloody face smiling against the ridiculous pain. Marina pulls him through the plane's choking carcass because he can't manage to help in the least. She is saturated top to bottom in her own sweat, her heaving lungs full of smoke.

"Ha!" the commander cries as Marina works him, inch by inch, through the hatch, where smoke pours upward like an inverted waterfall.

"She's going up," he mutters. "Leave me here."

The fire grows into an unbearable heat at their right side. She jumps over him, splashes onto the ground, and drags him down into the muddy grass. His face grins, head shakes. Marina's lungs burn as she pulls the commander through the mud with arms of melted rubber. She stumbles backward, and the ship explodes.

Flattening herself against the commander, a wall of heat smashes into them. Burning death missiles of debris blast all around. She lifts an eyebrow. Their much-loved Lisunov Skytrain is engulfed in flame. She sets to work with warmth and good light, examining the commander's chest wound while hot aircraft parts drop around them. She draws out her sad handkerchiefs and jams them into his chest.

"Press here," she orders, moving his hands to the wound. "I need to move you. I'll be right back."

Only twenty dense, smoky meters away, she finds the rest of her crew attempting to revive the engineer. "Get help!" she shouts and runs back to the commander.

"Leave me," the commander says, a pistol on his lap, ready to shoot himself when the wolfpack arrives.

Thirty minutes of blood-stanching, and the commander is out cold. Marina scrapes mud from her elbows, her face constricted by the stench of rotting flesh. But before she can understand this, the navigator returns with a horse and cart from a partisan-controlled village. This is luck so startling and fragile, she cannot speak of it—none of them do. They put the commander and engineer into the cart and hike toward the village.

In a candlelit farmhouse cellar, lacking anesthesia, the surgeon uses chunks of ice to freeze the commander's wounds, then extracts bullets and splinters. The commander grimaces with determination, tears soaking into his hair. Marina is glad she can't see well around this room of extractions, amputations, and worse; the floor is both sticky and slippery.

Later, in another dark room, Marina sleeps next to the commander, a sleep so deep she awakens in a stupor, fearful someone will ask her who and where she is.

The commander croaks, "My Defense of Stalingrad medal?" Marina is startled. "Where is it? I had it around my neck. Do you have it?" She has no idea what he's mumbling about. "Will you find it for me?"

How is he not dead? she thinks. *All that blood... he should be.* She shakes her head, rubs her eyes, and can't believe how thirsty she is. Her commander's wish, a dead man's wish, is *still* her commander's wish.

"Can you, please?" he says.

"Of course."

A tight conspiracy of black Stukas scream over the treetops. Marina watches them carefully, then steps gingerly over hastily buried anti-personnel mines and out of the trees toward the wreckage. Though its rear half is burned to its ribs, the cockpit is mostly intact—they are hopeful. After another hour, they find only exhaustion, hunger, and defeat. They walk without talking. Marina's family, her two young boys, her parents, and her Stalingrad-absorbed husband chatter inside her with heart-aching familial rhythms. This is overwritten by cost-to-benefit calculations of her failed resupply mission, failed medal hunt, booby traps in her trail, and imminent Stuka assaults. Just how will she get back to her regiment?

"But what do we tell the commander about his medal?" Navigator queries.

"I don't know," she says and thinks, *Critical partisan resupply run for the collapsing Central Front, and her flight commander wants his medal. They don't seem remotely equal. They are not. Should the desires of the dying put the living in peril? But Marina, this is the army—you're not here to think.*

R E P L A Y and H O L D

Lewis's Hellcat slings low, touching lightly back home on the deck of the *Enterprise*. It gathers back toward the launch line, past scores of head-socked deckmates, signalers, and metal-hatted, twenty-millimeter gunners. Boonville Redhead jerks to a standstill, and wheel chocks slide into place.

At wingtip, Wiley "Heelch" Felton, outfitted in his leather deck-crew helmet and goggles, salutes, flips two birds—accompanied by a sloppy raspberry—and helps push the aircraft off the line and fold back its wings. He climbs aboard and slides open Lew's cockpit, yelling, "Captain Llewellyn, did you know when you say Twy, you're actually saying *my* name, but with a 'T'? See that? See, it's Wy, but with a 'T' added for Twy. I know you miss her. So do I. I mean, you could call me Twiley… but that wouldn't be regulation. But if it helps?"

Lewis pulls down his goggles. "You looking for a fight with the entire ship, blabbering like a schoolgirl?"

Wiley thrusts out his chin, gesturing to the hectic flight deck, and says, "As you can see, Gasoline Alley is overrun with customers. I can't help you any more than this. Doc would offer this to Walt as long as it required no physical help. Doc is here to supply an expert stream of second-guessing."

Lewis understood this to be Wiley's way of saying, *"Please come back from this mission. Please don't get killed."*

"Wiley, you nut tree!" he replies. "If you don't quit your bawlin', I'm gonna do a double wrap around this boat and lever my drop tank on top of your head." Wiley salutes. Lewis pulls a letter from his jacket and says, "Though you're a useless mechanic, you are an accomplished postman." He shoves a letter into Wiley's wind-warped face. "And one more thing, Twiley, bring me a fresh piss bottle."

The best pals squint at each other, holding firm, as neither wants to break first. Finally, laughter and lung-ratcheting hoots broadcast unheard across the flight deck of the Grey Ghost. The Big E. The *USS Enterprise.*

HERE… HOLD RIGHT HERE… please.

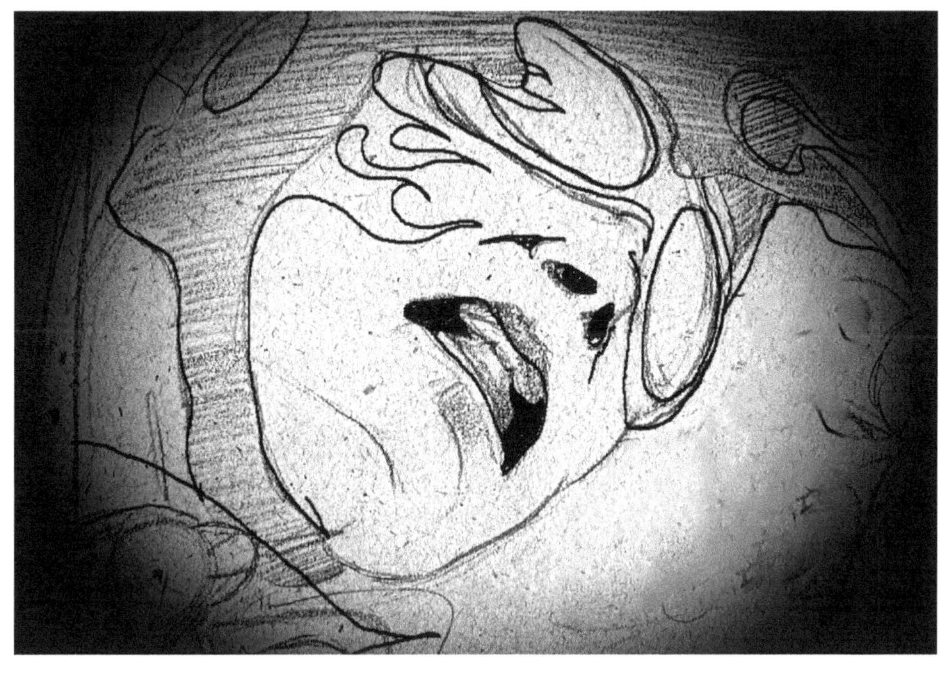

fourteen

Wolf Eats Rabbit

Five hundred shards of idyllic Austria were scattered around Gram Gram's coffee table and beyond. The other five hundred pieces obediently formed a rectangular frame of cloud, stone, and water.

The widow, Twyla Campbell, was locked in place by a long-standing grief; a fossilized amber grief between which years could pass without feeling its surge and sting. Tears tumbled and streamed through her spotted, bony hands. Her granddaughter leaned into her and said, "Grandpa Lewis was a hero."

The puzzle formed slowly, the afternoon passing with few words. Twyla's physical therapy was a success, and she often left her walker behind. She continued to grouse about her hip, yet it slowed her little. The blight in her lungs, however, had other plans. She considered life under more chemo and radiation. *Such a ham-fisted approach, like precision daylight bombing against the Third Reich—anything but precise. America's vaunted Norden bombsight system wasn't precise; it was just better than anything else. Chemo carpet-bombing.*

Inside carpet-bomb HQ, Little Twyla wheeled around the nurses' station, showing off her history report titled, *The Many Lives of Crissy Field, San Francisco.* Gram was grateful for this distraction while a nurse laid the needle into her chest port.

"You can't stop now, Gram Gram! Pilot Twyla is… is in serious trouble! Where is she going? Corny crashed! Marina crashed, and so much yucky stuff! Lewis left Whole Cheese all alone! Naomi is the only person who is… Don't you dare stop!"

Gram reclined her chair, glanced at her Molly Stark, and said, "Good debate, my bantam barnacle. Fair warning, more yucky stuff abeam."

*

Dim, bluish particles of a drained twilight barely illuminate two combat planes with red stars on their tails as they land on a dirt field.

Twyla lowers herself down from a window set high in a gray wall onto the oil-stained floor of a maintenance shop turned prison cell. Obliquely aware of her ruined party dress, she's more surprised by the volume of her own breath. Sharp, cold moonlight slips in, bouncing around her cell. Hastily welded bars separate her from crude tools, truck axles, and oxidized sheet metal. Her body aches from prolonged confinement in the Skytrain, and she's worried her feet will never be warm again. She absently stares at her destroyed French-heeled slingbacks and realizes she is thirsty and hungry beyond reason.

But why were the pilots so angry at me? Why take my snowsuit? Aircraft engine noise is interrupted by a pleading voice escaping from a black and severely scratched door just a few feet outside the bars. Something in the muffled speech focuses her mind, sharpens the Russian words.

"*Pozhaluysta!* Please! Only hours… Hitlerites' prison… *bol'she ne nado* was *borba…* fighting… escaped… wounded… no… *Net ne promyli mozgi, bol'she ne nuzhno…* clean… I escape. Please medical… please doctor."

Then another voice, this one hoarse and bitter. Twyla whispers her translation: "In-insul… insulting… coward. Russians never caught… capture… brainwash… report, no good… not trust… inform… Nazis aware!"

Twyla closes her eyes. The voice is stripped and gravelly. She replays each word. *Insults my intelligence, coward. How… you be captured? Your report not be trusted. Nazi dogs aware of our position. You should… have… killed yourself!* Twyla's eyes shoot wide. *I've got it!*

The first voice comes again, "Please let me explain!" Then, a bright gunshot and a thud, like bones against a wall, propel Twyla to her feet. "Oh, shit." Her empty stomach spasms.

The black door opens. A Soviet marshal not more than five and a half feet tall, wearing an unbuttoned khaki green tunic and trousers, steps over a collapsed body. The Army officer is pale, skinny, and holding a glass of clear liquid and a cigarette in the same hand. As he steps into the jail room, his piercing, ratty eyes absorb her. "Who are you?" His voice comes like cracking cement as he moves slowly toward her. His uniform collar has a red diamond shape with two marks, and his shoulder displays a double gold and red chevron.

"I-I… I'm lost," she stammers in Russian. A dry whisper is all she gets out.

He steps up to the bars and gestures her closer. "Who are you?"

She clears her throat. "Sir, I lost. I am ferry pilot. Got wrong plane back in—"

"Mmm, I understand that to be your story. My comrades tell me you're a Fascist sniper." He eyes her carefully for any reaction. She doesn't move, yet something about this outlandish misunderstanding is encouraging. His bloodshot eyes glisten over dark rings. He smiles and sips through dry, cracked lips.

Twyla shakes her head. "No, sir. You see—"

"Not a sniper. You are a spy," he interrupts with a casual gesture. "Stalingrad, they say. But I tell them the vodka has slowed their brains. No! Stalingrad is a dead city, maybe Kursk? Not again. Kiev? Moscow? Hardly. They tell me no more grand targets, the Nazis are done with that. Instead, they will fight us with small actions designed to slow everything down—the French way." He tips back his glass and wipes his mouth with the back of his hand. "Not possible. They are Germans. Why use tweezers when there is already a hammer in your hand? Don't worry, you are just an unlucky *Amerikanets* who happens to speak in my tongue in the wrong place at the wrong time."

Twyla nods vigorously. "Yes, sir. I just—"

"You know…" He starts unlocking her cell door. "I tell them they should believe you. Much stranger things happen in war than this." The door opens, and she steps out, cautious optimism unknitting her brow. He raises a pistol to her face, "We are Russian—we don't believe anybody," and pulls the trigger.

The End

ABOUT THE AUTHOR

T.W. Bellen is a filmmaker and cinematographer. He wrote the feature film *Turret*, (about a WWII, B-17 Gunner) and directed photography on Apple tv's, *Dear Edward*, Amazon's, *As We See It*, HBO's *VEEP* (season five) and Netflix's *Good Girls*—among many others.

T.W. is also an illustrator and author of the series *Twyla and the Warbirds -Family Lost*, and *Twyla and the Warbirds – Family Found.*

An aviation nut since childhood, T.W. grew up near Edwards Air Force Base, in California, attended many airshows, and was present at Kitty Hawk, NC for the 100th Anniversary of Powered Flight celebration.

He lives with his beautiful Stenographer wife in Northern California. They accuse each other of having weird jobs.

Twyla & the Warbirds: Family Found

Book One of the *Twyla & the Warbirds* saga, Family Lost, traces a difficult path for an American-Ukrainian rural girl from Boonville California.

At a tender age, Twyla Campbell loses her family in a freak aeroplane accident. Her young life is salvaged from indenture by the neighbor boy, who teaches her to fly.

Stationed in Honolulu with her fiancé, she narrowly escapes certain death while flying above Pearl Harbor. Twyla lucks into a slot with the W.A.S.P., women's ferry pilots training program in Texas, where "the girls" have no business in the Army Air Force. Twyla transports fighter planes to Alaska for Roosevelt.

There, she befriends Marina, a Russian pilot with indefatigable courage and odd sense of humor.

When tragedy strikes, Twyla boards a transport home, only to find herself arrested on the Eastern Front and scheduled for execution...

CLAVIS

Ace. Five aerial victories "kills." An enemy plane shot down regardless of pilot survival.

Aerodrome. A small airfield of flight operations.

Airacobra P-39. A small, single seat (mid-engine/tricycle gear) fighter, produced by Bell Aircraft, for the U.S. Army Aircorps during WWII. Quickly out of date and sent overseas, it became a popular fighter on the Eastern Front.

ATC, Air Transport Command. A worldwide air transport system, and United States Air Force unit, created during World War II as the strategic airlift component of the United States Army Air Forces – including ferrying of aircraft from the factories to air bases for operational use and combat training.

Boontling "Boont" A local, partial dialect spoken in and around Boonville, Anderson Valley (a small Mendocino County Appalachia in Northern California) in the 19th and 20th centuries. A local slang rooted in an object, animal, or a person's characteristics.
Read, *Boontling: An American Lingo*, by Charles Adams.

"Captain Eddie" Rickenbacker. Famous race car driver, Ace of Aces in WWI. At one time he owned the Indianapolis Speedway, Eastern Airlines and the Rickenbacker Automobile Company. Check out his autobiography *--astonishing.*

Cornelia Fort, a Southern Belle from Nashville Tennessee, was one of Nancy Love's "Originals." Cornelia was giving flight instruction in a small plane while over Pearl Harbor on Dec, 7 1941, when she was fired upon by Japanese aircraft. She made an emergency landing with her student and went on a vigorous war bond tour, then joined Nancy's ferry pilot program. Cornelia became the first American aviatrix killed in WWII. Read **Daughter of the Air**, by Rob Simbeck --*Heartbreaking.*

Curtis JN Jenny. 1915-1927. A training aircraft for the US Army in WWI, it became the backbone of American postwar aviation –a starring role if you will --to the barnstorming era that helped promote civil aviation throughout the 1920's

Easter Front. Home to Germany's war of annihilation and scorched earth policies, it held the largest military confrontations in history. Wholesale terrorism and massacres, staggering human atrocity and suffering. Tens of millions dead, wounded and missing.

Fascism *–Harmful to people.*

General Henry "Hap" Arnold. One of the first military pilots trained by Oroville Wright, senior bomber boss, and leading proponent of the 8th Air Force precision daylight bombing effort in England, 1942-45. He became the first five-star general in American history—and survived several heart attacks.

Lend-Lease Act (1941) The US aided its Allies China, France, UK and USSR , with material assistance in the form of aircraft, tanks, trucks, guns, naval ships, technology and food --and untold billions of rounds of munitions of all types.

Marina Raskova. Hero of the Soviet. Mother, Navigator, head of the all-female fighting units; ground attack, light bomber and fighter regiments. Brave, smart, and even though she didn't "feel the part," she was a natural leader.

Jaqueline "Jackie" Cochran. Self-made beauty-products businesswoman, and the fastest female on earth. Air racer, test pilot and head of the Women's Airforce Service Pilot's program during WWII. Two decades later, she would attempt to become an astronaut.

Jiminy Cricket. Widely known as the lead puppet's conscience in the Disney animated film, Pinocchio.

Key System (streetcar and bus routes) was a privately owned company that provided mass transit in the cities of Oakland, Berkeley, Alameda, Emeryville, Piedmont, San Leandro, Richmond, Albany and El Cerrito in the eastern San Francisco Bay Are, from 1903 until 1960

Nancy Harkness Love. Pilot, businesswoman and champion of female ferry pilots. She oversaw the first women transport pilots, the "Originals," before J. Cochran took over the program.

Spad XIII fighter. SPAD company's single seat fighter of 150 hp, introduced in 1917. Many Aces flew this fighter.

Sweetwater, Texas/ Avenger Field. The Central Texas training base for the Women's Air Service Pilots (WASP) training detachment. Also used by Canadian and RAF flight training.

Taylorcraft B (L-2H) A small high wing aircraft powered by a Continental 65 hp engine. A very popular aircraft manufactured in Ohio.

US Army Air Corps (1926-41) After June, 1941, it became the US Army Air Forces. During WWII, although not an administrative echelon, the Air Corps (AC) remained as one of the combat arms of the Army until 1947, when it was legally abolished by legislation establishing the Department of the Air Force.

James Lick Telescope, the "Great Lick Refractor" or simply "Lick Refractor," was the largest refracting telescope in the world until 1897. The University of California observatory sits atop Mount Hamilton at 1,283 meters elevation. On May 21, 1939, during a nighttime fog that engulfed the summit, a U.S. Army Air Corp Northrop A-17 two-seater attack plane crashed into the main building.

Yakovlev "Yak" single-seat aircraft were a famous line of front-line fighters, alongside, MIG, LaGG, and Lavochkin.

A hearty "thank you!" to the many writers whose works of global history have contributed to my understanding of 20th century aviation and war.

---T.W. Bellen

T. W. Bellen

Copyright © 2024 T. W. Bellen

www.ingramcontent.com/pod-product-compliance
Lightning Source LLC
Chambersburg PA
CBHW051121300726
48981CB00021B/498/J